HOSPITAL CIRCLES

Bill Francis was dangerously ill when Nurse Jo Dungarven was given the task of nursing him. And it was not surprising that, during the fight for his life, they fell in love. But Bill, a young and handsome journalist, took love very lightly, and Jo was destined to be bitterly disappointed before their friendship finally came to an end.

*Books by Lucilla Andrews in the
Ulverscroft Large Print Series:*

THE PRINT PETTICOAT
THE FIRST YEAR
A HOSPITAL SUMMER
MY FRIEND THE PROFESSOR
NURSE ERRANT
FLOWERS FROM THE DOCTOR
THE YOUNG DOCTORS DOWNSTAIRS
THE LIGHT IN THE WARD
HOSPITAL CIRCLES
THE HEALING TIME
EDINBURGH EXCURSION

◆

This Large Print Edition
is published by kind permission of
GEORGE G. HARRAP & CO LTD
London

LUCILLA ANDREWS

HOSPITAL CIRCLES

Complete and Unabridged

ULVERSCROFT
Leicester

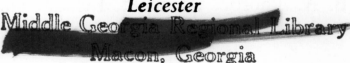

Originally published in Great Britain
in 1967 by
George G. Harrap & Co. Ltd
London

First Large Print Edition
published November 1971

SBN 85456 080 7

This special large print edition is
made and printed in England for
F. A. Thorpe, Glenfield, Leicestershire

CONTENTS

1. One Saturday Night in Hospital
2. A Very Special Patient
3. Reunion in the Car-park
4. One Morning on a Bypass
5. The General comes to Tea
6. Casualty has a Nautical Air
7. A Letter from Margaret
8. A Caller in Casualty
9. Margaret comes back to Benedict's
10. The Accident Recovery Room Unit
11. A Letter to Bill
12. The Unit is a Factory-belt
13. A Visit from Richard
14. The Sleeper Wakes up

CHAPTER ONE

ONE SATURDAY NIGHT IN HOSPITAL

I SLEPT through our floor maid's call that evening. I was still asleep when Aline came in with my postcard from Margaret.

"Jo, it's a quarter past. The first supper bell'll go in ten minutes." She shook me. "Can you hear me?"

I groaned. "Aline, be a dear sweet girl and go away and let me die in peace. If only for another five minutes."

"Mind you only make it five. Don't forget what the Night Super. said to us last night about the next girl to come in after she's arrived to read the register."

"The woman's a sadist." I turned on my face. "She beats us up for kicks."

"She's not beating me up. I'm going over now." She put my card on my dressing-table. "Don't go back to sleep."

"I won't," I promised, and was asleep again before the door closed after her. The next thing I knew was Gwenellen, shaking me violently.

I

Aline and Gwenellen were in my set. They were my greatest friends in Benedict's, and had rooms on either side of mine. "Jo, it's twenty-five to!"

"It can't be! Aline was only in five minutes ago!"

"Aline's over having supper. She said you'd woken, but when you didn't turn up I thought I'd better come back to investigate." She shook me again. "Up love! Don't forget Night Super.'s warning to send the next late-comer straight to Matron."

"Must you remind me of that traumatic experience?"

Gwenellen said placidly, "There's another you've got coming, love," and heaved up the side of my mattress. I landed on the floor. "With luck, you've fifteen minutes before she gets in." She made my bed for me and wound Little Ben as I hurtled into uniform. "I'll now return to my shepherd's pie."

"Gwenellen," I said breathlessly, "thanks."

She handed me Little Ben, advised me not to let Home Sister catch me leaving it so late, and took herself off.

Little Ben was an aged, ugly, and

apparently indestructible pocket watch that had cost my paternal grandfather five shillings when he was a Benedict's house-man. He had given it to his youngest daughter, Margaret, when she trained as a nurse at Benedict's just after the last World War. When I started in the Preliminary Training School two and a half years ago my aunt had passed Little Ben on to me and had my name engraved beneath hers and grandfather's on the back. I was very attached to Little Ben, and even more so to Margaret. I looked at her card as I did my hair.

It read: "Should be off my case and home in six days. Dickie breaks up Monday week. Is it that Monday or the one after your holiday starts? Either will suit us fine. Love. M."

Yawning, I pushed the card into my apron bib to answer during the night. I was night relief nurse in Hope, a women's acute medical ward, and tonight was one of the rare nights when all three Hope night nurses were on together. Hope was generally busy, but with the three of us I should be able to snatch the time for a letter in the small hours.

Margaret was a widow. Dickie, her only child, was twelve. Being another only child, and as my father's job had kept my parents in Singapore for the last two years, I now spent most of my holidays with my aunt and cousin, timing them to come in Dickie's school holidays. My coming summer holiday started on the same day as my cousin's, and I was much looking forward to it. I had enjoyed Hope and the work we did at night, but I detested working at night, as I had never managed to sleep well during the day. Usually it was late afternoon before I tossed myself into the near-coma from which Gwenellen had just woken me. I was tired of feeling tired.

I was ready inside the fifteen minutes. The unnatural silence in the Home showed I was last out. I should make the dining-room before the Night Superintendent, providing, as Gwenellen had advised, I escaped Home Sister. She was a nice old soul, but she had once been Sister Hope for twenty years, as she never ceased to inform us. If she caught me now in the front hall she would waste a good ten minutes warning me that I was risking tuberculosis and a gastric ulcer by being too late to eat a proper meal quietly, and probably throw in the chances of my poisoning a patient with the wrong drug before the night was out through carelessness induced by my own lack of blood-sugar. "Believe me, Nurse Dungarvan, I well remember a sad case in Hope. Such a nice girl, but . . . "

I went down the back stairs, meaning to use the back door. It was never locked before 9 p.m. It was that night. I cursed, crept towards the front hall, then stopped dead as I heard voices. They belonged to Home Sister and, of all people, the Night Super. Hell, I thought, now what? Then I remembered the new subway.

This was being built under the main road that divided the three nurses' homes and the medical-school library from the hospital. One of my Hope patients was married to one of the subway workmen. She had told me the tunnels had now been connected up and the workmen used the subway constantly as a private short cut. On the hospital side it opened into the basement under the Out Patients Department, which itself stood directly opposite our dining-room. It would save me minutes.

I hurried back softly to the basement stairs.

Our basement had been out of bounds since the work started, as a large sign on the stairs informed me. The stairs were roped off. I climbed over and went on down. The new tunnel opened on the left a few yards from the foot of the stairs. It was lit by hurricane lamps, and it too was roped off and had another "No Entry" sign. I patted it as I went by. The air smelt of damp and cement, but was not unpleasant, and round the bend from our tunnel where it was joined by the library tunnel the air was much fresher. In the main subway itself, a few more yards on, there was much more light, as there were lamps hanging from hooks on the walls as well as lining the floor. Despite my soft soles, my steps had an extraordinary echo. It so fascinated me that I stopped in the middle of the subway. The echo went on. Then a man's voice behind me called, "One minute, please, Nurse."

I did not recognize the voice. I recognized the man in the long white coat directly I turned. I took a deep breath. "Good evening, Mr. Leland."

"Evening." He caught me up.

6

"What are you doing down here?"

"Taking a short cut to supper."

"Supper?" He held up his wrist to look at his watch by the nearest lamp. "Night nurse?"

"Yes, Mr. Leland."

"Why come this way? Surely you know this subway is out of bounds?" His tone was mild, but, having heard of his reputation, I did not let that deceive me.

"Yes. I'm afraid I do." I looked up at his face and braced myself for the inevitable blast.

None came. He merely looked back at me in a rather peculiar silence.

He had been our Senior Surgical Officer for about four months. He was a Benedict's man, and, as was a Benedict's custom, had spent some years in other hospitals before returning to his present appointment. As I had been on the medical side since he came back, this was the first time he had spoken to me, or probably seen me. I had seen him around, frequently. Taking note, and stock, of new senior residents was something all nurses did within twenty-four hours of that resident's arrival in a hospital.

7

He was a tall, thin man, but with the shoulders to carry his height. He had a strong-featured face that was attractive without being strictly good-looking, and hair that was the colour of deep copper. As a student he had been nicknamed Red Leland. He was now Old Red to all Benedict's—behind his back.

When he first returned, my friends on the surgical side had made themselves fresh caps daily and spent hours on their faces before going on duty. A couple even went on diets. When he first returned. Now, when the surgical girls mentioned him, it was usually between their teeth.

I wished he would get on and get it over. And then, since weeping was something I could do fairly easily, providing I thought hard enough on a sad theme, I should see if a few womanly tears would be a good ploy. Despite his reputation and the general theory that doctors were impervious to tears because they saw so many shed, I had noticed that the way our men reacted to weeping females depended mainly on their ages. Roughly, those over thirty-five, and I put him in that group, reacted with a mixture of

8

impatience, embarrassment, and guilt. Those under, as likely as not, burst into tears themselves. I had been wept on by so many boyfriends that, had Home Sister known, she would have warned me of the dangers of pneumonia every time I went out on a date.

It might work on Old Red, I decided, summing him up. He was looking correctly grave, but his mouth was sensitive and he was a lot bigger than I was, in addition to being years senior. As any girl knew, with any normal man, that gave her the ace.

He broke the silence to ask, still mildly, if I had previously used the subway. "No? Good. Don't use it again until it's open and properly lighted. It's far too lonely. We've had the occasional report of undesirable characters lurking round the hospital. One could easily get down here. That's actually why I'm here now. Not that I've seen anyone. Have you?"

"No. I never thought of that angle."

"You will," he said, "next time. What's your name, Nurse?"

I stiffened. Was he going to report me? "Nurse Dungarvan."

His quick smile was astonishingly

attractive. "I thought so. Obviously related to Margaret Dungarvan?"

"Her niece." (God bless Margaret!) "You knew her?"

He said he remembered her well, hoped she was flourishing, and had I not better get off to my supper?

"Yes, Mr. Leland." I smiled. "Thank you."

Nine struck as I reached the dining-room. A junior Night Sister frowned, but by some miracle the Night Super.'s chair was still empty. I had time to eat my shepherd's pie and tell my table about meeting Old Red before she appeared and apologized to us all for being late. "You'll forgive me if I have a cup of tea before reading the register, Nurses?"

"Just this once, Sister," I murmured. "Well, girls?" I asked the table. "And what's all this codswallop you've been feeding us about Old Red's being foul to nurses? He's not. He's cute."

"Cute!" Aline choked and had to be banged on the back. "Jo, are you sure you haven't dreamed all this up? We know what your imagination's like. And we girls in the surgical block know our Old Red!"

10

Aline worked in Stanley, Gwenellen, in Marcus. Stanley was male general surgical. Marcus was a male major-accident ward. I said, "I have not imagined this! He honestly was cute! He asked if I was related to Margaret."

Aline said, "Maybe you reminded him of his long-lost youth."

"That's it! I awoke an avuncular instinct!"

"Well, don't count on it," she warned, "if you meet him on duty. He'll never let you get away with anything in a ward even if he's been pining with unrequited love for your aunt for God knows how many years."

I nodded absently, thinking of Margaret. "I wonder why he's never married? He's no queer."

Almost reluctantly, the table agreed. Since most men had acquired wives before they reached the stage of being an S.S.O. —and Benedict's having yet to appoint its first female house-surgeon, never had any but male S.S.O.s—a bachelor S.S.O. was regarded as an unexpected bonus and fair game for the entire nursing staff. In his four months in residence Old Red had done a great job of dashing girlish hopes.

Gwenellen hopefully suggested he might have a secret mistress. Aline disagreed. "Mistresses demand time and money. Where's the hospital resident with either?"

I sighed. "Poor Old Red. What a grim life!"

"No-one has to be an S.S.O.," protested Aline. "The grind may be tough, but it doesn't last for ever. Couple of years from now he'll be a pundit surgeon. Think what pundits earn and dry your tears."

"But think of the way pundits have to work for years and years to earn that money. Time they get it they're good as past it! No, I still think Old Red has a tough life. I must ask Margaret if she remembers him."

"Do that," urged Gwenellen, "and ask if she knows why he's never married. A man his age needs a wife."

That had already occurred to me. The Night Superintendent clapped her hands for silence. Before she reached my name I had chosen the wife for Old Red; when Gwenellen Jones answered I had also chosen my bridesmaid's dress, asked Matron for an extra holiday, coaxed our fare money out of my father, and was flying out to Singapore with Dickie.

Margaret had married one Simon Ellis, a junior orthopaedic registrar, in her fourth year. I barely remembered my uncle, as he had been killed rock-climbing when Dickie was a few months old. I had never understood why Margaret had not re-married. My mother said that was because one married whom one met. "And whom does Margaret meet? Her patients, whom she is far too much of a professional nurse to regard as anything but patients, married couples with children of Dickie's age, married G.P.s, and your little boyfriends, Jo. If only she could meet some really suitable older man. Trouble is, of course, they're already married. It's only the oddities who make elderly bachelors."

Old Red was no oddity. Nor was he really all that elderly. Middle-aged, per-haps, but so was Margaret. And very suitable. Also, the biggest point in his favour was the way he remembered her so well that he not only had not minded admitting it to me, but had been very nice in the process. I claimed no personal credit for that, since, like most girls, I could always tell when I had lit a spark in a man at sight, and vice versa. Nothing like that had just happened in the subway. Though Old Red had looked at me so keenly, I would be prepared to swear on oath that he had not seen me at all. Margaret and I were still very alike. I had been wearing the uniform in which he must remember her. He had looked at me and seen her. And God bless him for that.

I hoped Margaret liked red hair. I thought his a fascinating colour, but personally preferred dark-haired men, even though myself a brunette. Should I ask Margaret outright? No. Too obvious. I must get them together again first. I had no idea how, yet. I would work on it. Right now I was too busy working on where he could take her for a honeymoon. Spain? Italy? Ireland?

Aline kicked me under the table. "She's talking about you," she murmured, without using her lips.

The night's ward-changes were being announced. I just caught " . . . from Hope Ward to Marcus Ward as special."

"Me—?" I mouthed, and my table nodded.

I was furious. I had to wait until after grace. "What's the old bag playing at, Gwenellen? Aren't there three of you in Marcus tonight, and one a senior staff nurse? Why can't you special your own patients? I belong to Hope!"

"Have you forgotten it's Saturday night, Jo? Mid-July? And that we've had no rain since Tuesday, and it started getting hotter yesterday?"

"I had. I never remember what day it is on nights." I calmed down. "Any notion whom I'm to special?"

"We'd six on the D.I.L. [Dangerously Ill List] last night. By now we could have six more. Take your pick."

"How long do you think I'll be with you?"

"Most likely, just tonight. Our Marcus men don't linger on the brink like your Hope females. They may come in in little pieces, but if the pieces can be stuck together the results usually show inside of their first forty-eight hours. If not, they're usually dead. But why so incensed? You love specialing."

"I do," I said, "in my own ward and when I can special a patient right through, as I did my classic pneumonia girl in Hope a few weeks ago. What I detest is being a one-night special in a strange ward and then being whisked away. One can't special anyone without getting fond of 'em. I love fussing over patients. When I have to leave one in mid-air I fuss to myself for days after. That's why I object strongly to the Office's plugging me in as an Automatic Nurse for one night!"

Aline laughed. "Little Miss Nightingale's off! I know what, Jo! You'll just have to sweet-talk your new chum, Old Red, into requesting the Office to leave you in Marcus for more than one night."

"Oh, no! I'd forgotten Marcus is one of his wards. I wonder now, is that good or bad?"

Gwenellen thought neither, as if Marcus tonight was anything like Marcus last night Old Red would be far too busy to remember meeting me in the subway.

Aline disagreed. "He is the S.S.O., and he did catch you breaking a rule. He won't forget that. He doesn't forget things. Look how he's remembered your aunt. And even though you do look like her, and probably even more like the way she did at our age,

I can't see that being enough to inspire him with over-confidence in you as a special. Face it, Jo, you were a nut to use that subway! Specials aren't supposed to be nutty. Watch it with him, Jo, and watch it with Humber. She gave me hell when I was her junior in Cas."

Humber was the name of the Marcus Night Staff Nurse. When we left Aline at Stanley and went on up to Marcus on the floor above I asked Gwenellen how she got along with Humber.

"I play her by ear, love. She has her dodgy moods. She's a good nurse. The men like her. They feel safe with her—and she can be quite human." She un-hooked her cloak collar as we had to wait at the outer door of Marcus whilst two porters wheeled out an empty accident trolley. "You'll get on with Humber, once she gets used to you."

"Thanks, chum." There was an open red screen across the open door of one of the two small wards. "Think that's for me?" I asked, following her into the small corridor we called the ward 'flat'.

"Ten to one." She took me into the nurses's changing-room.

17

Staff Nurse Humber was waiting for us. She was about twenty-seven, tall and very slim. She wore glasses with brown-winged frames that suited her pointed face and enhanced the impression she gave of being about to become airborne. "So you are here to special our Mr. Francis? H'm. From Hope? That's something."

I was puzzled. "Is he medical, Nurse Humber? In Marcus?"

"Nurse Dungarvan, this may have slipped your notice, but patients are human beings and not machines to which one can fix tidy little labels. Mr. Francis is in Marcus because he was knocked down crossing a road this morning and has a double fracture of the right tib. and fib. He was conscious on admission, explained he had felt unwell for the last few days and had intended seeing a doctor today. He wondered if he was getting appendicitis. He has acute lobar pneumonia. I take it you do know the symptoms can be similar?"

"Yes. Sister Hope told me she'd known a couple of pneumonias opened up by mistake."

"Who, with any experience, hasn't?"

demanded Staff Nurse Humber coldly. She looked me over with an expression that matched her tone. "I've been told you've recently specialed a similar medical case, but as Mr. Francis is an accident case in addition to being allergic to antibiotics, personally I would have considered him a case for a trained special. However, as the Office seem to have decided otherwise, let's get in for the report."

Sister Marcus gave me a rather warmer welcome. "I am most grateful to Hope Ward for sparing you, Nurse Dungarvan. Sit down, my dears." She blotted her final entry in her vast, diary-type report book. "Another heavy night for you, I'm afraid, Nurse Humber. We've been admitting and transferring all day. This weather, of course. Now." She sorted some notes. "As the general report does not concern Nurse Dungarvan, I'll deal with her patient first. He is in Small Ward Two. His name is Mr. William Charles Francis; age 26; occupation journalist; religion Church of England; next-of-kin father; addresses of both in the Admission Book;

admitted to Casualty at 10.20 a. m.—" and she went on to tell us all I had heard from Humber. "After his pneumonia had been diagnosed by the Senior Surgical Officer the diagnosis was confirmed at Mr. Leland's request by the Senior Medical Officer," Sister added, then broke off to explain to the night junior, a second-year, that this was routine hospital etiquette when a surgical patient produced a medical complaint, or vice versa. The patient then came under both the S.M.O. and S.S.O.

Mr. Francis's fractures had been reduced and set, and a plaster splint applied by the S.S.O. under a local anaesthetic in the ward that afternoon. Sister Marcus said the condition of his injured leg was satisfactory. She regretted she could not say the same about his chest and general condition, and explained why in detail. "The major complication," she continued, "is his total inability to tolerate antibiotics. We have checked with his own doctor. It would be highly unwise to attempt using them, and in consequence we have on our hands what I can only describe as an old-fashioned case of acute lobar pneumonia. In the pre-penicillin and pre-antibiotic days, which none of you will remember, pneumonia was a very dangerous illness." Sister looked at me. "As you have recently seen for yourself."

"Yes, Sister."

"Then you will know what is required of you." Not that she left it there. She went, point by point, through the medical and nursing treatment. "You must particularly encourage him to drink, Nurse Dungarvan. He is too restless for a drip, and fluids are essential. He has found that a little hard to understand."

Nurse Humber looked up from studying Mr. Francis's oxygen-intake record. "Forgive my asking, Sister, but why is he using a mask? Have we run out of tents?"

"No. We put him in a tent, but he found the sensation of being, as he put it, sealed up so distressing that the idea had to be abandoned. He's none too happy with a mask, but happier. As the peace of mind of all patients is important, but never so important as in pneumonia, the compromise was essential."

Humber voiced the thought in my mind. "Is he difficult, Sister?"

"I wouldn't say that, Nurse Humber.

I think he is just an ill and shocked young man with the highly strung temperament of so many artistic people. Very reasonably, he is worried about himself. A vivid imagination can be no help to a sufferer from serious illness, unless we can help that sufferer to use his imagination as an ally." Sister turned to me once more. "That'll be another of your jobs, Nurse Dungarvan. Keep him calm, cheerful, and above all convinced he can recover. Staff Nurse Humber will give you all the advice and assistance you need. Throughout tonight you are not to leave your patient unless you are properly relieved. If you want anything, ring. And before you leave us I want you all to hear what the Senior Medical Officer said to me half an hour ago. He said, "Sister, that boy has got to run his course to crisis, and whether he survives or not depends not on myself or on any other member of the medical staff of this hospital. His life hangs on two things—his own will to live and good nursing.' " Sister Marcus paused for a few seconds. "All right, Nurse Dungarvan. You may leave us."

Humber shot me a worried glance.

Suddenly she looked older than twenty-seven. I knew how she felt. That girl in Hope had recovered, but the night before her crisis she nearly died. As I walked out of the ward and round the red screen I felt as old as Humber and as worried as she was about my not yet having been fully trained. It was one thing to talk tritely about holding life in our hands; it was a very different matter to find oneself on the point of doing just that. Momentarily, I was dead scared. Then I adjusted the red screen behind me and went into Small Ward Two.

CHAPTER TWO

A VERY SPECIAL PATIENT

MR. FRANCIS was asleep. His day special, a girl called Daisy Yates, was taking his pulse. She was a fourth-year, already an S.R.N., and due to take Hospital Finals shortly. We had worked together in a couple of other wards. She acknowledged this with a raised thumb, but when she showed me the assortment of charts on the bed-table pushed against the wall she gave a thumbs-down over his fluid-intake. I mouthed, "I've been warned," and we changed over without uttering a word.

He was on a fifteen-minute pulse and respiration chart. I took his pulse again directly I was alone. It was as she had recorded. His skin was dry and hot, his breathing rapid and jerky. Occasionally, on expiring, he gave a queer little grunt that I did not like. At least he only grunted occasionally. I had heard those grunts before with every expiratory breath. Yet he looked much worse than my Hope girl

24

at this same stage, probably owing to the shock of his accident. He had been sedated and was propped in a sitting position with his plastered leg stretched out under a large bed-cradle. The plaster was quick-drying and only slightly damp. The sickly-sweet smell of plaster and ether hung in the air and struck a false note. It was like looking at one of those pictures in a children's book in which there was a glaringly obvious deliberate mistake. Marcus Small Ward Two had turned acute medical, but it smelt like a plaster theatre.

I checked the oxygen. His mask fitted well, the valve worked properly, the large cylinder in use was two-thirds full. A spare full cylinder stood against the wall behind his bed. In our medical blocks oxygen was laid on in pipelines, but as surgical patients seldom needed continuous oxygen for long periods, the surgical side still used cylinders.

I looked at his plastered leg. His toes were warm and a good colour, and there was no sign of swelling above or below the plaster. I stood looking him over for about a minute and then went round the room.

An extra bed-table had been brought in.

It was as lined with trays as the other table was with charts. I examined them one by one—drinks, thermometer, stethoscope, blood-pressure machine, plaster cut-down setting, emergency transfusion setting in a sealed tin, emergency tracheotomy setting in another, emergency hypodermic setting on the final sterile-towel-covered tray. I looked at each phial of heart stimulant in turn, the files, the needles in their sterile jar. If any of those emergency settings were needed they would be needed in a hurry, and it was the special nurse's job to know where everything was. If anything was missing it was the special's responsibility to ask for it, and ask fast.

On her way off, Sister Marcus came in with Humber. Shortly after Humber returned alone and toured the room, as I had done. Once satisfied, she took his pulse again, then watched him for a while. She said very quietly, "I'm glad he's so thin," and took herself off.

His sleep was restless. He kept twisting himself on to the side of his affected lung, but did not wake when I altered his position. His hair was dark and long enough to fall over his eyebrows when it dropped forward. When I pushed it back, as it made him look so hot, the skin of his forehead was burning.

A spasm of coughing woke him. His cough was short and harsh, painful for him and to hear. He stared at me blankly as I held him forward until the spasm passed. "Another new face," he muttered when back against his pillows. "Hello."

"Hello, Mr. Francis." I explained about my taking over from his day nurse. "I'm Nurse Dungarvan."

"Pretty name." He breathed carefully. "Irish?"

"Half." I shook down the thermometer. "My mother's English."

His eyes were brown and dulled by drugs, his temperature, and anxiety. When the thermometer was out he wanted to know his temperature.

"Up a bit."

"Don't be so bloody silly, Nurse! Not being a moron"—he coughed—"I can tell when I've got a fever. I want to know how high I've gone. I don't want to be treated as if I'm three years old and backward at that! What the devil is it?"

I hesitated. I was going to have to

manage him, and whether I was able to do that successfully depended very much on how I managed this moment. I could not possibly tell him the truth, as that would scare the daylights out of him. I did not want to lie, as I was sure he would see through that and in future mistrust me. Nor could I let him bully me. The consequences to any patient-nurse relationship once a nurse allowed that could be as disastrous, if more excusable, as when bullying took place the other way round.

I took refuge in the truth, if not with the truth he wanted. It had worked with other patients. I just hoped it would with him.

"Look," I said, "I do see your point, and I'm not trying to talk down to you, but if I went round telling you, or any other patient, their temperatures my bosses would kill me. I know it's your temperature. It's also my neck."

"Truly? You're not just stalling?"

"No. I'm being honest."

He blinked as he thought this over. He had long and thick eyelashes. "Point taken. Are you going to stay with me? Like that other nurse, today?"

"Yes."

"All night? Does that mean I'm very ill?"

I hedged that one. "It's more because you're in this little room by yourself. You're in here because there's no room in the main ward. Incidentally, in there they've got a senior staff nurse to look after them, plus two other nurses. You've just got me, and I'm only a third-year student nurse."

"That means I'm not too bad?"

"Indeed you're not. You're doing fine."

He said slowly, "I rather think I am." His eyes suddenly smiled. "If all I have to do to get a girl with your looks to spend a night with me is bust a leg"—he stopped for breath—"soon as I'm out of here I'm busting the other."

"A trifle drastic, Mr. Francis, but a new approach. Now, how about a little drink?"

"Christ! Don't you start that! I'm not thirsty. Just hot."

"A drink'll help cool you down."

"How?"

That was an answer I could give in medical detail, and so I did.

"See here," he protested when I had

finished, "there's nothing wrong with my kidneys."

"There will be, if you don't drink." I slid a hand beneath his head and raised the drinking-feeder to his lips. "Be a pal, Mr. Francis. If you won't consider your kidneys, just consider my neck."

He looked up. Our faces, of necessity, were close. "That's no hardship. You've a beautiful neck—among other things. You realize you are taking an unfair advantage?"

"It saddens me deeply, Mr. Francis. Ready?" I tilted the feeder. "Cheers."

It took a little time, but he drank the lot and went back to sleep. He woke from time to time and on each occasion drank a little more. Humber kept reappearing and checking his charts. After a couple of hours she stopped scowling over his fluid-intake.

The Senior Medical Officer came in with the Thoracic Registrar. The Night Superintendent with Humber. A junior night sister alone. The General Surgical Theatre was working late. It was after midnight before Tom Lofthouse, the G.S. houseman and Gwenellen's fiancé, was the first of the surgeons to arrive in Marcus for his night round. Humber brought him into the Small Ward to look at my patient's injured leg. Tom caught my eye behind her back and winked to acknowledge my presence on alien territory.

Mr. Francis was awake again. He saw Tom's wink. When we were alone he asked if the fair doctor in the short white coat was my boyfriend.

"No. He's a great friend engaged to another great friend."

"How cosy!" He yawned. "You engaged to one of his great friends?" I shook my head. "Why not? Don't you like doctors?"

He was very drowsy, and as I had no intention of letting him wake himself up with a conversation on my private life or anything else, I said I did not believe in mixing business and pleasure, and, as I hoped, the cliché put him to sleep.

Behind the screen Marcus settled into the night. The occasional murmur of a man's voice, the swish of a nurse's skirt, the creak of bed-springs, the chink of slung-weights shifting, the clink of a glass being replaced on a locker-top, floated in over the screen. I was conscious of these familiar night sounds without actually listening to them. I was too busy listening to my man's breathing. Those expiratory grunts were slowly increasing. Sometimes he winced in sleep. I found myself wincing with him.

Special nursing affected most nurses I knew the way it did me. One arrived at the bedside of a total stranger, and inside of a few hours that stranger became not merely the most important person in the world, but one's entire world. Mr. William Charles Francis was now "my man" to me, and "Dungarvan's man" to the other Marcus nurses.

That even included Humber. She sent Gwenellen to sit with him, because she wanted to tell me about a telephone call from General Francis.

We talked in the flat. "Your man's father, Dungarvan. This is the second time he's rung tonight. Night Super. took the first call, but I've just been speaking to him, and you'd better have the full picture." She went on to explain that General Francis was a widower, and semi-invalid. He lived in Devon. He had made arrangements to drive up to London tomorrow. He had suggested coming to-night, but Humber had explained that that was not necessary. "I offered him a bed in our relative's hostel, but he prefers to stay at his club, and, as he has this spinal arthritis, is bringing his own car and the man who looks after him. I think he'll probably be more comfortable in his club. He sounded very nice."

"Any others in the family to be contacted, Nurse?"

"No. The only other son, the younger one, is in the Army in Hong Kong. As your man is single and hasn't given us any name apart from his father's, I take it he's unattached. Or doesn't want his girlfriend worried—though that I doubt."

I asked, "Why, Nurse Humber?"

She shrugged. "In my experience patients who worry plus about themselves always enjoy the drama of spreading the worry around, particularly to their beloveds. But I could be maligning the lad. I haven't seen all that much of him awake, and God knows he's got good cause to worry. I don't think he looks at all well."

That final remark was hospital jargon for

"I think he looks close to dangerously ill."
A dangerously ill patient, in jargon, looked
"poorly".

Gwenellen relieved me again for my
night meal at one-thirty. On my return
she said my man had not woken and the
S.S.O. had been in. She told me this with
her lips, not her voice. Lip-reading was an
accomplishment we all acquired on nights.

I mouthed back, "He say anything?"

"Not to me. He never does. Maybe I
should use the subway?"

The last few hours had so driven my
off-duty life from my mind that, momentarily, I had no idea what she was getting
at.

I wrote a long letter to my aunt next
morning. "I've decided I must have
schizoid tendencies. When I switch off
my lamp I switch on me, and vice versa,
with no trouble at all. And though this
may sound macabre, I did enjoy last night
once it got going. I like my sick to be sick."

I asked if she remembered Old Red,
and described meeting him in the subway,
but not his current reputation, for that
would have been less than tactful, as I

34

hoped one day to marry them off, and unfair, since he had been so pleasant to me.

I was early for supper that night and on edge until I heard, "Nurse Dungarvan to Marcus Ward as special nurse for tonight." The Night Super. lowered her list. "Nurse Dungarvan, when are your next nights off?"

I stood up. "Tuesday, Wednesday, and Thursday, Sister."

"And your holiday starts tomorrow week?"

"Yes, Sister." Across the dining-room I saw Humber whisper something to one of the junior sisters and that sister nod in reply. Humber smiled in a relieved way. I sat down again longing to hit something hard.

Walking up with us to our wards, Aline said, "I guess they'll keep you in Marcus until your nights off, and then shove one of the day staff nurses on nights."

Gwenellen looked startled. "That a guess? Or have you heard something?"

"Only that Humber's been raising Cain all day about having to carry D.I.L.s in Marcus proper and Marcus Small Ward,

35

and how, though she's willing, she can't be in two places at once." She turned to me. "I know you specialed that girl in Hope, Jo, and right through, but she was in the main ward, wasn't she?"

"She was."

"Well, then," said Aline, "you must see Humber's angle."

Gwenellen and I said nothing. Gwenellen was a kind and tactful girl. I was a girl in a flaming temper.

Daisy Yates was waiting outside the red screen when I left Marcus main ward after the report. "His father's still with him. I've moved out to let them say their private good-nights."

"How is he?" I asked. Though I'd just had the official report, I wanted the inside story.

"Not too good." She sounded and looked weary. She was a large-boned girl, attractive rather than pretty, with a beautiful skin and naturally curly, short hair. On duty she strode about looking as if she could not wait to get off duty and chuck a discus. Yet out of uniform she looked like a fashion model. She had the best dress sense of any girl in Benedict's and a passion for altering the colour of her hair. She did this subtly, so as not to offend authority. She was now a discreet auburn, which suited her, but tonight enhanced the whiteness of her face. "The lad's spirits have been flagging somewhat. After supporting them all day I could use some support myself."

"I can imagine. How'd he take his father's arrival? Didn't scare him too much, I hope?"

"I was afraid it would make him turn his face to the wall. Then, luckily, Old Red had the bright idea of suggesting General Francis used his spinal trouble as his main reason for making this un-expected trip to Town. Our boy was quite bucked about that. Apparently his papa loathes hospitals and doctors, having had a bellyful before he had to leave the Army, and since than has flatly refused to discuss his back. But he's agreed to let Old Red fix him up with an appointment to see Mr. Remington-Hart, which is sensible, as nothing sounds so truthful as the truth."

"Remington-Hart? A neurological surgeon for arthritis? Why? Surely he needs an orthopod?"

37

Daisy smiled. "Surprisingly enough, Old Red has not given me his reasons. No doubt he has 'em."

"No doubt." I glanced round the screen. General Francis was now standing by the bed, leaning on his two walking sticks. He was a tallish, spare man. His eyes were the same amber-brown as his son's, but looked lighter, as his face was more tanned. His dark hair was heavily streaked with grey, but still very thick. "I hope someone can do something for him. He's so crippled." I had another look. "Much younger than I expected. He doesn't look anything like my idea of an old soldier. He looks more like—what? I know! A weary poet."

Daisy said dreamily, "I think he looks a dish. He must have been a knock-out when he was young. And though he's anti-hospital, his manners are out of this world."

She looked over my head and smiled. "Ah, here's Corporal Wix. Come for the General, Corporal? He's just leaving."

Coproral Wix was the retired soldier who now worked for General Francis. He was about fifty-five, short, sturdy, and very neat. His handshake made my knuckles ache. "How is Mr. Francis tonight, miss?" he asked Daisy.

"A little tired."

Apparently Corporal Wix understood hospital jargon. "Like as I said to the General, miss, the young gentleman'll have to be worse afore he's better."

Bill Francis looked so much worse in twelve hours that I had to control my expression when I went back to him. He was much more restless than last night, and, despite sleeping drugs, much more wakeful. He wanted to talk. As talking had helped Violet, the girl in Hope, I thought it a good idea to let him talk himself to sleep. Humber disagreed. At eleven she sent Gwenellen to take over temporarily and took me into the duty-room. "Why isn't he asleep, Dungarvan? His leg hurting?"

"Not since that injection he had an hour ago."

She frowned at his prescription sheet, which she had removed from the bed-table when she called me out. "He can't have anything more for at least three hours. He must sleep. Insomnia can be a dangerous symptom in pneumonia. It's your job to cope with his symptoms. You are letting him talk far too much."

I explained my reason. She was not impressed. She was saying so forcibly when the telephone interrupted her. She dismissed me with a jerk of her head and took the call. I had not been back with Bill Francis two minutes before she appeared. "Time I took the weight off my feet." She took my chair by his bed. "Telephone, Nurse Dungarvan. S.S.O."

God, I thought, and what does he want?

He told me. "I've had a general report on Mr. Francis. I now want to know about his fractured leg. How is it?"

"Comfortable, Mr. Leland."

"Nurse, I want a report, not a placebo!"

I grimaced at the wall. This was the Old Red I had heard about, and not the man I had met in the subway. I gave him a detailed surgical report.

"I gather he's not sleeping? Why not?"

I resisted the urge to retort with his curtness, "Because he's not sleepy," and gave all the medical reasons I could think of.

"He's got to sleep. But he wants to talk?"

"Yes, Mr. Leland."

"Then let him. It'll probably unwind him better than anything else." He rang off.

I assumed my best dumb-brunette expression when handing this on to Humber. I had no idea how she would take it, but on past showing from other senior staff nurses I suspected badly. Trained nurses, in general, object strongly to being taught their jobs either by their juniors or by doctors. Nursing was a matter for nurses. This was a nursing point.

Humber soared in my estimation. "Well, I'm damned! I don't hold with this therapy, but if the S.S.O. is backing you up, keep on your way. But it had better work."

It was another hour before it worked. In that hour I heard about life on a London newspaper, the great novel that was one day going to be written, the shock to the Francis family when the General's eldest son refused to go into the Army. "After four generations of soldiers on both sides the boy cried halt! My mama took it hard, but the old man was very decent. He's a decent old boy, is my old man.

We've never seen much of each other, but we have each other's number. Old Wix, of course, has never forgiven me. Have you seen old Wix?"

"Yes. When he came for your father. He looked sweet."

"Solid wood, you mean." He chuckled and started coughing. "I'll say this for old Wix," he went on when the spasm had passed, "though he doesn't approve of me for not toting a gun, he's bloody good to the old man." He was silent. "Think they can patch up his back?"

"I don't know enough about it to answer that honestly. I hope so."

He was silent for a little longer. He lay watching me with eyes that were at last getting drowsy. "You're very honest, aren't you, Nurse?" He reached for a corner of my apron. "You're the first honest girl I've met. Now I've met you"—he gave my apron a little tug—"I'm not letting you go." His voice was much slower. "Any objections?"

I smiled in answer. A minute later he went out like a light. He did not wake when the usual procession of night sisters and men in white coats came in and out.

They were careful not to disturb him. The Senior Medical Officer murmured, "Listening in to his chest can wait. Sleep's the main thing."

He had not woken when I returned from my meal at two. Gwenellen and I changed places soundlessly. I took his pulse, then sat back in the chair by his bed, my hands in my lap.

The uneasy silence of the small hours fell over the hospital. Uneasy, because during those hours so often the dying became the dead. That night, as on every night in Benedict's, in some ward in every block at least one patient was hovering on the outer edge of life. Sitting alone in that darkened little room, I could sense the shadow of death lying over the hospital as tangibly as I could see the shadows of night in the corners of the room and outside the window.

Bill Francis was not yet dying. His illness had to run its course to the crisis that would come any time between the fifth and the ninth day. The S.M.O. was of the opinion that this was the third, not second night, and that for twenty-four hours before he was knocked down the patch of consolidation had started forming in Bill Francis's lung. The S.M.O. said it was not unusual for normally healthy people, particularly young people, to misjudge the gravity of their own symptoms and write off feeling so ill as a hangover. "That's partly because, being unaccustomed to serious illness, they can't believe something like that can happen to them, partly because they don't want to believe it. Subconsciously they're frightened, so they put off seeing a doctor."

If the S.M.O. was right, which he was bound to be, being a very experienced physician, then the crisis would come any time from the day after tomorrow—when I would be on nights' off. Hell, I thought, hell! That was not only for selfish reasons. He had now grown accustomed to me, and, as he was too ill for any kind of polite act, had left me in no doubt that he liked me. Sister Hope always said that a sympathetic nurse-patient relationship was essential in any severe illness. "Picture yourselves, Nurses, feeling ill and wretched and having to put up with someone you disliked touching you, attending to you. It would be enough to send your temperature up each time that someone came on duty."

All patients disliked staff changes. If he had a new night special, even if he later grew to like her, he would start by trying to play her up just as he had me, and, since she had told me herself, Daisy Yates. That was not going to help him at all, even if it made Humber happier. God damn Humber, I thought, and got up to write on the charts on the bed-table. My move woke him, and he did not see me. "Nurse," he gasped, "where are you?"

Quickly I returned to him. "I'm here. It's all right, my dear." He clutched me like a terrified child waking from a nightmare. "I won't leave you. There, there." I held him against my shoulder. "Go back to sleep."

"Not yet. I daren't." He began to shiver. "Hold me, Nurse, hold me! I feel so queer. I feel I'm going to float away. Nurse—am I going to die?"

"Of course not! You just feel queer because you're packed full of drugs and you've got a bit of a temperature. Who wouldn't feel queer with that lot?"

"It's not that." He was calmer, with the

calmness of cold fear. "I just have that feeling—this is the end of the line. This is where I get off. It's nothing to do with those drugs you gave me. They made me feel muzzy. I'm not muzzy now. I feel"— his voice broke—"I can't die! Don't let me die! I want to live—" He began to cry.

"Now you listen to me." I held him in my arms. "There's no question at all of your dying—do you understand me? You're going to live. You're going to do all the things you want to do. You may feel queer for a while longer, but that's only because you're ill, and illness makes people feel queer. But you are not dying now, and you are not going to die."

He lifted his head to look at me. "How can you be so sure?"

I was not sure. There was no time for working on the right, soothing words. I used the first that came into my head. "For a start, because I'm not going to let you die—nor is anyone else in this hospital. This is the best hospital in the country. We know our stuff. We're tough cookies here, and so are you. You've got a long and full life ahead of you, chum, so you must now stop worrying and go back to sleep and catch up on the strength you'll need for living it up when you're better."

He said, "I never normally trust women. I trust you. Do you know why?" He reached up to touch my face as he answered himself. "I love you, Nurse Dungarvan. Isn't that something? I don't know your first name, but I love you. Do you mind?"

I was so relieved to see the fear that left him that I would not have minded had he asked me to get into bed with him. Nor would I have taken that any more seriously than I took his actual words. He sounded coherent, but he was too ill and doped to have any idea what he was saying. "All I mind is that you should tire yourself staying awake. Will you try and sleep now?"

"You'll stay?"

"You know I will." I helped him lie back. "Have one little drink and then off to sleep." I reached out behind me for the feeder on the locker-top. I nearly dropped it when I felt it being placed in my hand. I glanced round. Old Red stood by the locker. His nod told me to ignore him. I did so, outwardly. When I next looked round he had gone.

CHAPTER THREE

REUNION IN THE CAR-PARK

A JUNIOR night sister was waiting at the dining-room door that next evening. "The Assistant Matron wishes to see you straight away, Nurse Dungarvan."

I did not know if Matron was on that evening, but I did know she invariably did her own dirty work. That was no help to my instant gloom. Before I knocked on the Ass. Mat.'s door, in my own mind I had been slung out for encouraging unseemly behaviour from a male patient and was miserably working on the choice of my next career.

"Come in! Ah, it's Nurse Dungarvan!" announced the Ass. Mat. as if life was full of jolly little surprises. "Good. Close the door, Nurse."

A closed door in a hospital was an ugly sign. My gloom grew gloomier. "Good evening, Sister."

"And such a lovely evening! Did you sleep well?"

"Yes, thank you, Sister," I lied.

"Good." She smiled briskly. "Sleeping on night duty can be so difficult, particularly in warm weather. Sit down, my dear."

I sat on the edge of a chair. Had she been Matron, her telling me to sit down would have told me immediately that whatever her reason for wanting to see me it was not to sack me. When Matron had to be tough she kept a girl on her feet. But our Ass. Mat., though not as young as Matron, was great on being all-girls-together and thrashing things out across a table. Her opening remark now increased my gloom. "Matron has asked me to have a little talk to you about your temporary position as a special nurse in Marcus Ward. I understand you have been nursing"—she glanced at a note—"Mr. William Charles Francis since Saturday night?"

"Yes, Sister."

"A most interesting case."

"Yes, Sister."

"And tomorrow night you are due for nights off?"

My gloom vanished. Suddenly I recognized her attitude for what it was. That had taken me a little time, partly as I

49

was still sleepy, partly as I had so convinced myself Old Red had reported me. I saw now she was softening me up just to ask me a favour. "Yes, Sister. I should be off tomorrow night—"

"But you are not too happy at the prospect of leaving your special patient at this stage? How well I understand that, my dear! When I was a special nurse in the final year of my training . . . "

Ten minutes and five anecdotes later she returned to my nights off. Providing I had no objection, Marton wanted me to work on until my holiday and have three extra days tacked on the end. I had no objection at all. It was another ten minutes before the Ass. Mat. let me go. When I did, being a very experienced Ass. Mat., she had managed to give the impression authority was granting me a great favour. "Such an invaluable and very rare nursing experience, nowadays. You are very fortunate!"

In the dining-room Aline grunted. "Huh! Matron can't have any spare staff nurses. Humber'll create."

Humber was too busy to create that

night. In the evening rush-hour a lorry had skidded into a car and jammed it up against one of the pillar-boxes outside the hospital. There had been four men in the car. Three of them and the lorry-driver's mate were in Marcus when we came on. The lorry-driver had escaped with slight shock. The fourth car passenger was still too injured to be moved from the Accident Recovery Room in Casualty.

Sister Marcus said Mr. Francis was rather poorly and had been moved from the Seriously Ill to the Dangerously Ill List. The General was with him. "I expect he will stay a little longer," continued Sister. "His son likes having him there."

It was a Benedict's rule that the close relatives of a D.I.L. must be allowed unrestricted access to their ill relative. Some people took full advantage of this; quite as many others did not. "I mean, it's not as if there's anything I can do, is there, Nurse? He is in the best place, and I'm sure I'd only be in your way. You'll let me know if anything—well—happens—won't you?"

That had shocked me until I heard it

too often to remain shocked. It still left me feeling sickened by the whole human race, until some devoted parent, husband, wife, or adult child of an elderly parent put things right for me by spending days and nights at a bedside.

There was nothing General Francis could do, and because of his arthritis he could only sit with any comfort on a hard chair. He sat still and straight-backed, where his son could see him and exchange an occasional word or smile, but well out of my way. He did not move until Bill slid into a heavy sleep after midnight.

The S.S.O. arrived as he was leaving. Old Red watched the older man's slow movements clinically as he held aside the red screen, then followed him out to talk. I thought the S.S.O. seemed puzzled, but as the light was dim I could have been mistaken.

On his return he puzzled me by behaving exactly as I expected an S.S.O. to behave. If he remembered our meeting in the subway or my relationship to my aunt, very correctly, he gave no sign. He ignored me until forced to ask a professional query, and then asked it of my cap. Having received identical treatment from rows of Benedict's men on duty, I could not conceive why Old Red should be the object of so much wrath from my fellow nurses. Certainly his terse telephone technique had annoyed me last night, but not enough to make me want to spit at the sight of him. What was there about him? I wondered, watching him brood over the row of charts. At face value he was quite a man. He lacked General Francis's extreme, if ageing, good looks and enchanting manners, but take him out of his white coat and he'd be dead sexy. That, of course, was the answer. The girls would forgive fat little Dr. Curtis, the S.M.O., with his thinning hair and glasses for ignoring them, as who wanted to be noticed by Chubby Curtis? Also Chubby Curtis had a wife. Old Red was another matter.

Dr. Curtis came in with Humber a few minutes later. The two senior residents frowned in unison at the rising temperature chart. "He's a good age and build," said Dr. Curtis. "Let us thank God for youth when the antibiotics fail us. How's the leg shaping, Red?"

53

"Fine. He'll be in a walking plaster in a few days. I think I'm right in saying the plaster theatre's booked for him on Tuesday afternoon next week." He glanced briefly at Humber. "Will you tell Sister Marcus?"

"Yes, Mr. Leland." She caught my eye expressively as Dr. Curtis voiced our thoughts.

"Bit of an optimist, aren't you, Red?"

The S.S.O. was now watching the rise and fall of the little green rubber bag attached to the oxygen mask. "I don't think so."

Humber returned momentarily after the men had gone. "Old Red stuck his neck out all right. Hope to God he's right."

"Yes," I said, "yes."

She looked hard at me, and then at Bill Francis. He was so far under as to be very near coma. "Seeing 'em like that always ties my inside in knots, too. Oh, well, this won't soothe any fevered brows. I must get back to my poor mangled sods. I'm very much afraid one can't last the night, and I've ugly doubts about another. Ring if you want me."

No-one died in Marcus that night. In

the morning Humber, Gwenellen, and the night junior looked exhausted and triumphant. I was glad for them, but I only felt exhausted. Bill Francis had woken at dawn. He had been perfectly coherent and much too bright. He had insisted I call him Bill. "The day nurse does, so why not you? You'll have to get used to it when we're married. You do know you're going to marry me?"

"Frankly, no, as the question has not yet arisen."

"You mean I haven't asked you? My dear sweet angel, Nurse Dungarvan, I'm not that much of a mug! If I asked you now wouldn't you have to say 'no'? Hospital ethics and so forth?"

I did not take any of that seriously, though I would have had to be ice all through to hear it with utter indifference. I was slowly coming to realize that I was not at all indifferent to my patient. That was one reason why I was so exhausted that morning. He was a patient. Every Benedict's nurse was warned of the consequences to herself if she were fool enough to let herself get emotionally involved with a male patient, before she left the P.T.S. Briefly, it was the quickest way out.

Sister Marcus had looked perturbed by my night report. That was her half-day. She was still on duty when we went on that night. A coach filled with holiday-makers returning from a day-trip to the sea had hit a double-decker bus on a new clearway two miles from Benedict's. There were four emergency beds up in the centre of the ward. One of the coach passengers died just as we arrived on duty. Sister Marcus gave us the report with her sleeves rolled up. I had never before seen any Benedict's sister do that. But until last Saturday night I had never seen how a major accident ward looked directly after a major accident.

"Mr. Francis," began Sister Marcus, "is poorly."

General Francis spent all that night on his hard chair on the other side of the bed. Corporal Wix stayed as well. The duty room was lined with armchairs borrowed from other wards for the relatives of the crash victims. Humber offered the Corporal one of the armchairs. He barely used it. He removed his jacket, rolled up his sleeves, buttoned his tie inside his shirt, and, according to Gwenellen, took over Marcus ward kitchen. He made countless pots of tea, set and washed up tray after tray, helped the night junior hand round tea to the stunned, grey-faced rows of waiting relatives.

I told General Francis this in one of the quiet intervals when he and I were alone with his sleeping son. "The night staff are so grateful. They say he's as good as an extra night nurse."

"Wix is a good man. He'll be happier if he can make himself useful." Another theatre-trolley returning rumbled by on the far side of the red screen. "Do you have many nights like this?"

I explained my not being a Marcus regular nurse. "I gather this is bad for a mid-week night, but typical of any summer week-end. Bank Holidays, of course, are hospitals' nightmares."

"And I presume this sort of thing goes on all over the country?"

"I believe so. Particularly in hospitals near motorways. Ever since they opened our new clearway our accident intake has soared."

"It must place an intolerable burden on the staff. You work in shifts?"

"We—the nurses—do. The men do what is to all intents a twenty-four-hour shift seven days a week. Officially they get here one half-day and one free evening a week. Both have to end by eleven for their night rounds. Then they have alternate week-ends from Saturday afternoon to Sunday night. Again, they have to be back by eleven. How they stand—" I broke off to get up, quickly. "No, Bill, no! Don't try and pull off your mask. I know it's hot and uncomfortable, but it is helping you— that's it." He had stopped fighting me as my voice got through to him. "That's better." I turned his pillows, propping him higher. "Another drink, Bill?" I had to use a teaspoon. "Swallow, now. Good. Another swallow. Another."

Dr. Curtis had been in four times. He was still up when the theatre eventually stopped at three-forty, and returned with the S.S.O. The latter was in theatre clothes, with his green cap pushed back on his red head and his mask limp round his neck. He looked as tired as a man could be and still stand upright.

Bill did not recognize either man. "What's the bastard trying to do, Nurse Dungarvan?" he mumbled as Dr. Curtis tried to listen to his chest. "Tell him to get the hell out of it."

"Take it easy, son," said Dr. Curtis. "I'm a doctor. I only want to help you." He waited while I soothed Bill. "All right, son? Do you understand now your nurse has explained? Good. Good."

When I went off that morning Bill did not recognize me. He did not even know his father. I left the General sitting stiffly in his hard chair, one hand on one stick handle, the other resting on his son's bed. His set face was grey as the sky at dawn.

All the Marcus night nurses were late for breakfast. Sister Dining-room was annoyed. "Really, Nurse Humber! I do not expect to have to remind a senior staff nurse that she should have more consideration for my dining-room staff!"

The tables were nearly empty. We broke with tradition, and all four sat together. The Marcus night junior, though at the start of her second year, was on her first spell of nights. (No Benedict's first-year student nurses did night duty.) She fell asleep over her sausage and bacon. Humber shook her. "Wake up and eat, Lewis. You've one more night before your nights off, and tonight can be as bad or worse. If you don't eat you'll be ill."

Gwenellen's chubby and normally highly coloured cheeks were sallow with fatigue. "I haven't had a chance to ask anyone— how's Bill Francis ?"

"Still with us." Humber answered for me. "At the rate he's working up he's heading straight for a crisis some time today."

Nurse Lewis had been chewing with her eyes shut. She roused herself. "What happens then ?"

Humber raised one hand, stiffening her fingers and slicing the air sideways. "He'll shoot upwards, 105°, 106°, maybe higher. Then at the crucial point which only his body can decide, either he'll drop"—she slapped the table—"down to normal inside of a few hours, or his temp.'ll shoot even higher." She did not raise her hand again. "That, of course, will finish him."

"How high can a temp. go ?" asked Lewis.

Humber shrugged. "Kids can reach fantastic heights and live. I've never myself known of any adult getting away with going over 107. Have you, Dungarvan?"

I was finding this academic discussion unbearable. But as it had to be borne, I shook my head. "There was a woman in Hope who touched 107.8. She died. She wasn't young. My pneumonia girl, Violet, hit 106.8 plus at her peak. She was down to 99 in two hours. She did very well."

Nurse Lewis was keen and persistent. "But aren't women stronger than men?"

"Yep," grunted Humber. I said nothing.

Gwenellen said gently, "There's no question of his temp. coming down by lysis?" And before Lewis could ask what that was Gwenellen explained. "That's when the symptoms subside gradually over several days."

"Could that happen?" demanded Lewis.

"Not in this case." Humber and I spoke together, and then we were all silent.

Humber did not speak again until Lewis left us. "I'm sorry to have given you so little help last night, Dungarvan. I didn't dare leave my poor sods for more than split seconds."

"I knew that. I managed all right—I think."

"If I hadn't known you could by last night," she retorted, "I'd have got me a spare staff nurse even if it had meant taking this bloody hospital apart. If I had still thought you as slap-happy as I originally assumed—and bluntly, my child, you gave me the impression of being incapable of specialing a cold in the head—if the Night Super. had let me down I'd have gone over everyone's head and rung Matron's flat. I've done that once. It wasn't popular. Nor is the death of a patient through incompetent nursing, as on that occasion I pointed out. Matron herself was sweet." She grinned quickly. "The Night Super.'s never forgiven me. But as she needs me a hell of a lot more than I need her, we get along." She paused. "I suppose you heard I asked Sister Marcus to get you replaced?" I nodded. "Know why you weren't?"

"Matron had no spares?"

"It didn't get to Matron then. Sister Marcus first had to talk to the S.M.O. and S.S.O., as inevitably their views mattered. The S.M.O. said you had been a very good night special in Hope. The S.S.O. said he'd no complaints, and he was dead against changing specials, as that always upset the patient. Sister told Matron, and you stayed. I'm glad about that. I was wrong and I don't mind admitting it. To be fair to myself," she added with a faint smile, "if you will insist on looking like the original swinging teenager it's small wonder that the thought of trusting you with a really ill man put the fear of God up me." She jumped up, yawning. "I must go to bed before I fall asleep here like that child Lewis. See you both"—she corrected herself—"I hope we see you back with us tonight, Dungarvan. I hope your poor sod makes it."

Gwenellen and I sat on drinking tea while the dining-room was cleared around us. Gwenellen remarked suddenly, "She always calls 'em sods when she wants to weep about them."

My body was in the dining-room. My mind was in Small Ward Two. I blinked. "What's that?"

She repeated herself, and added, "She cares about 'em."

"I know. You said she was good. She

is." I stared into my empty cup. "Why didn't you tell me she wanted me out?"

"Why hand on bad news? Anyway, I thought she'd change her mind."

"Aline didn't."

"Aline's a born Cassandra, and she doesn't like Humber."

"I wonder why not?" I murmured, without really wondering or caring.

Gwenellen realized that. "Humber told me Red Leland thinks he'll make it."

"He's only a surgeon."

"An M.Chir. and F.R.C.S. picks up some medicine. I back him."

I looked up. "Honey, you didn't see what Bill Francis looked like this morning."

She had no answer to that. And since she shared Humber's and my attitude to our job, she did not give me the kind of pep-talk Aline would have come up with in these circumstances. Aline was probably the most efficient girl in our set, and unquestionably the cleverest. If she did not marry directly she finished training, which was highly probable, as she liked the lads as much as they liked her, before long she would be a Sister Tutor. She had the right academic approach to nursing to make a first-class tutor, but not ward sister. Patients, to Aline, were fascinating mental problems to be picked up each time one walked on duty and put down directly one walked out of the ward.

Up to a point we all learnt to do that. It had to be learnt, if we were not to turn into nervous wrecks. But every now and then some patient managed to break through the mental barrier erected by training, habit, and self-defence. Several times I had seen Gwenellen with that barrier down, but never Aline. Mine was down, now.

The dining-room staff were getting impatient. Gwenellen rose slowly, patted my shoulder. "Come on over, love."

I expected to lie awake for hours. I fell asleep as soon as I got into bed, then woke to full wakefulness at three that afternoon. The weather had changed; it was much cooler, the sky was overcast, and it was trying to rain. I stuck it out for about an hour, and then could not stand another minute. We were not allowed to get up early without permission, but I didn't give a damn for that. I got up and dressed in a sweater and pants, made my bed, then sat on the end and shook physically with anxiety. Then I faced the thought that by now he could be dead.

I neither knew nor cared whether my distress for him was based on love for a man or love for a patient. I had loved other patients. A few men, more women and children. There was Violet, young Mrs. King, old Mrs. Evans, and all in Hope. Georgie, Marion, Paul, Linda—the children's faces floated through my mind. David Grant in Arthur. He had been twenty-one when he died of leukaemia, and I had had to help with his last offices and was then sent to escort his body to the mortuary. I had then been a night junior. My senior had not been a Humber. She had been furious when she saw my mask was wet. "A good nurse learns to control her emotions, Dungarvan!" In the mortuary the night porters had swung open the huge white doors of the refrigerator and lifted the shrouded, stiffened body on to an empty shelf. The refrigerator had ticked loudly. The senior porter had said, "Sign here, please, Nurse," and been kind when he had to wait until I could see well enough to sign that No. 4 was David Alistair Grant from Arthur Ward.

I could not take any more thoughts, or my room. I let myself into our corridor, soundlessly, and crept down the back stairs and out of the back door without hearing or seeing any member of the Home staff.

That door opened into one of the staff car-parks that lay between the medical-school library and our Home. I stood looking round vaguely and trying to decide what to do. Being off duty, I was forbidden near Marcus in or out of uniform. If I rang the ward and gave a false name someone might recognize my voice. But there must be some way—there had to be some way of getting news. I'd go crazy if I had to wait until supper.

"Jo, darling! What on earth are you doing here and up? I was just about to go round and ask Night Home Sister if there was a chance of your being called early."

I gaped at the speaker as if she were a mirage. She was a youngish woman of my own height, build, and colouring. She wore a cream lined suit, a black straw boater, and black gloves. The fact that I had never seen my aunt looking so elegant added to my impression that I was imagining this. She never visited Benedict's. She said she didn't hold with looking back.

"Jo, what's up?"

In answer I did something I had not done in years. I flung my arms round my astonished aunt's neck and burst into tears on her shoulder.

She asked no more questions. She swept me away from the door, along a line of cars, into her aged scarlet mini, gave me a handkerchief, and let me cry it out. Then she said, "You've been on nights too long."

"It's not that." I sniffed. "What are you doing here?"

"I'm on my way home from Oxford, and thought this time I'd come through London and look you up." She handed me her powder compact, lipstick, and a comb. "Do your face, darling. Then tell me."

She listened without interrupting until I had said all I wanted to say. Her vivid blue eyes appraised me kindly and keenly. "I'll find out how he is for you. I'll ring Richard Leland." She looked at her watch. "Is tea still served in the Doctor's House?"

I was too rapt in my own problems to remember anyone else's. "Yes, but you can't ring Old Red! He's S.S.O.!"

"So you wrote in your letter, darling."

That did rouse me slightly from myself. "You do remember him?"

"Of course! Very well! Richard and I trained together. We're old friends. I haven't seen him in years, but he won't have changed. He's not the type. He was a sweet boy."

"He's no boy now! I can imagine what he'll think if you ring him up and say you've found me weeping over my special patient! What excuse could you give?"

"Jo, I told you, he's an old friend. I don't need any excuse. Nor will he think it odd if you are a little het-up. Everyone gets het-up over their special patients. Or are you rather more than just het-up?" I did not answer. "Darling, you are not imagining yourself in love with this young man?"

"Don't ask me what I'm imagining!"

"Jo, be careful! Remember, he's a patient."

"Like to bet?" I replied savagely.

She touched my hand. "Let's face

things one by one. Where are the nearest outside phone-boxes? Still in Cas.?" She jumped out of the car. "You wait here. If authority wants to know why, blame me. Say you were too tired this morning to remember to ask for permission to get up early to meet me and then woke at the right time and didn't want to let me down. As I'm not only an Old Benedictine, but was in the same set as Matron—God help me!—no-one'll object after that. I'll be quick as I can."

"Hold on—" Her back was to the car-park entrance. She did not see the S.S.O. coming quickly out of the library and crossing the entrance. "He's over there—he'll be across the road before you catch him."

My aunt swung round. She was twelve years younger than my father, and for years now I had called her Margaret, but until that moment I had always thought of her as firmly fixed in the older generation. She was by far the quietest, as well as much the nicest, of my four aunts, and normally a rather shy woman. Her reactions momentarily startled me out of my anxiety. Startled and enchanted me.

She seemed to shed ten years in one second as she hollered, "Oy, Richard!" at the top of her voice across the car-park.

His reactions affected me exactly as hers had done. His head jerked round. He stared at Margaret, then bellowed back, "Maggie!" He came to meet her so fast that the skirt of his white coat floated out behind him. "Maggie Dungarvan! I can't believe this!" He put his hands on her shoulders and kissed her, then held both her hands and smiled down at her as I had not seen him smile since I mentioned her name that night in the subway. "Maggie, you haven't changed at all! What are you doing here? How long are you staying?" he demanded eagerly.

His gaiety jarred. My anxiety had returned, and I hated him for being so happy. I almost hated Margaret. How could they both stand there smiling when Bill might be dead?

My aunt was explaining that she had come up to visit me. It was only then that Old Red noticed me in the car. He glanced at me as Margaret went on, "I feel very guilty at getting the poor child out of bed, as I know she's specialing a D.I.L. and worried stiff in the process. And how one worried as a special, I well remember." Her smile had vanished. "How's he doing, Richard?"

He went on smiling. "Well." Still holding her hands, he spoke to me over her head. "Dr. Curtis is well satisfied with your patient's chest, Nurse Dungarvan. His temperature dropped just over six degrees this morning. When I was in Marcus just now he was normal. Dr. Curtis expects him to stay there, so you may find yourself out of a job tonight."

I was smiling and smiling. "Mr. Leland, that's fabulous!"

"Very pleasing indeed. I'm sure you can appreciate his father's relief."

"He was there?"

"Yes. Sister Marcus has finally been able to persuade him to go back to his club for a short rest." He returned his attention to Margaret. "How long are you here for? Do you have to hurry off, or can you stay and have dinner with me later? As this is my free evening, I'm sure I can get away by seven. Can you wait?"

I was too happy to hear her answer, or even recollect they were there. Later she told me she was going to accept his invitation. By then I was hearing wedding bells, and not only for Old Red and Margaret.

CHAPTER FOUR

ONE MORNING ON A BYPASS

I WAS well into my holiday before I learnt Margaret's real reason for looking so elegant that afternoon. She had come on to Benedict's from an interview with her bank manager. "When father opened an account for me in that branch just across the river from the hospital in my P.T.S. days he advised me, if possible, never to move my account. I've made an arrangement with the Downshurst branch which is now years old. I'm now far too devoted to my Mr. MacQueen to consider depriving him of my overdraft."

"Do you always dress to kill for him?" I asked. "Isn't he married with four kids?"

"He is." Margaret smiled. "But if you ever need to borrow money, Jo, don't forget this; look as if money is the last thing you need. As Tom MacQueen himself once told me, banks will always lend you an umbrella, when it's not raining. I'm not saying getting all dressed solves

74

the problem, but, as bank managers are human, it does make 'em that much more willing to help try and solve it. With the Ellis family finances being in a perpetual state of crisis, I'm something of an expert on the subject of raising an overdraft."

Her husband's pay as a junior registrar had died with him. He had had no private income, pension, or—which had surprised me in the last few years—life insurance. After his death Margaret had had only a widowed mother's pension to support Dickie and herself. My paternal grandparents had died within a few months of each other whilst she was training, and as Grandfather had tied up all his savings in annuity for my grandmother, none of his children had inherited anything from him. Simon Ellis had lost both parents before he married, and his only brother had been killed in the last War. My father had helped Margaret during the early years, but directly Dickie had been old enough to board at his preparatory school Margaret had insisted on returning to nursing and becoming sole breadwinner. A gloriously unexpected legacy from a great-aunt had allowed her to use half to start buying her cottage and bank the other half for Dickie's education. It had not been a large legacy. My father frequently said he did not know how she managed. Margaret gave all the credit to her Mr. MacQueen. "A dour Scot. But his mother was left an impoverished widow. He sits there looking like John Knox being unimpressed by Mary Stuart, and just as I think he'll never let me increase my overdraft he says, 'Aye, life's not easy for a woman alone with no head for business. I'll do my best for you, Mrs. Ellis.' And I could willingly kiss him, if I wasn't sure that would shock him to death!"

I said smiling, "If you always look as fabulous as you did on Thursday when you visit him I wouldn't bet on that reaction. How did you make out then?"

She closed the living-room door before answering, even though Dickie had long gone to bed. "He thinks I can manage the first two year's bills at Dickie's new school, but after that I'll be cleaned out, so God alone knows what'll happen. Unless Dickie has passed in well enough to get a scholarship."

Dickie had just taken the entrance

examination required by his father's old public school. The results were due next week. Dickie's place had been booked at birth.

I said "He's a bright lad. Isn't there a good chance he may get a scholarship?"

She shrugged. "His present Head is hopeful, but, as he told me, no-one can predict exam. results. It's tough enough to get into that school. To get in on a scholarship means passing little short of brilliantly. Dickie realizes that. He took the exam. very seriously—in fact, far too seriously. He's always set his heart on going to Simon's school. He's trying to pretend he's not worrying about the results now, but I know he is."

I had noticed this. I did not say so.

She went on, "At least twelve is one year older than eleven. I've seen how Dickie's pals look when taking the eleven plus, and it makes me so mad, Jo! No child of that age should have to face something which they've the intelligence to realize can affect their whole lives, even if they are too young to appreciate, mercifully, just how much. The poor little things look white and strained and old. Yet don't ask me how else they can sort out the bright from the not-so-bright, as I don't know. I don't even know it's a good idea they should be sorted out. Personally, I'm not sure it is, though Dickie's Head insists it is, and he should know. I've got to leave that problem to the experts. The problem I can't leave is what do I do if Dickie just passes? Break his heart now by saying the school's too expensive? Or wait two years and break it then?"

I said tentatively, "Suppose in two years' time the situation was different?"

"In what way?"

"You might have more money."

"How? Think they'll raise our pay? Darling, we are nurses, not doctors."

I was on thin ice, and I knew it. Though she had dined with Red Leland that evening and had seemed as pleased to meet him again as he had been to see her, though I had frequently brought up his name since my holiday started, each time she had immediately changed the subject. I had not yet been able to fathom why.

"Well"—I was intentionally vague—"by then you might have won a football pool."

"Don't do 'em. I don't know how. Do you?"

"No. So that's out. Well, then how about —if you marry again?"

Her expression was thoughtful as well as amused. "Are you suggesting I remarry to pay Dickie's school bills? An idea. I can't say I like it."

"But wouldn't you like to marry again?"

"In theory, yes, very much. In practice, I'm not so sure it would work out."

"Why not?"

She took her time. "Lots of reasons."

"Such as?"

"To begin with, I've been on my own a long time, and the longer one is alone the more used to it and the more choosey one becomes. Also, the more independent. I never aimed to be an independent, career-woman type, but on being jerked into it by Simon's death I've had to become one. It would be folly to pretend that at least part of me doesn't love independence, or that very independent women make the most adaptable of wives. And wives, my child, to make a success of marriage, must adapt."

"Surely, with the right man that would work out?"

She said, "Sweetie, don't forget I not only need the right man for me, but the right stepfather for Dickie. Ready-made good fathers who are free to marry and in my age-group aren't easily come by. Then there's another snag. As far as I'm concerned, Dickie must come first. Now I know the love for a man and the love for one's child are two totally different things, but it's not always simple for the father of one's child to understand that. To expect a man to understand it about another man's son is expecting a very great deal."

"But lots of second marriages are happy."

"And lots are not, particularly for the kids. No father's tough on a kid, but the wrong father can be far worse. I might take a gamble for myself. I'd never risk gambling Dickie."

Old Red was in the right age-group and free. As he had no children, how could anyone say what kind of a father he would make until given a chance to prove it himself?

"Margaret, I hope you don't mind my saying this, but aren't you forgetting that in a few years Dickie'll be grown up? And what then?"

"He'll move out and live his own life."

"And you'll be alone."

"Yes, dear. But if you're about to suggest I marry now for companionship later, don't. Though I may well seem aged to you, Jo, I'm not yet that old." She smiled self-derisively. "Or if I am I don't feel it. At the same time, I'm a long way from being young enough to imagine, as you do, that marriage is the answer to all life's little problems. On the contrary, and if this is corny I can't help it, as it's still true, it's when one marries that one's real problems start. I think I've enough of my own without looking round for a few more."

"But if you did you'd have someone to help with your problems! And, Margaret —don't you get lonely?"

"Obviously, Jo. Who, on their own, doesn't? But there are worse things than loneliness, and I'm old enough to have seen 'em. I've often come home from a job, or visiting so-called happily married friends, and thanked heaven fasting for my lot. I'm not complaining."

"I know!" I snapped crossly. "But it's time you did!"

"Phooey! You've got marriage on the brain tonight, darling. Must be this wedding you're going to tomorrow. What time do you want the car?"

"Ten-thirty-ish do?"

"Fine." She stood up. "Let's go to bed."

I knew when I was beaten. I went glumly upstairs. Fond as I was of Margaret, I could willingly have shaken her. She was behaving like an ostrich about Old Red—and a stubborn ostrich at that! From what I had gathered of her dinner with him in town, despite her obvious pleasure in meeting him again, she had given the poor man a straight brush-off. She had told him she was unlikely to be in Town again in the foreseeable future, and was sure he was far too busy to have time to drive down to Sussex. I had asked, "Why not?" She had laughed. "Where's the S.S.O. with energy for a one-hundred-and-twenty-odd-mile drive there and back?"

To comfort myself I reread Bill's letter. He had got my address from Aline, who had moved to Marcus to replace Gwenellen, who had flu. I had returned to Hope from the night after Bill's crisis. He wrote: "I nearly died again when you didn't appear." His plaster had been changed, and he had written whilst it dried. Once dry, they were letting him up. He hoped to join his father in Devon next week. General Francis had seen Mr. Remington-Hart on Monday. "He has not said anything about it to me," the letter continued,

but as he is making plans to leave Town this week-end, I fear the result was no dice. I know he would like me to send you his regards. He took quite a shine to you, did my old man. Like father, like son.

I now want to thank you. How the hell can I? Even though words are my trade, I don't know the right words. You may think you just nursed me. That I was just another job. Maybe. I think you saved my life. I think that had you not been with me on the black nights I would have died. You may forget me, though now I hope you won't! I'll never forget you. I want to see you again just as soon as they let me out of this hospital. May I, please, please, please?

I realize you can't write me here. I'll be in touch, my love—as you must know you are.

Yours—and this is no euphemism.

BILL FRANCIS

Dickie had just collected the afternoon post from the postman in the lane and given me my letter before taking in the rest to his mother. I had not yet told Margaret it was from Bill. It was bound to worry her, as he was still a patient and I felt she had more than enough on her plate already without my adding anything. Or, rather, that was my excuse to myself when the letter first arrived and sent me sailing up on to Cloud Nine. Reading it again that night, I discovered that, as usually happens, my motives were mixed. I did not want to worry her, but neither did I want to discuss him, even with Margaret. I did not really know why not.

I suspected it was because I had never been properly in love with anyone before, and the sensation was too strange, too pleasant, and too personal for sharing.

Margaret and I were very alike temperamentally. Suddenly it occurred to me to wonder if this was her real reason for refusing to discuss Red Leland. I was very much happier by the time I went to sleep.

The wedding to which I had been invited was taking place in a village church ten miles the other side of Downshurst, a market town eleven miles from my aunt's cottage. Dickie wolf-whistled when I appeared in my fine clothes. "I say, Jo, you look smashing! I dig that hat! Is it going to stay on?"

"Honest to God, I hope so! I've fixed it with two cap-pins." I turned round. "Do they show?"

Margaret examined the pale-blue Breton sailor hat with the enormous upturned brim that by sheer luck exactly toned with my dress and jacket. "Not a trace. You look a dolly. Careful with that hat when you get into the mini."

85

Dickie studied my skirt. "Is that a proper mini-skirt, Jo?"

"No. It's only two inches above my knees; a proper mini should be at least six. I thought with this hat this dress was short enough. Anyway, it's my best."

"Can you sit down in it?" asked Margaret.

"With care and a large handbag to slap on my knees." I picked up my bag and gloves. "What's the time? Twenty to? Hell! I'll be late."

"The bride'll be later, darling. Take it easy on the roads. And don't forget to wear my safety-belt, or your aged aunt will never lend you her car again."

"Don't worry, I won't. Having just spent a few nights in a major-accident ward, I'd rather be late than hurry."

They came out to the car with me. Dickie wanted to know who was getting married. "No-one's told me."

"Yes, I did, muggins! Yesterday, when we were doing the lawn. I was at school with the bride. Her name's Gillian, and she's marrying a schoolmaster. A David Benson." My cousin was groaning loudly. "What's up now?"

"Who'd want to marry one of that lot? Ugh!"

It was a lovely day and high summer. The traffic was quite heavy on the country lanes to Downshurst. On the Downshurst bypass there were six steady lanes of vehicles coming and going between London and the sea.

I had to travel about five miles on the bypass, and as the mini was elderly used the slow lane, to be sandwiched between a milk lorry ahead and a crowded estate-car, roughly as old as the mini, behind. On the upward curve over the first down the lorry was forced to a crawl. Margaret's mini was passed soaring up hills, so I changed into low gear and closed the windows so as not to be suffocated by diesel fumes. In the driving mirror I saw the driver of the estate-car was growing restive. Twice he attempted to overtake, but we had reached the top of the hill before a gap in the stream of cars streaking up on our right allowed him to slip in between the lorry and myself.

The lorry speeded up on the downhill run to the next roundabout and the huge road-signs giving warning of the end of the twin carriageway and the start of two-way traffic. Directly we reached the single main road the estate-car's off-side indicator began flickering. The driver had five passengers—three women and two men. From the stack of suitcases strapped on the overhead rack and the fact that they were driving away from the coast I guessed they were returning from a holiday. They were not very young and from the back-slapping and laughter I could see through the glass rear doors in fine form.

The lorry-driver had not waved the estate-driver on. The latter sounded his horn impatiently, and without waiting for any sign nosed his car into the middle lane, accelerating as he did so. Instantly, urgently, the lorry-driver's arm appeared to wave him back. The lorry-driver's reactions were quick, but not quick enough, as the estate-car-driver's acceleration beat him to it. He was abreast with the lorry when I saw the oncoming small black car overtaking on the other side, and overtaking fast. It took a conscious effort to resist the urge to close my eyes, while

I signalled to the traffic behind and made an emergency stop. The safety-belt held me back as I jerked forward and at the same second heard the ghastly clash of metal hitting metal.

The estate-car reeled drunkenly, shot sideways across the road and oncoming traffic, and came to rest with its bonnet jammed in the sloping grass bank edging the road on the other side. It only missed hitting an oncoming white sports-car by inches and by the swiftness of the young sports-car-driver's reaction. He swerved across the road between my mini and the car behind without touching either of us, and stopped his unharmed car on our grass verge about fifty feet away.

I realized all that later. At the actual moment I was transfixed with horror by the antics of the small black car. The impact had caused it to buck like a frightened horse. It turned right over backwards, spun briefly upside down like a top, then, still upside down, skidded into the back of the now stationary lorry. The jolt dislodged the back row of heavy milk-churns. They topped over the chain holding them in place, spilling themselves and their contents into the road. Within seconds the road was white with milk. On the driver's side of the wrecked black car the whiteness was turning red.

The lorry-driver jumped down as I leapt out of the mini and ran to the black car. At the back of my mind I was conscious of feeling very cold and of legs heavy as lead.

"I warned the bugger!" gasped the lorry-driver unsteadily. "I warned the bugger to stay back! Didn't you see me, girl?" He shook his fist at the driver of the estate-car, who had climbed out and was staring blankly across the road. "See what you done?" he shouted.

The estate-car-driver's stare did not alter. His passengers were filing out in a dazed little procession. There was no movement from the little black car, and the stain on the road was spreading.

I heard my voice say, "I can't get this door open." It did not sound like my voice.

The lorry-driver was about forty and powerfully built. He tried, failed, cursed. "Jammed. Let's have a go at that other, mate." He pushed aside another man.

90

"One of them's cut bad from all this bleeding blood—my Gawd!" The door was open, and the crumpled figure of a man had toppled from the passenger seat into the road. "Look at the poor bugger's face—" His arm hit me across the waist. "Keep back, girl!"

"No." I ducked under his arm and went on my knees. "Let me see if it's him that's bleeding. I'm a nurse."

A small crowd was round us. A woman screamed. "His face!" Somewhere close I heard someone vomiting. I nearly did so myself. I had to force down the wave of nausea. It was impossible to tell the age of the man who owned that face, what he had looked like five minutes ago, or even that that was the face of a man. But he was breathing, and he was not having an arterial haemorrhage. "See he's able to breathe and don't move him," I said, to no-one in particular, pulling off my hat before half-diving, half-crawling, into the upturned car.

I concentrated now on the driver. His legs were jammed. He was hanging upside down, and he was so soaked in blood that it was a few more seconds before

I discovered the severed artery was somewhere in his left leg. I used his own tie as a tourniquet. "Anyone got a pen? Or pencil?" I called. A hand offered me a ball-point pen. I pushed it into the tie-knot and twisted, hard.

"Stopped it, have you miss?" The lorry-driver's face appeared briefly on a level with mine. He had taken charge outside. He had sent the young sports-car-driver to ring for the police and ambulance at a phone-box a mile or so back. He had detailed another man to direct the traffic. I heard him growling at the crowd. "You heard what the lady said. You let that poor bugger be. Gawd knows how he's breathing proper, but he is, so don't you go shoving him around. Do more harm than good, see. Like the lady said."

A police motor-cyclist arrived first. "Stand back, please—back you get, sir—madam—let me get by." He crouched in the doorway, pulling off his leather gloves. "That one still alive, miss?"

"Just. His pulse is very poor."

"Reckon from the state of this car it would be. You a doctor, miss?"

"A nurse in training." I jerked my head. "I was in that mini."

He nodded and crept forward carefully to examine the driver. "Lost a good bit, hasn't he? Only the one leg as is bleeding?"

"Far as I can tell. From the feel I'd say both are broken. Ambulance coming?"

"On its way. We'd best not try to shift him out until it gets here in case we start up more bleeding. Will you be all right with him while I take a better look at the other bloke?" He touched the unconscious driver's head. "Don't much fancy leaving him hanging like this."

"At least it's keeping what blood he's got left in his head."

"True, miss. Too true." He uncurled himself and disappeared.

A police-car had arrived. Suddenly the wrecked car was surrounded by uniformed figures. Two ambulances came together. One of the ambulance men crawled in to take my place whilst his colleagues consulted with the police on the best method of releasing the driver.

There was so little space in the car

and I was so cramped that one of the policemen lifted me bodily out on to the road. He set me on my feet. "All right then, miss?"

"Yes, thanks," I lied. I was now shaking with delayed-action shock.

I did not fool him. "You best sit down, miss. I'll fetch one of the ambulance lads to take a look at you soon as we get this bloke out."

"You leave the little lady to me, mate." The lorry-driver was at my elbow. "I'll keep an eye on her." He sat with me on the grass verge and with unsteady hands rolled a cigarette. "Give you a fag, miss?"

"Thanks, but I don't smoke."

"Me daughters don't neither. Me lads —Gawd—like chimneys they are, the silly young baskets!" He inhaled gratefully. "Not that I can't be doing with this now."

"I can imagine," I said, and we were silent.

It was around fifteen minutes before the combined efforts of four policemen and two ambulance men succeeded and the driver was lifted from the wreck.

The lorry-driver had offered his help. A police-sergeant told him to stay where he was. "You look as if you've had your lot for today, mister."

"He can say that again," the lorry-driver confided to me. "Gets me in the guts, this does. Always the way of it."

"You've seen a lot of accidents?"

"Ten years," he said, "ten years I've had on this milk run, see, and I see more accidents than I've had Sunday dinners. But I not seen one yet as you might call a proper bleeding accident, if you takes my meaning?"

"Yes. Yes, I do."

Across the road a large grey car suddenly pulled out of the Downshurst-bound traffic and stopped on the grass verge beyond the estate-car and the police busy with tape-measures and notebooks. I noticed it vaguely. The lorry-driver was more observant. "What's this, then? More top brass?" he inquired of the policeman standing over us as he wrote down our names and addresses.

The policeman glanced round. "Not one of ours. 7 Oak Cottages, Hurstly, did you say, Mr. Jemps?"

The wedding was at Hurstly. The name reminded me of that, but the peculiar detachment of shock prevented the reminder from disturbing me in the slightest. I stared at the road and was not really surprised by the discovery that I recognized the man in a grey suit crossing with a police-sergeant. I did not even wonder mildly what on earth the S.S.O. of Benedict's was doing on the Downshurst bypass on a mid-week morning. It was my first personal experience of the extraordinary anaesthetizing powers of physical shock. I felt as if my brain and body were stuffed with cotton-wool. It was a rather soothing sensation.

The police-sergeant told his junior the gentleman was a doctor and a friend of the young lady's and returned to the other side of the road. The lorry-driver was now my mate. He said he was real glad to meet any friend of the little lady's, and weren't it a turn-up for the book the gent. should be a doc.? "Just passing was you, like? Could've done with you earlier, mate."

"So I've heard. A very unpleasant experience all round." Old Red was studying me clinically. "I've been told you're un-hurt, but I see you've picked up plenty of gore. How do you feel?"

"I'm all right, thanks, Mr. Leland."

"Good." He smiled professionally and took my pulse. "Rightish, if not quite right. Why not lie down?"

I lay back, listening to Mr. Jemps, the lorryman, giving the policeman a very clear and fair account of the accident. Old Red offered cigarettes all round. Only Mr. Jemps accepted. Red lit one for himself. I had not seen him smoke before, and did not know he did. The sight of him standing there smoking made me realize how little any of us in Bene-dict's knew what he was really like as a man, once out of the defensive armour of his white coat. I had seen him turn human with Margaret, but that glimpse had not been enough to tell me now whether he had stopped on recognizing me for her sake or because I was a Bene-dict's nurse. Either way I thought it a nice gesture, and when I next caught his eye I smiled. He smiled back, not pro-fessionally, but rather shyly.

The policeman had finished with Mr.

Jemps. He apologized for having to trouble me. "Best to get these things down straight away, miss. Care to tell me what you saw?"

"One moment, Officer." Red took my pulse again. "If you don't feel up to it you don't have to talk now, Nurse Dungarvan. You can make a statement later."

I sat up. "I'd rather get it over. I'm much less muzzy now."

"Right." He sat beside me and lent me his shoulder as a back-rest. My detachment was breaking up. Momentarily I realized exactly what I was doing. When I tell the girls, I thought, they'll not believe one word of this. I would not blame them. It was hard enough to believe now, myself.

At last the policeman shut his notebook. "Much obliged, Miss Dungarvan, Mr. Jemps. We'll not need to detain you any longer, so when you feel like moving off you do that. We'll be in touch with the two of you later." He turned to Old Red. "I take it you'll be seeing the young lady's looked after, Doctor? Nasty. Very nasty. Still, I reckon it could have been worse. No stiffs."

"And you know who you got to thank for that, mate, don't you?" Mr. Jemps got on his feet belligerently. "This pretty little lady here. Quick as a bleeding flash she was, the way she bunged herself head first into that little black job and stopped that poor bugger who was bleeding like a bloody stuck pig, afore any of your lot got here. But for her he'd be a stiff this very minute, and I'm not telling you no lies! Proper bleeding little heroine your young lady is, Doctor!" he informed Old Red. "You mind you look after her real good. Cruel shook up, she is now, like as you don't need to be no doctor to see, but she weren't shook up when she got a job to do!" He rubbed his hand on the seat of his pants before offering it to me. "I'd best get what's left of my milk on the road, or I'll have the Guv'nor after me. See you in court then, eh, miss? I'll fetch the wife along. Always had a hankering to be a nurse, she did. Real keen, she'll be, to meet you."

"I should like to meet her, Mr. Jemps. And thank you very much. You were wonderful."

Old Red waited until the Jemps-Dungarvan mutual-admiration society had broken up and Mr. Jemps was climbing into his lorry. "Where were you off to, originally?"

"A wedding." Normality had returned, but without affecting the conviction that I now shared with my mate Jemps and the cops that the S.S.O. of Benedict's was my official source of strength and comfort. "Do you know, I'd forgotten all about it?"

"I believe you." I had moved from his shoulder, so he got up and retrieved my hat. It was now lying higher up the bank behind us. "This yours?"

"Yes. Thanks." I looked it over. "It'll do again—" I looked down. "God! My dress won't. What time is it?"

"Ten to twelve."

"Then if I go back and change I can still make the reception."

He considered me curiously. "You feel up to facing a wedding reception? After this?"

"Quite honestly, no. But there's no more I can do here. The bride is one of my greatest school friends. We always promised to be at each other's wedding, and if I don't turn up she'll be upset. If I ring and invent some excuse she knows me too well not to see through it. But how can I tell a girl this sort of truth on her wedding day? It'll cast a hellish blight. Talk of accidents always does."

"But how will you explain matters when you do eventually arrive?

"I'll think of something. I'll say I forgot the time or date or way, or something. Gillian's always been convinced I'm a complete nut, and one of the advantages of being a known nut is that one can always get people to believe one's acted in a nutty way."

"Is that so?" His eyes were amused. "I can see that could be useful. You don't object to being a known nut?"

"I used not to. I used to think it a big giggle. Now I find it gets a bit tedious sometimes." I thought of Humber. "My own fault, of course, for always acting first and thinking later."

"Not always a fault, as your friend Mr. Jemps would most forcibly agree." The faintly rigid lines of his normal expression in Benedict's had relaxed. He looked and sounded so unlike his Benedict's self that once again I forgot his alter ego. He was just Margaret's old chum who had loaned me a shoulder and was still metaphorically holding my hand. I was grateful for that invisible handclasp and for his last remark.

"Well, thanks. There certainly wasn't time for thought just now, and had there been I'd probably have been sick." I looked at the mini. "I'd better move if I'm going to go back and change."

"Staying with your aunt, aren't you? Right. I don't think you should drive yourself yet. I'll run you back to Maggie's, and when you've changed we can come back here and pick up your mini. I'll have a word with the cops about leaving it here. I doubt they'll object."

I was relieved for myself, as I had been dreading driving again so soon. I was delighted for Margaret. I had to make a polite pretence at reluctance. "Won't it take you very much out of your way?"

"A little, but that's not important. I'm not due in Downshurst for another hour. I'm lunching with Mr. and Mrs. Remington-Hart. I hoped I'd have a chance to call in on your aunt some time today, and thought I'd ring from Downshurst to ask if it would be convenient. Is she home this morning?"

"Yes. She'll be in all day, as I've got her car." I stood up eagerly. "Thank you very much. I'd love a lift back."

"Good." He spoke to one of the police-men. "Your car can wait," he said on returning. "Let's go."

We had to wait before crossing the road. As we did so he explained he had taken the day off, instead of next Sunday, which would have been part of his free week-end. He wanted to see Mr. Remington-Hart about some patient and to spend next Sunday catching up on "cold" cases. These were the patients with non-acute surgical conditions on the long waiting-list for non-acute—*i.e.* cold—beds. "We haven't a free surgical bed today, and, by some chance, today we are quiet. So I gave myself the day off."

I looked at the empty estate-car when we reached the other side. "I wonder what happened to them?"

He knew the answer from the police-sergeant to whom he had first spoken.

"They had a few minor cuts and bruises and slight shock. They went in the first ambulance with the man with the facial injuries. The second took the man you dealt with."

"Do you think they'll do?"

It was a stupid question, as he had not seen any of the victims. Instead of slapping me down, as any surgeon could quite reasonably have done in those circumstances, and particularly a surgeon with his reputed bite, he said simply, "Not having seen them, I can't truthfully answer you, but from what I've heard the two in the black car should have a fair chance. How old were they?"

"I've no idea at all about the man with the face. The other"—I hesitated—"well—not young, definitely. Thirty-fivish —forty. About that."

"I see." A smile flickered over his face. "Though definitely not young, that's still not too old for there to be a considerable amount of resilience present. That's the vital element, and whilst it remains the human body can survive the most amazing injuries. As a general rule, the very old and the very young have the least in reserve, though one meets the occasional nonagenarian with the resilience of a twenty-year-old." He stopped, smiling apologetically. "I beg your pardon. I'm riding a pet hobby-horse."

"I wish you'd go on. I'm interested. I love 'shop' talk."

He looked at me hard, realized I was being honest, and did as I asked. I guessed that was in part to help me over my shock, in part as I was Margaret's niece, but also, as I was now discovering, because, though a naturally reserved man, having once forced himself to open up, in common with most reserved people, he was now having no difficulty in talking. As hospital 'shop' fascinated him, he was very interesting, and surprisingly amusing. I enjoyed that drive, and when it ended was more anxious than ever to shake some sense into Margaret. I thought he would make me a delightful Uncle Richard.

CHAPTER FIVE

THE GENERAL COMES TO TEA

THERE were two cars outside the cottage
that evening—Old Red's grey and a new
black Rolls which I assumed belonged to
Mr. Remington-Hart. Whilst I had
changed into my second set of wedding
clothes Margaret had explained that the
Remington-Harts had bought a country
house in Downhurst in the last year.
They were childless. Mrs. Remington-
Hart was qualified and did public health
in London. Bernard Remington-Hart had
originally started at Benedict's in the same
year as Simon Ellis.

"In here, Jo!" called Margaret from
the sitting-room. "General Francis and
Corporal Wix have been hoping you'd be
back before they had to leave for London."

I was delighted to see the General
again, and not merely as he was Bill's
father. Though he did not make me as
starry-eyed as Daisy Yates, he was the
best-looking man of any age I had ever

seen, and I adored his old-fashioned manners. Though crippled, he managed to give any woman in his presence the conviction that she was delicate, helpless, and ultra-decorative, and could rely on him to shelter her from life's cruel blows. "General, how nice to see you! Hello, Corporal!" Rather unfairly, as he had been very nice that morning, it was a few minutes before I remembered there was a third guest present. "Hello, again, Mr. Leland."

He nodded amiably. "Good wedding?"

"Splendid, thanks. They've now gone on a fishing honeymoon. Not my idea of romance—takes all sorts."

Everyone smiled. Richard admitted he liked fishing. "Me too," put in Dickie. "It's smashing!"

General Francis said it so happened that he owned the fishing rights on a fairly respectable stretch of water. "As you're a fisherman, Mr. Leland, if you'd care to come down to Devon during this present season I'd be most happy to offer you unlimited fishing." He smiled at Dickie. "If your mother can spare you, boy, perhaps you'll visit us?" He turned to Margaret. "I feel sure you'll understand that it will give me great satisfaction to entertain your niece's young cousin. We can fit him out with rods and waders, and Wix'll look after him well. We'd enjoy having a boy around the house again, eh, Wix?"

"That's right, sir! Be like old times!"

Margaret said warmly, "This is very kind, General."

"It would give me great pleasure." General Francis looked from Margaret to Red Leland.

The latter had been watching General Francis and Margaret alternately. I amused myself watching all three and rather cruelly thanking God for the poor old General's disability. Margaret, out of uniform, was still shy with strangers. How she had survived a nurse's training and remained shy was beyond me, but the fact remained she had. I had seen shyness stiffen her into a quite absurd primness. Had General Francis not had his two sticks propped against his chair as a tangible reminder of his condition, and had he not, as had now been explained to me, been making this social call to thank me for nursing

108

his son after paying a second professional visit himself to Bernard Remington-Hart, his appearance and that Rolls outside would have frozen Margaret into a prissy caricature of her normal self. Fortunately, being a nurse, she had the built-in weakness for the sick that belongs to all nurses. I did not know if she was aware of the fact, but she was treating the General like one of her patients. She was an excellent nurse and sweet to her patients, which was why she was in constant demand in the neighbourhood as a private nurse. But for her insistence on being free for Dickie's holidays she could have had a ward sister's job in Benedict's by just picking up the nearest telephone.

I suspected it was Margaret, rather than the General, who was responsible for the continued mellowing of Red Leland. He looked and sounded now so unlike Old Red, the reputed scourge of Benedict's, that I couldn't wait for my holiday to end to let me get back and tell the girls. But before our guests left I had reluctantly decided this was one story not for telling. It could be a very important story, and, knowing the damage our grape-vine could do with any story, the only way to stop that was to keep this one to myself.

And they call the young mixed-up! I smiled grimly to myself, still watching the trio holding one conversation aloud and a second with their eyes. Compared to this little middle-aged lot, we didn't get to first base! It was so fascinating to observe that I was very sorry when the party broke up, and even more so when Margaret did not ask her old pal Richard to stay on for supper with us after the Rolls drove away.

"Why," I demanded as the grey car disappeared, "didn't you?"

"Darling, you know very well he's got to be back for his night round."

"That's not till eleven. Three hours."

"He's S.S.O. S.S.O.'s aren't supposed to cut things so fine." She turned to go inside. "Has Dickie told you yet you had a phone-call?" she asked over her shoulder.

Bill Francis had rung me from Marcus half an hour before I got back. Dickie said, "When I heard them say it was St. Benedict's Hospital I thought it must be for Mr. Leland, so I called him. But he said it was for you and gave me the phone back to take a message. Your boy-friend said to say he was sorry he had missed you, and he'd be writing and was doing nicely. He said he was a Bill Francis, so I told him we had a General Francis talking to Mum in the sitting-room, and he seemed ever so surprised! The General," he added chattily, "was surprised too."

"Honest to God!" I sat on the stairs. "Margaret, how did your chum Richard take my being rung up by a patient?"

"I don't expect he liked it, darling, but you are on holiday, and though it was very naughty of that boy to risk ringing you from a ward, you can scarcely be held responsible."

"I hope you're right. Luckily Old Red was in a very good mood." Bill's call had shaken me in more ways than one, so I dispensed with discretion. "Thanks to you. He likes you a lot."

"We've always liked each other." She went into the kitchen to prepare supper.

I followed her. "How well did you two know each other? Was he one of your boyfriends? Did he date you?"

"We went out together. He wasn't so much a boyfriend as a boy who was one of my friends." She began cracking eggs into a bowl. "He's nearly a year younger than I am, but we always got on very well. And that doesn't mean what it would mean if said by one of your generation!"

"Come off it, Margaret! You're not that old!"

"I feel it, when you tell me of the apparently acceptable behaviour amongst your contemporaries." She smiled. "I feel I must have trained in the Dark Ages. But when I started at Benedict's nineteen years ago, and during my training, though a few forced the pace, no-one thought one odd, or sick, if one didn't leap into bed with one's boyfriend, or indulge in violent necking sessions on every date. You may not believe this, but though Richard and I have now known each other for eighteen years on and off, the first time he kissed me was in the car-park last Thursday."

"You're not serious?"

"Perfectly," She laughed. "Shall I shock

you more with another truth? I was engaged to Simon for six months and a virgin when I married."

"You were? Wasn't it a hideous strain?"

"Possibly. But not unenjoyable. You kids must miss an awful lot in your eagerness to sip the heady cup of life, as your grandfather used to say. How can you get the taste at a gulp?" She beat the eggs. "Mind if I ask, have you gulped?" I shook my head. "Why not?"

I said slowly. "It could be because I've never been dated by anyone I liked enough." I winced at a memory. "It could be Rosie."

"Who was Rosie?"

"She was twenty-four. She came into Dorothy when I was on days there at the end of my first year." Dorothy Ward was gynaecological. "She had had a criminal abortion somewhere. She would never say where, or who did it. She collapsed, they turned her out of the house, and literally left her to die on the pavement outside. She was given five pints on admission. The cops searched the house. They found instruments, but were never able to pin it on anyone."

"She die?"

"Not at once." I stared out of the kitchen window. Dickie was standing on his head in the garden. I did not see him. "She was doing quite nicely when she suddenly developed gas gangrene. Dirty instruments. She was plugged with everything we'd got. It wasn't enough." I paused, looking backwards. "She was very pretty. She had long brown hair. We did it in two plaits with huge white bandage bows. I'd never met gangrene before. The smell was terrible. She wanted to live. She fought like hell. She's the only person I've seen die really horribly. We got rather matey. I don't know if this was true, but she told me she had only slept with the man once. He never came to see her."

"Could have been true. Once is enough."

I nodded. That was something else I had learned in Dorothy Ward.

Dickie appeared at the window. "I say, wasn't that Rolls a smashing job! Are all generals loaded?"

Margaret said she thought General Francis must have more than his pension to run a Rolls, own fishing rights, and

114

pay a full-time manservant. "Did you realize Bill Francis had a wealthy father, Jo?"

"No. Neither the General nor Bill gave me any hint of lolly."

"I think that reflects rather well on them both. Lay the table, children. I'm about to cook omelettes."

I had a postcard from Aline next day. She said she was enjoying Marcus, but not working with Humber again. "Gwenellen's on sick-leave and going to O.P.D. on days when she gets back. You are going to Cas."

I passed the card around the breakfast table. "Isn't that life? I detest departmental nursing, so whenever a department's short, there they send me!"

The following morning Margaret had two letters. The one in Richard Leland's handwriting she kept to herself. She handed round the "thank you" letter from General Francis.

Hoping for another letter from Bill, I began watching our post as closely as Dickie. Neither of us had had the letter we wanted when the penultimate day of my holiday arrived. Margaret and Dickie were in the garden playing badminton when Mr. Remington-Hart rang up and asked to speak to my aunt.

Dickie was taut as an overstrung violin that day. His examination results were now overdue. I took Margaret's place to keep him occupied. She was away some time, and returned looking thoughtful.

"What did he want, Mum?" asked Dickie.

"To discuss a patient I nursed for him years ago. Let's have that racket, Jo. I know you want to wash your hair for tomorrow."

She roasted a chicken and made a fresh fruit trifle for supper as it was my last night. Both were Dickie's favourites, and though normally he ate twice as much as his mother and myself put together, he refused second helpings. When Margaret said, "How about bed, darling?" instead of his usual protests he obeyed immediately, and even agreed to have a bath.

She was silent until we heard him upstairs. "Poor little thing, he's so on edge! Going to Simon's old school is his

Big Dream. I've been thinking, Jo. If I work through the holidays as well as the terms, and get another mortgage, perhaps I can manage those fees. It'll mean seeing so much less of him, and God knows I seem to see little enough already, but being an only boy I've felt I must pack him off to boarding-school to get some men in his life and break the apron-strings. I'll tell you this; every term when I watch that school train go out I feel as if it's taking two-thirds of me with it."

"I've always known that. But if you work in the holidays, what'll you do with Dickie?"

"Holiday camps or something. I dunno. I'll have to think about it. I'll get the coffee."

She was in the kitchen and Dickie in the bath when the telephone rang. I answered it, then put my head round the kitchen door. "Dickie's headmaster."

Margaret stared at me, then shot by me into the hall. I did not know how Dickie heard over the noise of the running taps, but at her "He's got it! Oh, Mr. Perkins, thank you for ringing tonight!"

he appeared swathed in a towel at the head of the stairs. Two minutes later, in damp pyjamas, he was swinging Margaret round and round the little hall. "Bully for old Perky!" he chanted. "Bully for old Pongy Perky! He said I'd be a sort of ape not to get a sort of scholarship as I sort of could if I sort of used my noggin! I say, Mum, I'm starving! Can we have a celebration nosh?"

He ate three-quarters of a two-pound fruit cake, six thick jam sandwiches, four apples, two oranges, and finished off the chicken and the fruit trifle. "That's better. May as well go to bed now."

Margaret went up with him. I heard yells of laughter. On her return she flopped into an armchair, and we smiled at each other.

She said, "I'm so glad to have you here to share this, Jo. I often think I miss not having someone with whom to share the joys of Dickie, far more than I miss having someone with whom to share my worries. I'm so proud of my son tonight! Bursting with pride, and I can say it to you! Think of this, darling! My son! And he's got the highest marks of any candidate taking that entrance exam.! In all England! My Dickie! His Head is as thrilled as myself. It's only a small prep. school. He said, 'Your boy obviously has the ability to give of his best when his best is required. A boy with that ability is a boy who should go far.' Oh, Jo!" Tears poured down her face. "I'm so happy. I feel twenty years younger."

She looked it.

Much later I asked, "Do you still miss Simon a lot?"

She hesitated. "Twelve years is a long time. There are times now when I can't even remember what it was like to be a wife. When I look back the me of those days bears no relation at all to the me now. It's odd how much one changes without being aware of it. I didn't realize how much I've changed, until I was back in Benedict's the other day. And seeing Richard in a white coat." She paused. "My God, how it all came back?" she added softly.

"Too much?"

"Much too much for comfort."

"I can imagine. Yet, is that such a bad thing?"

"That's roughly what Richard said when I dined with him. He asked why I never took a case in Benedict's Private Wing. I said I didn't hold with raising ghosts. He said nor did he, but sometimes one had to raise 'em to lay 'em." She fiddled with the arm of her chair. "He gave me quite a stern lecture on the subject. I don't know whether he's responsible for the offer I had from Bernard Remington-Hart this morning. I've a notion he is."

"Offer? I thought you said R.-H. rang to talk about an old patient?"

"He did. We discussed a man I nursed for him about seven years ago in a London nursing home. The man had an aortic aneurysm at the base of the spine. Bernard excised it and put in a piece of nylon."

"Automatic Heart job?"

"Of course. Bernard did a very good job. He's done some very good spinal work. He's got another spinal problem at the moment. He's not yet sure if it's operable, but if it is he wants me to take the case. It has to be in Benedict's Wing." She shot me an almost scared glance. "Can I face it, Jo? I don't know."

"Margaret, you must! After all, why not? Yes, of course, I know your reasons —but be honest! Is there a nicer hospital to work in? Haven't you always said the more you've seen of other hospitals the more you've realized there's only one Benedict's?"

"Yes." Again she hesitated. "You haven't asked who's the patient?"

"Should I? Anyone I know?"

"General Francis. That's why it has to be Benedict's. Bernard says he flatly refuses to be done anywhere else. He now trusts Benedict's. And that wretched Richard," she added impatiently, "has got me right in a corner by bringing that nice man here and letting him invite Dickie down to Devon. I'm going to feel so ungrateful if I refuse. As Bernard said, and I had to agree, private nurses with the right technical experience for such a case don't grow on gooseberry-bushes."

I said very carefully, "Yes, I do see that if your pal Richard is behind this he has put you in a corner. But it might not be his fault, and it would be wonderful if something could be done for that old

General. He is such a sweetie. When do you have to make up your mind?"

"Not for some time. Bernard won't be doing him until after Dickie's back at school. I promised to think it over and let him know."

"Margaret," I coaxed, "say yes, if only for the General's sake. Didn't you think him a doll?"

She smiled faintly. "No. Just a very nice man."

"Well, then! Oh, this is fab! Bill'll be so thrilled!"

"Hey, Jo! This is a strict professional confidence! No raising of false hopes. This is just for the trade, still all very much in the air," she warned, "and not the trade at large. You're not to say one word of any of this to your pals when you get back to Benedict's."

"I won't, I promise."

Before I left for London next day Margaret had the official confirmation of Dickie's examination results. The delay had been caused by one set of papers going temporarily astray in the post. Each of us in turn read aloud the splendid sentence. "The Board of Governors have pleasure in offering your son, Richard Simon Michael Ellis, the following School Scholarship."

Dickie read the figures and calculated fast. "Mum! In five years this'll come to over two thousand pounds! Gosh! I never thought I'd cost so much! Did you?"

"It crossed my mind, darling. More toast?"

I looked at the letter again. "Dickie, why are you Richard Simon Michael?"

" 'Cos my Dad was Simon Richard and Grandpa was Michael. Shove us the marmalade, Jo."

Margaret smiled at me over the table as if she had read my mind and was too happy to be anything but amused by the fact. I returned her smile. "I like the name Richard."

"Now there," said Margaret, "I do agree with you, Jo."

CHAPTER SIX

CASUALTY HAS A NAUTICAL AIR

SISTER CASUALTY had been two years junior to Margaret in training. After she had finished midwifery and two years as a Benedict's junior sister she had joined the Royal Navy as a nursing sister for a few years. She had returned to Benedict's and been appointed to Casualty after working for six months with the retiring Sister Casualty, five years ago.

She described her R.N. experience as "not her tot of rum". "Never seemed to nurse anything but gastric matelots. Nothing against matelots. Damn good chaps. Never much cared for gastrics. But admin., that's my right berth."

The Royal Navy had left its mark. In Casualty we did not report for duty, we came aboard; we worked watches, not shifts; when we went off duty we went ashore; on our days off we took the liberty boat.

Sister Casualty off duty invariably wore

a trouser suit, white shirt, and silk cravat in assorted colours. As she was just under six foot tall and very slim, wore her dark hair closely cropped, and her face though free of make-up was not unattractive, the result was certainly striking. In uniform she looked very dignified and very nice, and she ran Casualty so efficiently that without her various little ways her professional skill would have been enough to account for her already being a hospital legend in her own lifetime.

She was very kind to the patients, and for that they would gladly have forgiven her personal idiosyncrasies, if they noticed them, which was unlikely. She was "the Sister". To nine patients out of ten she was the first hospital sister with whom they had been confronted, and the great majority, when they walked, were pushed, or were carried for the first time through the double doors of our main entrance, were very apprehensive and trying to hide the fact. How they hid it depended largely on their education. The less-educated showed a nervous awe; the better, generally, open belligerence. They knew their rights and they were going to get them. The hospital belonged to them. Hadn't they paid for it with their National Insurance stamps, income tax, and rates? They had heard how hospitals messed people about with all that unnecessary waiting and medical jargon, and if anyone tried to treat them like illiterate peasants there'd be a letter in the post to some M.P. before the day was out!

Sister Casualty handled them all magnificently, each patient different, and yet each one as if he or she was her sole reason for taking up nursing. She had a remarkable memory for names and faces, which helped, but above all it was her genuine kindness that not even the most irate could withstand. "No question," they told each other in educated voices, "that woman's doing her best for us. One can't blame her for faults in the system." Which was true.

On my first morning she had taken one look at me. "Ah, yes, Dungarvan! Clearly a relation to Maggie Ellis, *née* Dungarvan. Your aunt, eh? God! That makes me feel long in the tooth, gal!" She patted my arm. "Welcome aboard!

In which other departmental establishments have you previously served?"

"Out Patients and the General Theatre, Sister," I replied, resisting the urge to salute by holding my hands more tightly behind my back in the correct position for any Benedict's nurse when talking to a senior.

"Both'll help you here, if not very much. You've been sent to join my Accident Recovery Room team as soon as possible, but I refuse to allow my gals near my A.R.R. until they've found their sea-legs. I'd say that'll take you around three weeks. It may have to be less if we are rushed. For today, Staff Nurse Fields will be your guide, comforter, and friend. What Staff Nurse Fields becomes tomorrow depends on you. Tomorrow you will do alone the work you've been shown today, but under her supervision. By the third day I expect third-years to work alone, and if you slip up, gal, I'll have your guts for garters! Got that?" That time I had to stifle an "aye, aye". "Yes, Sister."

"Good." She patted me again. "Now, your watches. You'll be on from 7.30 a.m.

to 4 p.m. this week; next week, 1.30 p.m. to 10 p.m.; third week, 3 p.m. to midnight. Then back to square one. Right?"

"Yes, Sister." It could not have suited me better. If Bill's leg went according to form he should be back in town for his first follow-up clinic when I started my second all-day shift with its row of free evenings. I had hoped there would be a letter from him waiting at Benedict's when I returned last night. I was a little disappointed it had not been there, but I was quite sure he would write again in the next few days. Having said so much in his first letter, he was bound to follow it up. If not, he would never have written at all.

Sister Casualty said now we had everything ship-shape, how was her old oppo Maggie Ellis. "Nice gal. Good senior. Did her own work and didn't expect me to clear up after her. You clear up after yourself, gal? You'd better if you know what's good for you! So your aunt's still nursing? Good. Always thought it a wicked waste of a good nurse when she chucked it to marry. Still, Simon Ellis was a Benedict's man."

She was voicing not only her own views, but those of authority at Benedict's. Authority never ceased to sigh when nurses left to marry, but if Benedict's nurses married Benedict's men, then authority sighed a little less loudly.

Staff Nurse Fields was the most senior of the five permanent Casualty staff nurses and Sister's official stand-in. She was in the same year as Humber, and had the same brisk efficiency, but was much more friendly. She was married, which probably explained that. Authority might prefer single nurses, but every student nurse I ever met preferred to work under a married senior. When Sister handed me over Mrs. Fields thrust a sheaf of lists of names at me. "Don't lose these. You'll need 'em. It'll be days before you remember who's who, but don't let Sister catch you checking up from your lists after your first week. That top list has the most vital names. Those in blue work in the Hall, those in red in the A.R.R. Unit. The most important name in the Hall is Dr. Jones, the Senior Casualty Officer. In the A.R.R. Unit it's Mr. Waring. He's the Senior Accident Casualty Officer."

Dr. Jones was a member of the Royal College of Physicians; Mr. Waring a Fellow of the Royal College of Surgeons. Both men were permanent members of the department with no ward responsibilities.

Mrs. Fields said, "As by some miracle the A.R.R. Unit is empty, I'll take you there first." She opened a door. "The Cleansing Theatre. This is where all bad accidents come first and have their clothes removed and first transfusions. It's really here that, if their lives can be saved, they are saved." She closed the door, opened another. "The Intensive Care Room. Accidents come here from the C.T. when they are not fit to stand the journey to the wards straight away." We moved on again. "This whole Unit has grown from the one room originally set aside for road accidents some years ago. Then there were no permanent senior residents in the department as now, and all the housemen had to double-up as C.O.s [Casualty Officers] here and housemen in the wards. They still do that in the Hall, but Mr. Waring has two registrars, two house-surgeons, and one anaesthetist on his permanent Accident team. Plus four nurses. It may seem a large Accident Staff. Often we could use double." She opened another door. "Burns."

Burns were my Achilles heel. I looked apprehensively at the five operating-type tables spaced far from each other round the wide tiled room. Each table was fitted with transfusion stands and connected up to the piped oxygen laid on throughout Casualty.

"Do you ever have to use all the tables at once?"

"Often enough for five to be necessary." She glanced over to the two male nursing orderlies testing an oxygen tent in the far corner. "Isn't that so, gentlemen?"

One of the orderlies was West Indian. His name was Nugent, and he had a beautiful voice. "So very right, Nurse Fields." He turned to his smaller, stouter colleague. "Isn't that the truth, man?"

His colleague, Luis, was a Spaniard. He had large, sad brown eyes. He raised them, expressively.

"Aie, aie aie. Remember, last week, no? Those children, no more than babies, and the mama had gone shopping and left on the oil-stove, no? Aie! How they looked!" He crossed himself.

I asked, "How did they do?"

The men looked at Mrs. Fields. She looked at the empty tables. "They didn't."

We were just finishing our tour of the many dressing, examination, and clinic rooms off the Hall when Mrs. Fields was summoned to Matron's Office to discuss her next holiday dates. Sister told me to wait outside her open duty-room door and watch all that was going on. "No better way of learning any new job." She turned as two uniformed policemen came in through the main entrance. "Have you gentlemen come to see the lady who fell backwards off a bus and hurt her knee twenty minutes ago? You'll find her in Room 3. Know the way?"

"Yes, thanks, Sister."

Sister explained to me, "The poor old dear's in a fine twitter as she thought the bus was stopping, not starting—" Sister shot off to meet an anxious young woman with a baby in her arms and a small tearful boy hanging on to her skirt. The boy had a messy bandage round his right knee. Sister crouched by him. "And what have you been doing to your knee, sonny?"

"He will climb that old fence back of our buildings, Sister. I've told him not to, and so has his dad," replied the mother, "but you know what boys are!" She stroked back her baby's hair. "I'm sorry to bring the baby, but I had to, as I'd no-one to leave him with."

"That's all right, m'dear. Very sensible of you to come up, as we'll need your consent for any treatment the doctor may decide on for your lad." She ruffled the boy's hair. "Like climbing, do you sonny? Jolly good fun, isn't it, when you don't fall off? Let's have a peep under that bandage—no—I won't hurt. Ah. Well, now, when you see the doctor, if he decides to mend you with one or two stitches, you tell him I said, could he please give you a stitch to take home in a matchbox? You'd like that to show your mates, wouldn't you?"

The child had been about to cry again. He stopped in mid-wail. "You bet! Smashing!"

Sister sent them off with one of the

Hall nurses and rejoined me. "I'm always glad to have mothers come up with their nippers. You'll be surprised at how many moppets we have bring themselves up. The very young have astonishing guts, but there's so little we're allowed to do for them without signed parental consent. Ah —an ambulance. This'll be another knee. You see."

She was right. A few minutes later a youth with a shattered left knee-cap was wheeled on a low-slung ambulance trolley into the Cleansing Theatre. He had come off his motor-bike.

Sister said, "Don't ask me why things always come in in triplicate. Can't explain. Fact remains, they do. Now what?" The oldest of the three porters running the glass-fronted lodge just inside the main entrance was putting a middle-aged woman with a blue hat into a wheel-chair. Sister returned after escorting the woman and porter into one of the examination rooms and leaving a nurse in her place. "Dr. Jones'll be in to look at that woman directly, Paddy," she told the old porter as he ambled up. "I've no doubt he'll ask Dr. Curtis to admit her to a cardiac ward."

"Sure, now, and there's no doubt in my mind at all, Sister! And hasn't she the very face of a heart?" He went on to his lodge.

Sister smiled at his blue-jacketed back.

"Paddy's an old salt. Knew directly I saw him put her in a wheel-chair that we'd a cardiac on our hands. Paddy doesn't put a patient in a chair at sight for nothing. He's far too good a diagnostician. Old Cas. porters get that way. You can always trust 'em gal. And what's he want now?" The old porter was returning, shaking his head gloomily. "Well, Paddy?"

"A bag, Sister. You'll be needing a paper bag."

Sister disappeared to talk to one of her staff nurses. Later she explained the reason for the paper bag.

"One of these." She showed me a large bag made of toughened brown paper with a sealing device at the mouth.

"These take the clothes of any vermin-infested patient." My expression amused her. "Did you think we no longer get 'em in alive?"

"Yes, Sister. My aunt has told me they still admitted quite a number of patients in that condition in her day, but I thought things had changed."

"Technique's changed, m'dear. So has treatment. We've new equipment, new drugs. But not new patients, because patients are human and human nature doesn't change. Some day, when you've time, ask one of the Sister Tutors to let you have one of the copies of the Casualty records for the last hundred years. You won't find very much difference in the type of patient we had in then, to now." She looked round the crowded Hall. "A hundred years ago they were carried in after coming off their horses, or being knocked down by carriages. There was a lot more tetanus, but no more than was carried in here fifty years ago in the First War. Twenty-five years ago they were knocked down by bombs. Now they get knocked down on the roads. The internal-combustion engine probably chews them up a lot more than anything that's gone before, but the patients themselves don't alter. The brave are still brave, the cowards cowardly, and the dirty are still alive from head to foot. So if you ever start scratching in Casualty don't dismiss it as the odd gnat-bite. Directly you go ashore have a bath, send everything you've been wearing to the laundry, and wash your hair. Mercifully, human lice still abhor cleanliness."

Gwenellen and I were the only members of our set on days. As Gwenellen now worked in the Out Patients Department, which closed at 6 p.m. from Mondays to Fridays and at 12.30 on Saturdays, she was enjoying one of the most envied and regular off-duty shifts in the hospital. Having all my evenings free that week, we spent most of them together. We agreed that without our set we felt as out of touch as two visitors from outer space. Gwenellen was seeing next to nothing of her fiancé, Tom Lofthouse, as the surgical side was having another of its regular breathless rushes. "Much more," said Gwenellen, "and I'll begin to wonder what my beloved looks like. Aline sees more of him on nights in Marcus."

"How's she getting on? I've not set eyes on her since I got back."

"When does anyone see the night girls, love? I've only run into her once when she was coming back from nights off. She was in fine form."

"Despite Humber?"

"They're still fighting it out."

"Poor Aline!" Gwenellen rolled her eyes.

"See here, I know you like Humber," I protested, "and so did I, eventually, but she's got a hellish bitchy exterior."

"Aline knows how to take care of herself. Talking of bitches, how are you getting on with old Sinbad in Cas.?"

I smiled. "I wouldn't call her a bitch."

"Indeed, nor would I, love," she replied in her most placid manner, and then we both laughed, rather unkindly. I said it was probably a good thing Cas. was always so busy, and Gwenellen, having already worked in Cas., advised me to avoid the splint room on the rare quiet night. "Have you heard Daisy Yates is joining you in Cas. when she gets back from holiday this week-end?"

"No. Good. I like Daisy. Why did no-one tell me? No-one ever tells me anything!"

"You're a fine one to talk!"

I thought of Bill. I had talked a great

deal to her about my nights in Marcus. I had tried to be discreet, as the subject was professional dynamite even when discussed in private with a great friend. I had had to talk about him to someone to ease my mind. He had still not written, and it was now beginning to worry me. "What's that supposed to mean?" I asked carefully.

She asked why I had said nothing about that accident on the bypass, or seeing Old Red and General Francis on my holiday.

I was astonished and relieved. For an ugly moment I had been convinced she had guessed the real reason for my avid professional interest in Bill Francis. As I did not now want her to guess my real reason for keeping quiet on this other matter, I used the truth, if not all the truth. "That accident was so bloody awful I didn't want to talk about it. How did you hear?"

"From Aline. She had it from your ex-special p., and he had it from his father. Old Red must have told the General. Ghastly, was it?"

"Yep."

"I should have worked that out for myself. I saw an accident at home once." She shuddered. "I can still throw up. I haven't Aline's academic approach either. She, of course, thinks you're just being dead crafty."

"Why?"

"Because she's still fixated with her idea that Old Red's been carrying a torch for your aunt for years, and it's now burst into a fine new flame. She thinks you don't want to spoil things with careless talk. I think that's a right load of old codswallop, and Tom agrees with me. If Old Red really wants your aunt, why wait all this time? They've both been free for years. Admittedly, he doesn't yet earn a fraction of the money a man of his age and experience would expect to earn outside, but he is on the way to the real big-time. And even now, as he never has time off for spending the twenty-something quid a week they'll dish him for the one-hundred and twenty-hour stint he puts in most weeks, he could just afford a wife and kid. Look at Chubby Curtis."

For once, I thought before speaking,

and so was able to refrain from remarking tritely that it took two to make a marriage. Aline's insight underlined my conviction on holiday that this was one tale not for retelling. If by one careless word now I backed up the rumours Aline was bound to be spreading at night, by tomorrow morning Tom Lofthouse, a chatty lad, would have it all round the Doctor's House. The men gossiped as much and as scurriously as ourselves. Any single senior resident had to accept as part of his job the fact that his juniors were going to speculate constantly on his lack of visible sex-life. If any gossip reached Red Leland I suspected he would shrug it off and forget it. But not Margaret. If she arrived in Benedict's to find herself established as his mistress, future wife, or both, she would promptly develop a new set of anti-Richard complexes to add to those she already had, and Heaven help his chances with her then!

I answered Gwenellen with a non-committal "Uh-huh," and, as I now knew the subject was safe, asked if she knew when Bill Francis was due in Out Patients for his first follow-up clinic.

"I'd like to know how his leg's getting on."

"I've not yet seen his name on the list. I'll let you know when I do."

"Thanks. I wish you would."

She went on to talk O.P.D. "shop". I did not hear much she was saying, as I was thinking of Margaret and how impossible it would be to get Gwenellen, or anyone else in Benedict's with the obvious exception of Old Red, to believe the real truth, if I attempted to explain it. They would assume, as I had until this last holiday, that Margaret was a widow from lack of opportunity, not choice, and must surely jump at the prospect of Red as a husband. He had so much to offer her, or any woman. Benedict's, like the world, was convinced every normal unattached woman wanted a man, and vice versa. I thought so, too. Yet I now had to accept, if not yet understand, that Margaret's fundamental reason for not remarrying was the plain fact that she did not want to. She did not want another man in her life. She just needed one.

The problem continued to bother me, and so did my lack of a letter from Bill.

One afternoon, a week later, I decided the time had come to stop dithering like a Victorian maiden and to write to Bill, when I got off at ten that night, asking if no news was good news. Daisy Yates showed me the postcard she had had from him that morning. "As he's sent his love to us all, take your share, Jo."

"Thanks very much."

When I got off, instead of letter-writing, I accepted a last-minute party date. I did not enjoy it much, but it was better than lying in bed feeling hurt, a failure, and gnashing my teeth in turn.

Next morning I continued to make excuses for Bill, but as I now know I was making them, they no longer soothed me. Some days later Gwenellen told me he had attended his first follow-up clinic two days previously. "Sorry I forgot to tell you. His leg's fine. He inquired after you and Daisy."

"How nice of him!"

The S.S.O. was crossing Casualty yard when I was going on duty that afternoon in a flaming temper. He was frequently in Cas., and generally ignored me, as he had done in Marcus. Occasionally he exchanged the time of day. Being in no mood for civilities, I was about to walk by with a brief "Afternoon" when he stopped. "I've just been talking to your aunt on the phone. She asked me to apologize to you, should I see you, for not having answered your last letter. Dick's off to Devon to fish on Monday. I'm driving him down. Any message for your aunt or cousin?"

On any day that would have pleased me. It now had the effect of a shot in the arm. I beamed up at my future Uncle Richard, asked him to give my love to Margaret and Dickie, my regards to the General and Co., and added my hope that he would have a good holiday.

"I hope so, Nurse Dungarvan. Thank you." He smiled and walked away. I went on into Casualty.

A junior C.O. called Robin Armstrong and a long, lanky student with a brown beatle-cut were leaning against the wall just inside the doorway. Robin I knew well. He was one of Aline's old flamers. "Hi, Robin," I murmured as I passed.

"Hi, Jo." He sounded faintly bemused. I guessed Sister had been beating him up again. She got on very well with most of the men, since, whatever their personal views on her, they admired and were grateful for her professional skill. But Robin Armstrong she did not like. She gave him hell at the slightest opportunity. As he was a rather slow and clumsy young man, he gave her plenty of opportunities.

He provided one now. Leaning against a Cas. wall when Sister was on the bridge was asking for an explosion. Sister suddenly spotted the pair and exploded. "Mr. Armstrong!" she bellowed across the crowded Hall. "If you have nothing better to do than prop up buildings, will you kindly go and find yourself a street corner and not clutter up my department! As for you, boy"—she bore down on the student —"are you one of my new dressers today? Then get your mask up and get into the Accident Unit! I am sure Mr. Waring requires your invaluable assistance!" Having dispatched them, she turned on me. "Back aboard, eh, Nurse Dungarvan? Deal with these." She handed me a stack of forms. "Quick Developing Unit, first. Take the wet plates for Christina Maris Anson straight up to Bertha Ward. Then get to the Out Patients Laboratory with this—" She paused as a police-sergeant appeared behind me. "Looking for your man, Sergeant? That petrol explosion? In the Burns Room of the Accident Unit, over there, third door on your right. And you'll need one of these." She gave him a disposable mask from the large glass-covered jar on a shelf by the door. "You know what to expect?"

"Aye, Sister." The man was grim. "It'll not be the first man I've seen after he's tried to fill up a car with a lighted cigarette in his mouth—nor the last. I heard as he was fried to a crisp."

Sister saw my wince as the policeman removed himself. "One way of putting it."

"Sister, such a cold-blooded way!"

"Cold-blooded words don't necessarily betoken a callous nature, as you should be well aware by this stage in your training. It's not what people say that gives 'em away, it's what they do." The Burns Room door had closed behind the police-sergeant. "I've had dealings with that man before. I've seen him crying like a child over a dead baby he carried in. His language would have made a Chief Petty Officer blush . . . But this won't get us out on the tide." She quickly finished all she had to tell me about my errands. "Cast off and don't dawdle!"

I did not dawdle, but as I had to pass our post pigeon-holes, from force of habit I looked in mine in case the second post had been sorted early. Mine was empty.

Hurrying on, I thought of Sister Cas.'s remarks, and then first of Violet in Hope. After her crisis she had said, "I'll never forget what you done for me, dear. I'll remember you all my life."

She had repeated those words when she said goodbye. She had gone to a convalescent home in Bournemouth. She had not even sent me a picture postcard. It would not be surprising if by now she had forgotten my name. After a dangerous illness few patients willingly looked back. The illness and those involved faded like a bad dream.

Bill had written one letter to thank me. He had rung the cottage.

Nice gestures both, I reflected bitterly, and both typical gestures of any young man in a hospital bed who temporarily imagines himself in love with one of his nurses as a form of occupational therapy.

My bitterness was directed solely at myself. How could I have been such a fool as to take him seriously? When all the time I had actually been with him I had always realized he was the type to make a pass at the nearest girl with his last gasp, and I had just happened to be that girl. Yet since leaving Marcus I had let my imagination blow it all into a Great Romance.

Yet it was not all imagination. At least, not as far as I was concerned. I could accept that I had been foolish, but that acceptance was not yet a sufficient antidote for the niggling little pain in my heart. I had just enough sense to appreciate that as a pain it rated no higher than a toothache. But a toothache can be a singularly uncomfortable experience.

CHAPTER SEVEN

A LETTER FROM MARGARET

IT was an unusually sultry afternoon, and Casualty on my return was emptier than I had yet seen it. Sister said she had no work for me for a few minutes, so I could direct traffic for her whilst she had a few words with Dr. Jones.

Mr. Wrigley, the head porter, fixed open the double-glass swing doors. "Quietish, eh, Nurse Dungarvan?"

"Very. What's keeping 'em away? The heat?"

"Nah. Thursday. Payday round here. When a day turns quiet, like, it's always on a Thursday."

I thought of the Thursday Red had given himself off. "Why's that, Mr. Wrigley? What's payday got to do with it? No-one needs money to come in here."

"And that's a fact, Nurse! But there's many a missus as needs to be home when her old man comes in from work on a Thursday, if she's to get her proper share of his pay-packet. Mind you, I'm not saying as that's what she'll get for the asking, and I'm not saying there's not many a man as'll hand over his pay-packet unopened, but there's enough of the other sort to give us a bit of a breather Thursdays." He surveyed the handful of patients waiting for attention outside the various Junior Casualty Officer's rooms. They were all elderly. "Proper Darby and Joan Club we run here of a Thursday. The old 'uns know if they come in now they'll be seen nice and easy and have time for a chat-up with their old mates."

He walked slowly back to the lodge. I watched the empty entrance and the yard beyond that for once was clear of ambulances. The heat was making the tar bubble up between the stone flags. The plane-trees by the main gates were limp with thirst. The iron railings were so dusty, they looked grey, not black.

The patients on the benches fanned themselves with newspapers. A bit of heat, they allowed, was all right, but this was no joke, it wasn't. "Be a storm afore long," announced one old man; "I can feel it in me knees."

"Never get a fine week like we just had," agreed his neighbour, "but we pay for it. I don't mind a good storm meself. Clears the air lovely. But my good lady can't abide 'em. Think old Tom'll be in there much longer? There's the three of you to go in before meself. Maybe I'd best push off home and look in again tomorrow."

The two ladies at the head of the little queue whispered together, then announced that if Mr. Carter had no objection they would be happy to oblige Mr. Mullings, as they did not like to think of Mrs. Mullings having to face a storm un-protected.

"Suits me, ladies." Mr. Carter was the first speaker. "I'm not in no hurry, neither." His smile was patient, peeved, and very sad. "You got to be young for that. Like them two lads out there, see? Having a race, I reckon! Strewth! In this heat!"

"And here comes another lad back of 'em!" Mr. Mullings heaved himself up by the back of the bench for a better look. "Student lads, you reckon?"

The two young men racing down the pavement by our railings had reached our gates. They tore in, up the yard, and towards the entrance. One carried his dark jacket in an odd kind of bundle under one arm. His companion had his on despite the heat and their speed. On reaching Cas. they ignored the porters in the lodge, the protests of the admission clerk at her desk, and Mr. Wrigley's stern, "Now then, you lads! What's all this?"

They charged at me. The one carrying his jacket produced from beneath a white paper carrier-bag. "Take it, Nurse!" he gasped. "We found it—in that phone-box, at the end of the road. Is it still alive?"

Sister had heard them from the S.C.O.'s office and was already beside me. "Let me see." She opened the mouth of the carrier-bag. Lying insde, wrapped in a clean woollen shawl, was the smallest baby I had ever seen. Its mottled little face was a mass of wrinkles. Its eyes were closed. It had strangely long, fine black hair.

Dr. Jones had followed Sister. As he was about to put on his stethoscope, she said briskly. "It's breathing, Dr. Jones. I think straight up to an incubator?" She phrased that as a question, out of respect for etiquette. She was actually giving an order. She did not wait for his nod. She whisked a blanket off the nearest trolley, wrapped it round baby and bag, and placed the bundle in my arms. "Up to the Maternity Unit, stat., Dungarvan. Run. Don't drop it, but run. Now."

I had never been told to run on duty. I ran out of the department, and was only vaguely aware of the sudden uncanny silence and the way legs were moved aside and doors held open. In the ground-floor corridor I found Dr. Jones was running with me. He grunted, "I'll get the fast staff lift to the Mat. Unit," and shot on ahead.

The lift was roughly two hundred yards from Casualty. It seemed more like two miles. It was just after four o'clock. Our ward teaching rounds ended at four. The corridor was crowded with students, with white coats, with nurses going to and fro from tea, and the occasional pundit. I bulldozed my way through the lot, including one outraged Office Sister. "Nurse Dungarvan! What do you think you're doing?"

I paused on one foot. "Sorry, Sister. Sister Casualty's instructions—" I ran on.

Dr. Jones had the gates open. He slammed them shut and kept one finger on the top floor button. With his free hand he reached inside the carrier-bag. "Still breathing, but growing cold and his muscle-tone's bloody poor."

I hugged the bundle more tightly to increase the warmth. "Think it's a boy, Doctor?" I gasped breathlessly.

"Don't waste my time asking me bloody stupid questions, Nurse!" he snapped. "How could I possibly tell its sex since, as you know very well, I've had no time to examine it? I just call all babies 'he' until proved otherwise."

The lift stopped. A waiting gowned and masked midwife took the baby, and Dr. Jones hitched up his mask and followed her into the incubator nursery. I waited in the corridor for our blanket and any message for Sister Casualty, and brooded on the baby's chances of survival, how any mother could have made herself pack her own baby in a carrier-bag, and what kind of thoughts passed through a woman's mind when she walked away after abandoning her baby in a telephone-box, or anywhere else. Or did she not think at all?

Or had someone else done it for her?

I wished I knew a few of the answers. I didn't know any. I felt lost and ineffectual, and Dr. Jones just now had done nothing to improve my morale. But I did not take his rebuff too personally, since, having worked with him, I was now accustomed to his habit of being unctuously civil to his seniors and much less than civil to his juniors. From Tom Lofthouse I had heard he was not popular in the Doctors' House, yet, conversely and amazingly to anyone who had been his junior, our Dr. Jones rated as a favourite pin-up in the Staff Nurses' Home.

In Benedict's the staff nurses set the tone, since they saw more of our men on and off duty than any other nursing strata in the hospital. Their views trickled down through the student nurses' years and were apt to be accepted as gospel, since that saved the students the bother of forming opinions for themselves, and also it was not often a student in her first couple of years, if not longer, had the opportunity to form any opinion on our men. In Benedict's, as in most hospitals, only the higher nursing ranks dealt directly with the residents. To deal with a pundit one had to be either a sister, senior staff nurse, or a rare fourth-year on nights.

The staff nurses called Dr. Jones "dear Jackie". He was tall, very fair, reasonably attractive, and when he made with the charm at hospital parties they lapped it up. One had to work under him to discover he never troubled with the charm unless he considered it worth his while. The staff nurses were prepared to forgive his short temper on duty, as he was "such fun on a party". But Old Red's silences they found inexcusable because he never attended our parties, or bothered to turn on the charm to anyone. Yet that he could talk, and well, I had discovered that day in the car. I had also discovered recently, again via Tom, that the men now liked him. "A tough but decent bastard" was their view, even if his inability to make small-talk still riled the staff nurses. Was he just very shy? Like Margaret? Did he turn silent where she turned prim? And was that such a fault? After Bill's chattiness I did not think so.

"Don't look so worried, Nurse." The midwife was back with the blanket. "He's breathing quite nicely and warming up

156

now he's in the cooker. He's small, but he should do."

I felt hideously ashamed, having forgotten the baby. "I'm so glad, Sister. Thank you. How old is he? And he is a boy?"

"Yes." She had a nice smile. Dr. Jones had come out with her and walked straight over to the lift. He had to wait. He behaved as if I were invisible as he did so. The midwife showed me a note that had been pinned to the baby's jacket under the shawl. "We'll keep this unless the police want it. Dr. Jones has a copy."

The note read: "No money, no husband, no home. I'm sorry. Please call him Patrick and be kind to him."

I grimaced. "The poor woman."

Dr. Jones glanced round. "Wouldn't you say she left her regrets a little late, Sister?"

The midwife merely shook her head sadly. I had never been so tempted to hit any man as I was at that moment. I went down in the lift with Dr. Jones in a blazing silence. I doubted he noticed. We were not at a party, he did not go in for brunettes, and I was very much his junior. On the ground floor he walked a few feet ahead, leaving me to trundle behind like a meek Arab wife.

Sister Casualty sighed over my report. "Oh, dear! The poor gals will do these things. We get so many of these dumped babies in."

"With notes, Sister?"

"More often than you perhaps expect. The umbilical cord isn't as easily severed as these unhappy mothers imagine. The maternal instinct can't be dumped, even when you've got rid of your baby. The only instinct stronger is self-preservation. At this very moment that little scrap's mother must be in hell, and part of her will stay there for the rest of her life. Society may or may not forgive her. Nature will never allow her to forgive herself. I hope she can be traced. She hopes so too, or she'd not have written that note, though she may not realize it yet. One can but hope. Now, go and get those three lads some tea. The police have finished questioning them."

The three young men were waiters off for the afternoon. Their names were

Kevin, Frank, and Trevor. Trevor had stayed behind to ring the police and explain their actions. "We were late off, see," explained Frank. "Gone spare, we had, as we'd missed our bus. So we thought we'd walk to the next stop, and then we see this bag on the floor. We thought some bird must've forgotten her shopping. Talk about giving us a turn when we saw it move! Doing all right, is he, then? Patrick, eh? Cor!"

Sister beckoned me. "Amon. aromat. and a wheelchair for that dresser over there. Get him outside."

The dresser with the brown beatle-cut was standing outside the Accident Unit. He looked dazed and pale-green. He slumped into the chair I pushed behind him and thankfully sipped the sal volatile.

In the yard I asked, "What was it? The man with petrol burns?"

"Yea." He screwed up his face as Dickie did when repulsed. Standing, he was about a foot taller than me. Seated, he looked not much older than Dickie. He was quite good-looking. He would be even more so when he was over the spotty stage.

"Poor you. Burns your weak spot? They're mine."

"Guess they must be. First I've seen."

"First—down here? I know this is your first day, but you've been in the wards?"

"Not yet."

I gaped. "You're not a pre-clinical?"

"Just finished that. My lot came back from holiday yesterday. The chap who was to have been my ward partner hasn't come back. Don't know why not. So this morning the fat little chap in the long white coat who was sorting us out in the Dean's Office said I'd better come along here for a few days until they got me organized with another partner. Don't know why we have to have partners. Do you?"

"Yes. It's a Benedict's rule that all students walking the wards must walk in pairs. That way you can chaperon each other."

"Why do we want to do that?"

This was not the moment to lecture him on the facts of hospital life, so I said briefly, "Patients prefer two to one," and asked if he had explained his position to Sister.

"No. What's it got to do with her?"

I smiled. "Chum, you'll find out. Never mind. Tell anyone?"

"That chap Dr. Jones, who runs this joint."

"I see. He can't have told Sister, or she'd never have pitched you straight into the A.R.R. Unit. Did you tell Mr. Waring?"

"He a big chap with red hair?"

"No. That's Mr. Leland, the S.S.O. You told him?"

Apparently he had talked to no-one in the A.R.R. Unit. A nurse taking him for a more experienced dresser had given him a gown and told him to go into the Burns Room. He said, "There was such a crowd round the chap on the table I couldn't see him at first. Then someone moved. I just came out in a sweat." He was doing that now from the memory. "I didn't know what to do, but this tall chap with red hair—what did you say his name is?"

"Leland."

"Leland. Well, he sort of noticed me and said 'Out, boy, fast.' I outed fast. And you say he's—what is he?"

"The Senior Surgical Officer. The fat little one who sorted you out this morning was the S.M.O. Get me? His name is Dr. Curtis. The S.M.O. and S.S.O. are our two most senior residents. They really run this hospital, and they'll be running your life for the next few years."

"Where does this Waring come in?"

"He's Senior Accident Officer."

"I say!" He regarded me respectfully. "You do know the answers. You a staff nurse?"

"No. Third-year student. Hence my dark-blue belt and blue dress. The second-years wear blue dresses and white belts. The first years, mauve. The girls in grey are staff nurses. And any female wearing a black belt with a silver buckle ranks as a sister. When in doubt call all women in uniform 'Sister' and men in white 'sir' and everyone'll love you!"

He leered. "That a promise, Sister?"

I smiled. "You're cured. I must go back in. Don't hurry, but bring that chair in with you when you come."

"Don't go yet. I like talking to you."

"Sorry about that, but Sister Cas.

162

doesn't hold with her dressers chatting up her nurses."

"Stuff the old bag!" he retorted cheerfully. "At least tell me who you are. I'm Charlie Peters."

"Jo Dungarvan." I stayed momentarily, as there was something I wanted to know. "How old are you, Charlie?"

"Twenty next month. Isn't it hell? A chap might as well be dead when he reaches twenty. You?"

"Twenty-one. Dead."

"Don't worry, Jo," he said kindly, "you don't look it. And, anyway, I think older women are much more interesting."

I went back inside. Sister's frown took the smile off my face. "Have you been taking a medical history, Nurse Dungarvan?"

"In a way, Sister, yes." I explained myself.

Sister was even more angry than I had anticipated. "Nineteen? Straight out of pre-clinical? And exposed unprepared to view a patient whose appearance caused me to warn a hardened policeman! Why was I not instantly informed of his true situation? Is Dr. Curtis not aware that

I refuse to have schoolboys or schoolgirls in my department! A major Casualty department is no place for children! Where is Dr. Jones?"

Dr. Jones had gone to tea. Staff Nurse Robins was in with Sister in the Hall. "I'm sorry, Sister," she apologized uncomfortably. "Dr. Jones asked me to tell you he was off to tea. I forgot."

Sister tapped her foot. "Were you aware the Senior Medical Officer had chosen to send us Mr. Peters, temporarily?"

"No, Sister."

Sister pressed her lips together. At that moment Red Leland came out of the A.R.R. Unit and towards us. "Sister, I had to send out a dresser. He all right?"

"We have attended to him, Mr. Leland," she replied icily. "He is now sitting in a chair on the deck and looks better. But whether an inexperienced schoolboy can be all right after the type of traumatic experience to which he has just been subjected I would not care to say. That is not my province. Running this department is my province!"

He looked thoughtfully from her to the

dresser. "I don't recognize the boy. New in casualty today?"

Sister told him how new. "I was not informed."

"Obviously not, Sister. I'm sorry about this."

"It's not your fault, Mr. Leland."

"Forgive my correcting you in your own department, Sister, but it is. Since that boy's a dresser, he's on the surgical side. When anything goes wrong on the surgical side the fault is automatically mine." He glanced round. "Is Dr. Jones available?"

On hearing Dr. Jones was at tea he accepted Sister's offer of a cup from our mobile canteen. She sent me to fetch two cups, and told me then to go to my own tea. She had disappeared with Old Red into her duty-room and closed the door before I left Casualty. On my way to the dining-room I passed Dr. Jones returning. He assumed a pained expression and averted his eyes. It gave me a great deal of pleasure to think how much more pained he was going to be in a few moments.

Gwenellen was at tea, and reading a letter she had had from Aline by the second post. Aline was now off nights, on holiday, and spending her first week with her grandparents in Cornwall before flying to join her parents in Majorca for the two following weeks. In the letter she asked Gwenellen to ask me if my aunt had at last decided to put poor Old Red out of his misery?

"Honest to God! Hasn't she changed discs, yet?"

"You know our Aline, love, once she gets a bee in her bonnet."

Unfortunately I knew Aline with her quick brain, and quicker tongue, very well. Margaret had now officially accepted General Francis as her next case. He was due in the Wing a few days after Dickie started in his new school, in just over three weeks' time. Aline by then would be back and on days. A flat denial might silence Gwenellen and Tom Lofthouse. It would have no effect at all on Aline, who could add two and two faster and get the sum right better than any girl I knew. I could hear her laugh. "Pull the other one, Jo, it's got bells on it. If Old Red's not gone on your aunt, why's he so decent to you?"

A possible answer hit me. I blushed

before I gave it to Gwenellen. I did not often blush, but generally did when about to lie. "Dear old Aline. It's obviously never occurred to her she could be barking up the wrong tree."

Gwenellen put down her cup to look at me, wide-eyed. "Don't tell me my Tom's going to be right?"

"Over what?" I tried to sound casual. I didn't succeed, which inevitably increased Gwenellen's curiosity.

"About you and Old Red. Tom says Robin Armstrong says Old Red's always chatting you up in Cas. Robin says he even waylays you on your way on duty. Didn't he this afternoon?"

I began to appreciate what I had started. "Yes, but that doesn't have to mean—"

"That you are anything more than good friends? Say no more! I understand!" She grinned. "I'll ask no leading questions, as I remember how I loathed them when I first started seeing a lot of Tom. But don't expect people won't notice, love. Old Red being S.S.O., and you're being only a third-year, of course they'll notice! Particularly as normally he'd rather run that mile than chat up a nurse! And to think you're in my set! I shall bask smugly in your reflected glory—but don't worry! I'll put Aline straight and try and get Tom to belt up about it when amongst the boys. I don't want anything to spoil this."

I was very touched and very guilty. "You approve? I thought you detested Old Red?"

She was honest. "I didn't until he hurt my pride by being impervious to my girlish charms. That riled me, just as it's riled the other girls. If he wasn't so attractive himself," she continued, echoing some old thoughts of my own on the subject, "who'd give a damn? But to be made to feel as if one's made of wood by a man who obviously isn't made of wood is too much for any girl's stomach. But now he's showing definite signs of not thinking you are made of wood I'm quite happy to stop taking violent umbrage and to start liking him. I'll tell you this, I've always had to like him on the job. I like the way he doesn't reach for his knife at the drop of a hat, and the way he doesn't give a damn about his statistics. Remember our last S.S.O.? When I was in Stanley last year, even though I was only in my second year, I knew as well as all the other Stanley staff that if we had in a dodgy case the S.S.O. would fix things so that someone else operated on him. He was taking no chances on having too many deaths to muck up his statistics. Old Red doesn't do that. Tom says he takes all the dodgy cases himself. Tom's getting quite attached to him in a macabre sort of way, so why shouldn't I? After all, I've got my Tom. I'll be delighted to dance at your wedding."

I was scarlet. "Hey, Gwenellen! Take it easy!"

She laughed not unkindly. "Joanna Dungarvan, don't try and kid me that with your imagination you haven't already picked your wedding dress? Or aren't you interested? Now, that would make this really interesting!"

I said, "I thought you weren't going to ask leading questions?"

"Hint taken, love. Hint taken."

It was a relief to get back to Casualty, and another to recollect Old Red's coming holiday. I refused to face the prospect of his return yet, since I seemed to have faced quite enough for one afternoon. Worrying ahead had never been one of my habits, which was why I had mentally allowed Bill's importance to get so out of hand. Thinking of him again made me so wretched that on my way back into the department I did not even notice the owner of the hand that held open the door for me, until I chanced to notice Dr. Jones watching from outside his office. When our eyes met he gave me a frigid little smile. Thinking it must have been aimed at someone else, I glanced behind me. "Oh. Thanks, Mr. Leland."

Old Red acknowledged that with a nod and walked on into the corridor. For the rest of that evening Dr. Jones astonished the Casualty junior staff by being, for him, an angel of sweetness and light to us. His new civility did not last, but, as Daisy Yates remarked one day in the following week, it had been pleasant not to have such a right little God Almighty in Cas., if only for a short time.

Though we worked in the same department, I saw little of Daisy, as we were always on different shifts. We met mainly at meals, which I enjoyed, not only because I liked her and could still indulge myself foolishly and talk with her about our special patient in Marcus, but also as Daisy, being so near the end of her training had several friends amongst the staff nurses. Nurse de Wint, the staff nurse in permanent charge of the A.R.R. Unit, had been at school with Daisy and was one of her greatest friends. Mary de Wint ranked with Mrs. Fields in seniority, though, as she never worked in the Hall, when Mrs. Fields was off Staff Nurse Robins, the next in line, took her place. From Nurse de Wint, Daisy heard all the hottest bits of inside Cas. gossip. Some of these she passed on to me.

That was how I heard Old Red had been angry at Sister over the Charlie Peters affair, and had said as much to Dr. Jones. He had then persuaded Sister to bend her inflexible rule forbidding raw nurses or students in her department. Daisy said, "He told Sister he'd like our Charlie to stay in the Hall to give him the chance to get his nerve back in easy stages. Not that the lad now looks as if he's got any nerves. He's as happy as a sandboy."

"Until an ambulance unloads an

accident. Then he turns pale-green again."

As Charlie was forbidden the A.R.R.U., he did not stay pale-green long. When Old Red returned from holiday Charlie, panting helpfully round the hall like an overgrown puppy, was part of the Cas. scene. He got on very well with the patients, and made them laugh without taking umbrage when they laughed at him. They all asked whether he played for the Beatles or the Stones, and were much amused to hear he had formed his own pop group with some of his fellow junior students. It was called The Benedict's Bones. It was a terrible group. None of them could play or sing in tune, and Charlie, who fancied himself on skins, had no real idea of rhythm. When he discovered I could play the piano, whenever we were off together he dragged me down to one of the older lecture rooms in the Medical School basement that happened to possess a piano, to thump out the background beat. Those sessions nearly wrecked my hearing for life, but they made me laugh so much and took up so much of my off-duty that, as time went by, sometimes, just sometimes, I was able to laugh at my one-time passion for Bill.

Eventually I felt strong enough to write the truth to Margaret. She replied by return.

Darling, I am sorry for you, but at the same time I am sure that one day you will be very glad things have turned out the way they have. I know I never met Bill, but from all you said of him he reminded me much too much of a man I once knew and loved. He was not right for me. I never felt Bill Francis was right for you.

That letter astonished me. I had never suspected she had ever loved any man but Simon Ellis, and I knew she could not have been referring to him since she had never spoken of him without affection and great kindness. One of the few occasions when she had been really cross with me had been when I suggested he might have been wiser to make some sort of provision for his wife and son. "Who thinks of death at twenty-eight, Jo? At that age one thinks one is going to live for ever!"

I guessed now that she had met this

other man during her widowhood. Was he the real reason for her still being a widow? It seemed probable. I wondered when they had known each other and why the parents had never mentioned the affair to me? Or had they not known about it? Recollecting the years my parents had spent abroad, it was very possible they had not. Poor Margaret, I thought, and then I thought, Poor Old Red. He's not only up against the ghost of Simon Ellis, he's paying this other man's bill.

Did he know that? If so, it could explain why he had waited so long for her, and why, now they had met again, he was handling their relationship so very carefully. Patiently, steadily, he was easing his way back into her life, seeing her regularly, but not too regularly, and taking pains to get to know Dickie and myself, which was sensible since we were both important to Margaret. His technique was beginning to pay off. Margaret had admitted Dickie liked him; I now thought of him as part of the family; Margaret herself had lowered her resistance enough to take his advice. Her last paragraph ran:

I hope I'm right to come back to Benedict's. As you know, Richard has done nothing but advise me that I must. He says I must stop running away from the past. He is a sensible man, so I am going to take his advice. Very reluctantly. I realize that is an admission of cowardice, but one of the few consolations of approaching middle age is the fact that one no longer objects to having to admit a weakness.

CHAPTER EIGHT

A CALLER IN CASUALTY

Mrs. Fields went on holiday. Robins became senior staff nurse, the other staff nurses moved up one, and the senior student nurse in the A.R.R. Unit came back into the Hall as an acting staff nurse. The general post this caused amongst the A.R.R. Unit nurses left a vacancy. Though I had been in Casualty longer than the three weeks Sister had talked of on my first morning, and by Cas. rules was temporarily senior to Daisy Yates, it was Daisy who was sent to join the Accident Nursing Team. Sister said, "Not too sure you've got your sea-legs yet, Dungarvan."

My reaction was mixed. Daisy, being a nice soul, was very upset for me. "I do hope you don't mind, Jo? I expect Sinbad feels that as I'm in the last few months of my final year, she'd better pack me with as much experience as possible before I get whisked away to act staff nurse in some ward. That's already happened to half my set."

"Well, thanks," I said, "for the kind words, Daisy, but let us not kid ourselves. You're a much better Cas. Nurse than I am."

"Scrub that! You're doing fine in the Hall."

"Sister obviously doesn't think so. I'll bet she thinks that directly she lets me into the A.R.R.U. I'll do a Charlie Peters! She may be right." I grimaced. "Every time I see those grey faces being trundled through Cas. on accident trolleys heaped with grey blankets, and know that under the blankets are mangled, bloody, and road-filthy bodies, I start shaking. That's why in one way I'm glad to have been passed over. Of course, in another way I'm not."

She said, "According to Tom Lofthouse, you didn't lose your nerve or your head when you ran into a real accident."

"That was in hot blood. Baby, did I shake afterwards!"

"Who wouldn't?" She eyed me speculatively. "Is it true Old Red just happened to pass by that morning?"

"Yep."

She raised an eyebrow. "Quite a co-incidence?"

"They happen sometimes."

"So I've heard." She looked as if she had heard a lot more, but was too tactful to say so. I cursed Tom Lofthouse. Several other Cas. girls had now started casting me speculative glances, but so far no-one had made any cracks to me, which was a relief. I was not sure whether I owed that to Gwenellen, the universal awe of Old Red, or Aline's being away. I suspected a bit of all three.

Charlie had not yet been found a ward partner and was still working in the Hall. When he heard about Daisy's move he was now sufficiently informed about Casualty to welcome me as a fellow-member of his L.M.F. club. "Like we lack moral fibre, man! Yellow, that's us!"

Luis was helping us clean the Plaster Room after a long session of plastering. "You call Nurse Dungarvan a man, Charlie? Aie, you English! In Spain for a man to call a pretty girl a man would be great rudeness."

"Luis," I said, "even in England, if a man called me that, I'd take it as great rudeness. But not from young Charlie!" I ducked as Charlie threw a wet sponge my way. It hit the wall. I picked it up and chucked it back. It caught Charlie's left ear.

"Nurse Dungarvan!" Sister was watching from the doorway. "May I remind you you are on watch? If I ever catch you indulging in horse-play again I shall refuse to have you in my department. Go and attend to Mrs. Scutt! Mr. Peters, I want you to escort a patient to X-ray! Luis, it's high time you were off watch! Cast off! Nurse Dungarvan must finish this clearing alone, later!"

Mrs. Scutt was one of our regulars. She was a large, cheerful lady with bad varicose ulcers which she was constantly banging against the furniture in her house on non-Varicose Vein Clinic days. Her house lay just across the road from the hospital. That day was not a V.V.C. day in Out Patients and, in any event, as it was after six o'clock, Out Patients had closed.

Mrs. Scutt loved to talk. In her loud,

squeaky voice she described at length the particular occasional table that had caused her present damage; she described her husband's hernia; her mother's left kidney; her daughter's twins. Charlie came in as she was in the middle of her obstetrical details, and, though now fairly accustomed to the patients he was slightly taken aback. "Sister's at early supper, and Nurse Robins thought you might like some help, Nurse Dungarvan. But would you rather I came back?"

Mrs. Scutt, being an old hospital bird, had no difficulty in translating Robins' euphemistic message, or in placing Charlie, though she had not met him before. "Lord bless you, duck, you don't want to go! Learning you to be a new young doctor, are they then?" She waved a huge and kindly hand. "You park your backside in that chair along of old Mother Scutt and watch how my little nurse finishes me leg real lovely. Now, like I was saying, duck," she continued to me, "they didn't spot as she was carrying the two until the first come on. Mark you, I said as she was too big, but they said as it could just be the water, as they couldn't hear no more than the one heart. But they was lying one on top of the other, duck—and the little lad was beneath and upside down. His sister's afterbirth was in the road—and the time they had getting it away!" Her voice rose even higher. "And then the little lad started to push his way out backside first. All black and blue his poor little behind was— and as for my poor Linda's privates!" She turned to Charlie. "A month back this was, duck, but she's not been right downstairs since."

Charlie was sitting on the edge of a dressing-chair, and his eyes above his mask were as wide as Gwenellen's at their widest. He said in a grave tone that would have done credit to the S.M.O., "So she is still having to stay in her bedroom? How inconvenient!"

Mrs. Scutt bellowed with laughter, slapped him hard on the back, and ex- plained herself so plainly that Charlie went purple behind his mask. I kept my eyes on the dressing as Mrs. Scutt produced photos. "Lovely pair of kiddies, aren't they? Andrew and Anne. And isn't their old Nan real made up with them, Doctor?"

She gave Charlie another slap. "Take a good look!"

That slap knocked him off his chair. He grabbed at one leg of the dressing-trolley to steady himself, forgetting his own weight and that the trolley was on wheels. The combination sent the trolley rolling across the room behind him. It hit the wall, and the enamel tray on the top shelf set with stainless-steel dressing dishes and bowls, slid off. Tray and contents clattered to the floor. The noise was shattering.

"Oh, God! Terribly sorry!" Charlie dived for the dishes. "Will you have to start all over again?"

Mrs. Scutt stopped squeaking "Save the pieces, duck!" to assure him her dressing was on real lovely, and all she now needed was her elastic bandage.

"Perhaps you can put that on, dresser?" suggested Old Red's voice. He had come in and was leaning against the closed door, surveying the chaos with an expressionless face. "A word, please, Nurse."

Charlie's mask had slipped down. I kicked his ankle as he opened his mouth. I said, "Yes, Mr. Leland," and hurried out of the door he was now holding open. Before he closed it we heard Mrs. Scutt's irate, "He's never going to tell her off, is he?"

As it was perfectly obvious what Old Red wanted to say to me, I did not wait. "I'm very sorry about that crash, Mr. Leland. I'm afraid there was a little accident."

He had moved a yard or so from the door. He said drily, "That's a weight off my mind. It sounded as if someone had suddenly gone berserk. I came in expecting to have to make speedy contact with the Relieving Officer."

"With whom, Mr. Leland?"

"The gentleman to whom we turn when one of our patients, or staff, turns into an acute manic. And if I don't have quiet now you'll probably have to get him for me. I've just wasted ten minutes trying to listen to a man's chest. I suspect he has a diaphragmatic hernia. I'd like a chance to confirm my suspicions. As I'm in the room next door to your present patient, you'll appreciate my difficulty."

"Some difficulty, Mr. Leland?" Sister

had come back and was beside me, looking very fierce. "May I help?"

"Well, thanks, Sister, I'd be grateful." He ignored me to smile at her. "As I have just been telling your nurse, I'm having trouble listening to a chest. Either my stethoscope has a fault or I'm going deaf. May I borrow your stock stethoscope?"

"My dear man, of course! Fetch it from my desk, Nurse Dungarvan!"

When I returned to Mrs. Scutt she was still indignant. "It's that red hair, duck! Always the sign of a proper Tartar!"

Charlie still looked upset, but Sister removed him before I could take him aside and soothe him. "Get this room shipshape! Get a mop to that mess on the deck! Isn't that a pair of Spencer Wells under the radiator?" She retrieved the instrument herself. "Good God, gal! Are you incapable of doing even a simple dressing efficiently? You are well into your third year! Surely you have learnt by now that care of equipment comes second only to care of the patients!" I had learnt that. I had also learnt not to waste energy making excuses, and to recognize the signs and symptoms of a sister suffering from an attack of acute haema-dementia. Sister Cas. was not often bloodyminded, and this was the first time she had been so with me. I hoped it was just a passing phase, sparked off by her catching me fooling around in the Plaster Room, and thanked my guardian angel for the way Old Red had just covered up for me. Had he not, by now I could be *en route* for Matron's Office. Sister Cas. was not a woman to make idle threats. God bless Old Red, I thought. One of these fine days, when he's my uncle, I would thank him for this.

Shortly after Sister sent me to chaperon the patient in Room Two. "Miss Flora Mackenzie. I trust you are capable of chaperoning, professionally!" Chaperoning was so easy, it was the job reserved for the most junior nurses.

Miss Flora Mackenzie was very old, very thin, very small, and very militant. She lived alone and had fallen off a ladder in her sitting-room. She had displaced backwards the lower end of her right radius and sustained a few other minor bumps and bruises, but was otherwise intact. She was more angry than shocked, particularly when Old Red suggested it was not wholly wise for ladies not in their first youth to climb ladders. "Then I would like it fine for you to advise me how I am to repaint my ceilings, Doctor! I cannot do a good job from a chair on a table! I have tried, but I am too wee to reach. I have not your inches, laddie, but I will not tolerate a dirty ceiling!"

"Forgive me, Miss Mackenzie," he apologized, "but you are eighty-eight."

"And I hope I may be spared to repaint my own house when I am ninety-eight, Doctor!"

He smiled at her as he smiled at Margaret. "I'm not a betting man, Miss Mackenzie, but if I were I'd put my shirt on your being able to do just that. However, I still have to say I do not approve of your climbing ladders."

"Aye. You've your job to do as you see fit." She eyed him sternly. "What now? I'd best warn you, I'm not staying in this hospital. I've my work waiting at home."

He knew she lived alone, and wasted

no breath reminding her there was no-one there to look after her. "I'd like to set your wrist and put on a small plaster, which will take a little time to dry. There's no question of anyone trying to keep you in St. Benedict's against your will, but if you would consent to remain with us, say, overnight I'd be very grateful. It would give me a chance to see your wrist plaster has dried correctly and give our students a rare opportunity to see how fit and active a lady of your age can be."

"I've kept my health. The Lord has been good to me." Her old eyes appraised him. "So you want me in just for the plaster and to give your student laddies additional geriatric experience? And not because you've a foolish wee fancy in your mind that I require cosseting?"

He hedged. "I'd like you to stay."

"Aye. No doubt, since you fear I'll maybe return to my painting before my plaster's dry."

"I don't fear that, Miss Mackenzie; I'm convinced you'll be back up that ladder before the ambulance has had time to drive away."

"Is that so?" Suddenly she smiled. "Aye, that's what I'd do. You're a good judge of character, laddie, and as I'm not so bad at that myself, I'll bide by what you say if you'll answer me this; what's your true reason?"

"I think you are more shocked than you realize and, for a day or two, need us to look after you."

She looked up at him in silence, then nodded. "Maybe you're right, laddie. I'm not as young as I was. I'll bide a wee while in your hospital, but there's to be no cosseting, you'll understand!"

He signed her admission form. I took it to Sister. She raised her eyebrows. "I never thought we'd be able to keep her. Go up with her to Bertha Ward, gal."

On my return Staff Nurse Robins was after my blood. "Dungarvan, you were supposed to have cleared the Plaster Room! It's still in chaos!"

"I'm sorry, Nurse Robins; I had to leave it. I'll finish it now."

"Not now you can't! There are two splinters waiting to be removed and one cut thumb soaking in the Women's Dressing Room. There are two dressers in there, but as one of the splinters is in the thigh, you'll have to get it out. Then do the Plaster Room."

Charlie was one of the two dressers. Three other women with minor injuries came in before the room could be cleared. Robins called away the other dresser to help the S.C.O. Charlie and I cleared up together.

He was still upset about Mrs. Scutt's trolley. "I wish you'd let me explain to Old Red. Was he foul? . . . Oh, Christ!" He had now knocked over a bottle of gentian violet. The sink he had just cleaned was stained badly. "I'll never get this muck off."

"Meth.'ll shift it, stat." I handed him the room's stock bottle of methylated spirit. "Don't work yourself into an acute anxiety state. Just pour on and watch. And don't worry about this afternoon either. Old Red wasn't foul." I stacked a large bowl-sterilizer, then turned on the water. "On the contrary, he was sweet—careful!" I lunged for the meth. bottle and caught it before it hit the floor. "Honest to God, Charlie, you need to do something about your reactions!"

"Sorry, Jo. But was he really sweet? Old Red? But everyone says he's an absolute swine to nurses."

"Everyone says—a right load of old codswallop." I replaced the bottle on the shelf, closed the lid of my sterilizer, and switched on the heat. "These things'll need twenty minutes as it's the end of the day. What time is it now?" I hitched out Little Ben. "It can't be ten? Hell! Robins is on until midnight with me, but Sister's off at ten, and if I don't get the Plaster Room straight before she does her final round she'll kill me. Will you keep an eye on this sterilizer and turn it off if I forget it?"

"Sure, but can't I help you in the Plaster Room?"

I did not want to hurt his feelings by saying I would manage far quicker alone, so I used an equally true reason for refusing his offer.

"As the other dressers have vanished, you'd better stay up this end and make yourself very visible. If not, in Sister's present mood, she'll probably send out a landing party of the Royal Marines to round you boys up. You show her there's one sterling lad on watch!"

"Aye, aye, sir!"

The Plaster Room lay beyond the A.R.R.U. It was quiet in there. I hung up the plastic sheet I had left soaking, rolled away those that had dried, scrubbed dried plaster from the table with the special remover, and wondered wearily how much longer it would be before the scent of wet plaster stopped reminding me of Marcus. I could now forget Bill for hours, even days, then one sniff of wet plaster and I went straight back to Marcus Small Ward Two.

"Excuse me, Nurse—oh, it's you!" Old Red had come in. "Have you seen a watch lying around? I've left mine somewhere; I thought in Cas. I've just asked Sister. It hasn't yet been handed in. As I put on a plaster in here an hour ago, I wondered if I'd left it on that shelf above the sink. No." He looked underneath. "Hasn't slipped down either."

I searched with him and in vain. "Sorry, Mr. Leland. Have you another?"

"In my room. I'll have to go up." He

turned round as the door opened again. "Wanting me, Peters?"

"Er—no, sir." Charlie looked startled. He turned to me. "It's that sterilizer you asked me to watch, Nurse Dungarvan. It seems to need some attention."

"Sounds ominous." Old Red smiled faintly. "Perhaps you should see to it before it blows us all up, Nurse." He held open the door for me. "Thanks for searching."

Charlie cantered after me as I hurried back to the Dressing Room. The sterilizer was bubbling quietly. "There's nothing wrong with this thing, Charlie!"

"I know that! But I couldn't think of any other excuse to get you away when I bust in and found Old Red chatting you up! Sorry if I put my big foot in it, but what else could I say? This chap with the leg or something who wants to see you said something about being or having been a patient, but not being here as one now, and as he's loaded with flowers for you and I didn't know how Old Red would take it, I used the sterilizer."

I stared. "Charlie, what are you

talking about? Who wants to see me?"

"This chap with the limp. He's got some flowers for you and was asking the porters, and I told him you worked here and I'd get you. As Sister and Nurse Robins are swigging coffee with that drag Jones, I took him down the short cut through Eyes and shoved him into 15. I've closed the door. Only the porters saw him come in, and they won't talk! His name's Francis, and he says you nursed—" His voice stopped abruptly. "Come to investigate the sterilizer, sir?" he asked of Old Red in a surprised squeak that was nearly as high as Mrs. Scutt's.

"No. As I heard no explosion, I presumed the danger had been averted. I just looked in to say I've found my watch, Nurse Dungarvan."

"Good." I was too shaken to ask where. "Shall I tell Sister, Mr. Leland?"

"Don't bother. I'll be seeing her." He walked off.

Charlie and I looked at each other. Charlie asked, "Think he heard about your chap with the floral tribute?" I shrugged. "Jo I'm sorry. I always seem to be landing you in it."

"It's not your fault if my old boy-friends choose to drop in at the wrong moments." He was groaning. "What now?"

"I've really done it this time, haven't I?"

"Relax!" I was trying to think fast and barely heard what he said. "I've got to get rid of this man before Sister or Robins finds him there. If not—" I slid a thumb-nail across my throat.

"They surely won't do you for this? How could you help it if some chap drops in with flowers?"

"Charlie, grow up! When something like this happens everyone always blames the girl!"

"Then how about Old Red? If he heard, won't he tell Sister?"

"Not him!" I was too concerned for caution. "Jackie Jones mightn't hesitate to run to Sister about something he only overheard by chance. Old Red is no smooth-talking, trouble-making sod. And anyway, he and I are sort of mates. If he did hear I'll bet he'll have another attack of deafness and maybe a touch of amnesia as well." Then I realized what I was saying. "Charlie, this is just between you and me. Promise?"

"Sure." He grinned. "I say, Jo! You're quite a bird, even if you do like 'em long in the tooth!"

That crack penetrated, but I had wasted too much time to deal with it. "I know! I'll get rid of my man, and you stay up here and create a diversion if anyone appears before I'm in the clear. Break something. Faint. Anything."

"Trust me, Jo."

I hoped I could, as I had to. I knew he now realized this was serious, but I was not sure I had got through to him how serious. For any Benedict's nurse to entertain socially on duty was, in nine cases out of ten, a sacking matter. The tenth case got off with a very stern reprimand from Matron and a very black mark against her name for the rest of her career. No nurse with such a mark was likely to get a reference from Matron when she left the hospital, or, which was even more important to Benedict's nurses, a Benedict's Training School badge. These badges were handed out only on a nurse's last day in the hospital, after she had taken State and Hospital Finals and accumulated a sheaf of satisfactory ward reports. One bad report could lose a girl her badge. We coveted these badges, and I never realized how much until that night in Casualty.

I crossed the length of the Hall in a raging temper with Bill Francis. Once I had longed to see him. Not half an hour back I had been dewy-eyed with nostalgia for him. Now I was about to meet him again, it was as if I had suddenly woken up from a syrupy dream. He was not worth my losing my badge! Why risk seeing him at all? Why not go back and Let Charlie get rid of him for me?

I had reached 15. I hesitated outside the door, and for just too long. Sister, Robins, and Dr. Jones came out of the latter's office

"And where are you off to, Nurse Dungarvan?" called Sister. Charlie did his stuff before I could answer. There was a crash of breaking glass.

"Not that boy Peters again!" Sister sent Staff Nurse Robins to investigate. "Now, Nurse Dungarvan! Why is there a light on in 15? Has another patient come aboard? If so, may I ask why neither the staff nurse nor myself have been informed? And why use 15 when you are well aware that room is only used at night when the department is crowded?" She swept by me and into 15. "Oh! Oh, it's you, Mr. Leland!" Her voice altered. "Nurse Dungarvan, why did you not explain at once that Mr. Leland was seeing a patient in here?"

Nurse Dungarvan was in no condition to explain anything. Fortunately, Mr. Leland did it for her.

"This gentleman is not a patient, Sister. There has been a slight, though not serious, misunderstanding. May I introduce to you General Francis. General, our Sister Casualty."

General Francis had risen from his chair by the examination couch and was supporting himself with his sticks. On the couch were two sheaths of flowers. The General wore white tie and tails that accentuated his normal elegance. He looked incredibly distinguished. In comparison, Dr. Jones seemed a scruffy, wishy-washy fair boy in a limp white coat, and even Old Red, one of the neatest men in Benedict's, looked a slightly untidy young man.

Sister Cas., in general, was impervious

to masculine charm, and yet she mellowed visibly as General Francis apologized for his presence. "As I have just explained to Mr. Leland, I returned to my hotel from a dinner engagement and discovered the flowers I had earlier ordered to be delivered here for Nurse Dungarvan and Nurse Yates had, by some misdirection, been left at my hotel. Since that is very near I came over with them. I was explaining this to your door porters when a most helpful youngster kindly took me in his charge and escorted me into this room."

Sister and the two residents exchanged resigned glances. Sister said, "I expect it was one of our students at present working here as a dresser. They are a willing bunch of lads, if occasionally over-willing."

"Precisely," said the General. "And, to be fair to the boy, I possibly confused him, since when he very properly inquired as to whether or not I was a patient, I had to admit myself in some doubt on the point." He turned to Old Red. "As I expect you are aware, Mr. Leland, my room in your Private Wing is booked from this evening, but as I wanted to attend a regimental dinner tonight, with Mr. Remington-Hart's consent I'm not moving in until tomorrow." He then explained why he had sent Daisy and myself the flowers in the first place. "I never anticipated the unlooked-for pleasure of being able to deliver one bunch in person. With your permission, Sister, may I do that now?"

Sister not only gave smiling permission, she allowed me to escort him back to his car. We walked the length of the Hall, instead of taking the short cut through the darkened Ophthalmic Department.

We walked very, very slowly. The deterioration in my companion's movements in the few weeks since I had last seen him was distressing to observe. He did not mention his health or coming operation, beyond asking if Daisy and I would visit him once it was over. "If that's permissible?"

"We'll have to ask Matron. I'm sure she'll say yes. I know we'd love to come and call."

"Splendid." His smile would have had Daisy weak at the knees. It did not affect mine, though I enjoyed it, vastly. Oddly, instead of reminding me of Bill, it reminded me of Old Red. Then I looked more closely at the General's face and realized the comparison was not odd at all. Both men in repose looked austere and even severe. Both, when smiling, underwent a total transformation that illuminated an unsuspected streak of gaiety in their characters as successfully as it illuminated their eyes. I saw now exactly why, when General Francis's name came up, Daisy bemoaned the fact that she had not been born twenty years earlier. Twenty years back he must have been the most exciting man any girl could hope to meet, in or out of the British Army. That had nothing to do with his still almost staggering good looks. It was just something in his eyes when he smiled and his voice when he talked to a woman. Even though he was old enough to be my father and now walking like an old, old man, every feminine instinct I possessed was reminding me most pleasantly that he was neither my father nor an old, old man. Ten minutes ago I had felt angry, rather tired, and very hard done by. I now felt fresh, gay, attractive, and very, very feminine. In fact, I felt so wonderful that I glanced back at Old Red. He did not notice, as he was talking to Sister outside 15. But it struck me then how very wise he was to keep his sexy side so firmly battened down on duty. Life in Benedict's might be more of a riot if we had an S.S.O. who lived up to his potential, but the effect on our work could be disastrous. All good nurses were trained to keep their minds on their jobs, but even good nurses were human. So it was just as well Old Red never allowed anyone on duty, including perhaps himself, to remember that he also was human—and still a good deal younger than General Francis.

We talked about Dickie's visit and success at winning that scholarship. "My aunt," I said, "makes no bones about it. She's bursting with pride!"

"With every reason. Raising a child alone, and particularly a boy, is no easy job for any woman. Mrs. Ellis has done very well by that boy. He's a good boy, and very much a boy. I much enjoyed having him as my guest. Unfortunately, being a serving soldier whilst my own boys were growing up, I missed nearly all their boyhood. Your young cousin's visit made me appreciate just how much I missed. However, if there is one occupation in life that is more pointless than others it is regretting the past." We were a few feet from the main entrance, but he needed to pause before moving on. He used the pause to say how grateful he was to my aunt for deciding to take his case. "I hope I won't prove a too impatient patient."

"General, I'm sure you won't!" I was about to add his son had been an excellent patient, and found I could not do it. That was not because Bill was Bill, but because it would have been such an outrageous lie, as Bill's father would realize. Bill, I suddenly saw with that horrible clarity of hindsight, had been a selfish and demanding patient. I took another good look at the General's face. There was no selfishness there and no weakness. He would not weep on Margaret's shoulder.

My impulsive remark amused him. "A snap judgment, I fear, but excellent for my morale. Thank you. Do you make many snap judgments?"

"Too many. I don't mean to, but keep doing it."

"One does, at your age. I used to pass judgment on sight. Paul, my younger boy, being quite surprisingly mature for his age, does take his time, but Bill takes after myself. I suppose you know he's now touring through France? I understand he sends regular postcards to his St. Benedict's friends."

"Yes." Surprisingly, I found I was not acting. "Nurse Yates has had a few. I hadn't heard he was in France. He still on holiday? And how's his leg?"

"Doing very well. The plaster'll be off in a week or so. I presume he'll come back for that. His paper have given him another six weeks' leave-of-absence, so he decided to see France and, I believe, Spain."

"How very nice for him!"

In the yard Corporal Wix was showing the finer points of the Rolls to one of our porters. He came over to shake my hand, but had the kindness and tact not to attempt to help his employer's slow progress. I waved them off, then went slowly back inside.

Sister, Robins, and Old Red were now standing by the lodge discussing the General's condition.

Sister said, "So Mr. Remington-Hart won't touch him for at least fourteen days?"

"No." Old Red frowned at the floor. "He'll never touch a back until it's been properly rested."

That explained why Margaret was not due for another ten days. It had begun to puzzle me.

Robins asked, "What's the prognosis, Mr. Leland?"

"I can't really answer that until we see what we find when we get him on the table. If it does turn out after all to be a growth, and the chances are high, then the chances of there being secondaries will be even higher. And an op. will almost certainly speed things up. He's willing to risk it, and he's been told the risk."

Sister sighed. "So when he signs his consent form he could be signing his own death-warrant. Poor man! A remarkable face," she added briskly. "Intelligent.

Sensitive. Pity he chose the Army. He would have done well at sea. I hope he does well in the Wing. I wonder who'll have him?"

Old Red looked up from the floor, and glanced at me before answering. "Mr. Remington-Hart is bringing in two private nurses who have worked with him previously. Both are former Benedictines, whom I think you'll remember, Sister. Miss Kateson and Mrs. Ellis."

"Kateson? Kateson? No. Before my time. But Mrs. Ellis, of course, I remember! If we are talking about Maggie Ellis, _née_ Dungarvan? That child's aunt?"

"That's right, Sister."

"Really? I am pleased! Such a charming gal and a very good nurse." Sister looked at me, meaningly. "Strange thing, heredity. Sometimes a trait gets passed on from generation to generation, and sometimes it can be missed out altogether."

It was rather a dirty crack to make in public. Robins slightly endeared herself to me by going a little pink and gazing at the ceiling. Old Red returned to frowning at the floor. I would like to have told them both that on that occasion the crack had sailed over my head. I had other things to occupy my mind. Things like General Francis's being a widower, and his only other son in Hong Kong, tonight his last night out of hospital, perhaps for ever, and Bill on holiday in France.

My mind flashed back to those nights in Marcus Small Ward. I could see the General now, sitting so stiffly and so still on that hard chair, with one hand on the bed and the other on his stick.

I could see Sister's point. Sometimes some trait got missed out altogether.

CHAPTER NINE

MARGARET COMES BACK TO BENEDICT'S

I KICKED off my shoes, stretched out on my bed, and watched Margaret light a cigarette. "Did I ever know this other man?"

She walked over to my window to get rid of her match. "I doubt it. It was all over years ago." She leant on the sill. "How this place has grown! And altered! Cas. seems the only place that's still where it was. Subway open yet?"

"Royalty's been invited to do that on the 14th of next month. New caps, aprons, white gloves, and toothy smiles will be issued to one and all." I watched her back. "What was his name? Or don't you want to talk about him?"

She turned, smiling. "Darling, I haven't your passion for P.M.s. Anyway, isn't one P.M. enough for one afternoon?"

We had been holding a post-mortem on my dead fixation for Bill Francis, and I had been hoping we could now resurrect her old affair with the man she had mentioned in that letter. I said, "Don't slap me down—but did Old Red ever know about him and you?"

"Oh, yes."

So that hunch was right. "Margaret, there's something else I've been meaning to ask you. When was the last time you saw Old Red before you two met up in the carpark? When you left Benedict's?"

"No. It was—when? Six or seven years ago, I think. It could be less. I do remember he was then a senior registrar here."

"You came up to Benedict's?"

"No. I met him outside a few times when I came up to the bank."

"Did you meet before that?"

"Sometimes. When he was an h.s. he used to visit the flat Simon and I had in Fulham. He came to Simon's funeral."

"You never told me that!"

"Jo, you were then eight years old."

"I don't mean then, I mean now."

She looked at me reflectively before answering. She looked older that afternoon than she had when I last saw her at the cottage. Her face was pale and unusually tense. "I know what you mean, but as this is probably the first time I've mentioned Simon's funeral to you, are you really surprised?"

"No. Sorry. We're so alike in so many ways that I keep forgetting you're not an extrovert nut like me."

"Is that what you are?" She sat on my bed. "And how does an extrovert nut get on in Cas?"

"Not so hot. I'm now the most senior Hall junior. At this rate my Cas. time'll be through before I'm inside the A.R.R.U."

"That the Accident Team? Richard explained it to me when he was down at the cottage this Sunday. It's news to me. Cas., as I remember it, was a free-for-all, with everyone sooner or later doing every job."

"But in those days there weren't millions of cars on the roads, we hadn't a spandy new clearway two miles off, and weren't the largest general hospital to the London end of a not so new motorway."

"So Richard said." Before I could ask her more about that particular visit she asked what was really wrong about Casualty. "Cas.? Or Sister Cas.?"

"Sister." I told her how Sister had seen me chucking a sponge at Charlie. "She's had doubts about me before. That convinced her I'm nutty as a fruit cake. She was so peeved she really went spare that afternoon! Since then—" I gave a thumbs-down sign.

Margaret remembered Sister Cas. from their mutual training as well as Sister remembered her. She said, "She was a good, if tricky junior. I can imagine she's now even more tricky, particulary to her juniors. I can understand her getting peeved at finding a nurse larking around, but I wonder which it was that really peeved her—your larking, period, or your larking with a young man."

"Margaret!" I shouted with laughter. "Not even Sister Cas. could mistake Charlie for a man! He's as young as Dickie, mentally! He's got a girlfriend at home, and she's all of fifteen! He doesn't even kid himself I'm his Benedict's girlfriend!"

"No? Then how does he regard you? Mother figure?"

"More like his passport to puberty."

"My poor aged niece! Is he still in Cas. ?"

"No. They found him a ward partner last week. He's now walking the medical wards, and by some miracle the medical block is still standing. Give Charlie time. He'll knock it over or blow it up yet. A nice boy, but a menace." I turned serious. "You don't honestly think Sister took him and me seriously?"

"That's not as improbable as you think. You're the type of girl most women'll take one look at and instantly assume there's only one thought in your head. I don't know the expression you kids now use. In my day you'd have been called a 'hot little number'!"

"Turn it up!" I flushed. "I'm no sex-pot! Now, Aline is! She looks so pale and willowy, but, baby, does she knock 'em flat! Not me. All they want to do is to tell me their problems and weep on my womanly bosom!"

"And do you really think the boys would want to weep on you if you'd a flat bosom, darling?"

"Candidly, I don't think my boyfriends

would give a damn! Anyway, if I was that sex-obsessed, why waste energy training? Nursing's hard work. There are hundreds of easier ways of hooking a man. Why embark on four years' hard for the doubtful joy of hooking a doctor?"

She said, "Jo, if you think the average woman indulges in logical thought when confronted with a very pretty girl, then you know even less about your own sex than you do about men. Oddly, as it's not the accepted notion, I've always found men much more ready to believe that a pretty woman doesn't automatically have to be on the make. Whether that's because men are more charitable, or can sense the fact, I don't know. I do know you should never expect any woman less attractive than yourself to give you the benefit of any doubt where men are concerned unless she knows you well—and not always then. This may be a man's world, but the sex toughest on women are women."

I remembered Staff Nurse Humber, and then those speculative glances I had been recently collecting. It had never occurred to me that Sister might have noticed them, or, having done so, given the matter two thoughts.

Margaret asked if I had acquired any other attendant dresser since Charlie was moved.

"No. Haven't looked at one. No virtue there, as we've not one worth looking at. They're all so young, and the C.O.s aren't much better. Most of them look as if they only need a shave once a week. The only man I ever talk to now—and when I say talk we exchange the time of day and sometimes, just sometimes, discuss the weather—is your old mate Richard. Surely Sister can't have objected? Seeing that he is S.S.O., and to treat the S.M.O. and S.S.O. with civility and respect at all times is firmly engrained in all good little Benedictines before they're let out of the P.T.S."

"That's true." She was very thoughtful. "Does he talk to the other girls?"

"To the staff nurses, sometimes. Not often. He's no great talker. He talks a bit to me as I'm your niece."

She pleased me very much by allowing that must make a difference. "Benedict's may alter outwardly, but not Benedict's traditions. The only person in the hospital to whom the S.S.O. can natter with as an equal is the S.M.O., and as Dr. Curtis is married and goes home whenever he can get off, Richard, when he has time to notice it, must be pretty lonely. Of course, he could talk to the sisters—"

"Do me a favour, Margaret! Have you seen most of our sisters?"

"Careful! Don't you realize that's what I am whilst I'm here?"

"You rank as one of our sisters? Blimey! What make?"

"Senior." She laughed at my reaction. "Don't forget I trained in the Dark Ages in the same set as Matron. I'm having supper with her tonight in her flat."

"Honest to God! Wait till I tell the girls!"

She said, "If you don't mind, Jo, I'd rather you didn't. I've been away a long time. I'm only here as a private nurse, even though, being an old Benedictine, I'm temporarily given this exalted status and lent a sister's uniform. But I feel I've no real right to it, or to throw my weight about because I happen to know

Matron, the S.S.O., and a handful of pundits by their Christian names." She hesitated and studied her hands. "Frankly, darling, old Auntie is feeling aged and dithery. You call your boyfriends young. My child, the lot of you look like children to me. When I stepped out of my taxi this afternoon I felt like a ghost from my own past stepping back into that past—until I saw my face in the mirror and realized it was the wrong face for this setting. I've now to grow accustomed to this face in this setting, to strange faces in well-remembered places, and to the well-remembered faces that only half-a-dozen people, apart from myself, in this present Benedict's will remember at all, and that are no longer present. I'm not only talking about Simon." She looked up now with eyes that looked backward. "I was very happy here. Happiness remembered can be as painful as an old pain. I'd like to be able to ease my way back in gently without too much of 'Do you really remember so-and-so?' and 'Was it really like that?' Understand?"

"Yes," I said, and thanked God I had at least had the sense to realize most of this in advance and put a stop to Aline's inspired guess. Luckily for Margaret and myself, if not Aline, the latter was still in Majorca. She had had acute food poisoning in her last week of holiday and had remained out there with her parents on sick-leave. There were now a few more of my set on days. Occasionally they teased me mildly about Old Red, but without Aline to lead, as she invariably did on every subject in our set, and with Gwenellen to keep them in her plump hands, on the whole my friends had been remarkably reticent.

At supper that night I told Gwenellen Margaret had arrived to nurse General Francis, since she would have thought it very odd had I not done so. She was momentarily interested, but more from the General's angle than any other. "There's such a nice man, Jo! Too bad so good a father should have so spoilt his son. A proper little 'I want' he was! But I expect his mother ruined him whilst his father was away fighting wars or doing whatever it is soldiers do in peace-time. But, listen, love—have you heard the latest? Tom vows it's true . . . "

She went on to enchant me with the hottest grape-vine story in weeks about one of the married theatre sisters who was separated from her husband and a married renal specialist who was not, yet, separated from his wife.

It was several days before I saw Margaret again. The Private Wing occupied a building set apart from the rest of the hospital and on the far side of Casualty yard. The Wing was staffed only by trained nurses who lived and ate with the sisters. The Sister's Home was out of bounds to student nurses unless going there on some official ward or departmental errand. Officially, we were not even allowed to ring up the sisters, though that could be got round by giving a false name. Of course, Margaret could ring me, but I was working an extra late, late shift her first week. She came off at nine-thirty each evening. She could not ring up for a chat after midnight when I got back, and though I was free every morning, she was off only from four to eight each evening. The Wing was not merely a building apart. The Wing nurses worked strange off-duty hours and often nursed a patient right through without a day off, taking all the time then due to them at the end of one case before starting the next.

One morning when I was back on the day shift we ran into each other in the ground-floor corridor. Margaret was out of uniform. The General's operation had been temporarily postponed for further tests, and she was having an extra two hours that morning to make up for time she had missed yesterday. She said she had nothing to do but sit and talk to her patient. "I feel such a fraud."

"I expect he's glad to have you there. This waiting must be hell. How's he taking it?"

"Very, very well."

"So he's a good patient?"

"To date, model. He had a card from Bill this morning. It was posted in Malaga."

"How the lad gets around! Daisy Yates had another a couple of days ago. Hers was from Gibraltar." We had reached the Out Patients Laboratory, my destination. "Must go in here. See you."

The pathologist on counter-duty pushed up his glasses to read my request form. "I presume Dr. Jones wants to use this in the next half-hour?"

"He didn't say, Doctor, but I expect so."

He took a small test-tube half filled with a colourless turgid liquid from one of his battery incubators. He held it enclosed in the palm of his hand. "We are making more, but the next batch won't be ready until two this afternoon. This'll begin to deteriorate directly its temperature drops below blood-heat, so hang on to it until it's wanted. And, please," he added, smiling, "don't drop it, or we will all be very sad here."

I smiled back. "I'll be careful, Doctor. Thank you very much."

He nipped round his counter to open the door for me. That was an unusual gesture for any stray doctor to any stray nurse in Benedict's, but not for a pathologist. For some peculiar and delightful reason which none of us had ever been able to fathom, our pathological department was staffed exclusively by polite and obliging individuals, whether doctors or technicians. Consequently, we all welcomed any chance to visit any of our Path. Labs., as the experience gave our morales such a boost.

Mine badly needed a boost that morning. Sister was being as tough as ever; Dr. Jones had already snapped my head off three times; Staff Nurse Robins was now fast moving in on Sister's act with me, and even Old Red when I wished him 'good morning' had looked as painted as Dr. Jones at his worst.

I had grown too accustomed to Sister and Dr. Jones to bother overmuch over them. Robins' attitude I could follow. As Sister's stand-in she had to back up every line Sister took, and this morning I had heard her confide to one of the other staff nurses that one of her migraines was starting. She was hoping to keep it off until lunch-time, as it was her half-day and she intended going straight to bed, but from the look of her just now when she sent me to the O.P. Lab. she was feeling wretched. No-one could blame a girl with a migraine for being peevish, particularly as Casualty Hall was having a busy morning.

Perhaps Old Red's got a migraine, I thought casually, and then, as I realized belatedly that for the past few days he had been much less forthcoming than previously, I wondered what I had done to upset him. Had he noticed other people noticing us? Had some word somehow reached his high-powered private sitting-room in the Doctor's House? Or was Margaret making his life tricky, and was he working off on me the irritation he would not want to work off on her? Just as before his feelings, whatever they were, for her had overlapped enough for him to include me in their aura? That seemed possible, but so was the fact, since I now knew how dangerously my imagination could mislead me, that being in a gloomy mood I was taking unintentional offhandedness for an intentional slight. Watch it, Joanna, I warned myself, or you'll find yourself with the best little persecution complex in the business.

I had left Robins with Dr. Jones in his office. On my return Old Red had joined them, and all three were standing in the doorway. Matron, had arrived for one of her regular but unexpected rounds, and was up the far end with Sister and talking to a waiting patient. A twitch of Sister's left eyebrow informed me Robins was now in charge of the Hall. I crossed to the S.C.O.'s office, and waited at Robins's elbow.

Old Red broke off his conversation. "Nurse, if you want Dr. Jones, Nurse Robins, or myself, will you please come back in a few minutes? As must be apparent," he added impatiently, "we're occupied."

Had Robins not been struggling with her headache, watching the Hall with one eye, and paying attention to Old Red with the other, she would probably have explained why I was there, since she knew very well. So did Dr. Jones, but he never explained away any actions of his juniors.

I apologized with the meekness expected of any student nurse by a senior resident who had suddenly decided to turn into a Big Doctor. Then I moved a few yards away to wait out of earshot.

The Hall was full. The warm, dry weather was still lasting and the heat-wave making headlines in all the newspapers the patients on the packed benches were either reading or using as fans. Every window and door in the department that could be opened was wide. There was not a breath of moving air about, and outside the noon sun had caused the ambulance men to shed their jackets, roll up their shirt-sleeves, push their caps back on their damp heads, and loosen their ties.

The heat made me feel for Robins. She looked a dirty grey now, and by the way she was blinking up at Old Red, who was still talking about some patient, she was having difficulty getting him into focus. Dr. Jones, being so blond, was scarlet in the face. Old Red, despite his flaming hair, was paler than normal, which accentuated the colour of his blue eyes. He was lucky, I thought, not to have the florid complexion that so often went with red hair and blue eyes. And then I thought, And so's Margaret, even if she doesn't realize it.

He glanced my way then, and briefly our eyes met. Instantly, and it was not my imagination, his expression hardened. Honest to God! I thought, looking away fast, *Et tu, Brute!* Foolishly, I nearly wept. I knew exactly how Julius Caesar felt.

The genuine Cas. Hall junior was doing the noon "re-stocking and testing". She had checked and replaced where necessary the drums of dressings used in all the dressing-rooms, the disposable mask jars, and the various stock lotions and emulsions in regular use. The solutions of double-strength sterile saline and hydrogen peroxide were literally used by the gallon daily. Three times each day and once during the night the Cas. junior refilled those particular bottles.

Throughout Benedict's every routine job had to be done in the approved way and order. When cleaning, we worked from clean to dirty, always clockwise, and if cleaning instruments, first the "blunts"—*i.e.* forceps—then the "sharps" —scalpels and scissors. In stocking and testing there was an official order in which one topped up bottles. First the "safe" lotions, emulsions, and solutions, then the "unsafe" spirits. The two of these in constant use in Cas. were ether methylated and methylated spirits. The "safes" were refilled in the dressing-rooms, but to avoid any danger of an explosion from the heat of the sterilizers the "unsafes" were refilled on a metal trolley parked outside each room in turn.

The junior jangled her metal trolley past me. "It's bad enough doing this with Sister watching, but with Matron as well I'm a nervous wreck," she muttered.

"Relax." I looked behind her. "They've gone into the A.R.R.U."

"They won't be there long. There's only one man in I.C. [Intensive Care] with a fractured skull, and he's only there until someone can find a bed for him. The S.C.O. wanted to shift him on, but the S.S.O. says we must keep him. That's what they're thrashing out now."

"How do you know?"

"Heard Sister telling Matron. What are you doing?"

"Keeping this tube cooking until the S.C.O.'s ready."

"I've got to say it: they also serve who only stand and wait." She pushed on.

By her next stop two small children

waiting with their mother had grown bored with looking at their comics on the bench and were sitting on the floor by their mother's feet, building a brick house. The boy looked about five and his sister a little younger. They were being very good, and far more patient than the youth sitting on their mother's other side. He kept shifting his legs, standing up, sitting again, and complaining to his neighbours. "When are we going to get some service, eh? What they need along of this joint is a spot of organization. Look at them all standing around yak-yak-yakking like a pack of bleeding old bags."

The children giggled together, then the boy tugged his mother's skirt. "Mum, the lady's trolley goes yak-yak-yak too, don't it, Mum, don't it?"

"Now, Barry, you be a good boy and stay nice and quiet like you been doing."

"Mum, no, Mum, you listen!" He shook the trolley gently by one leg, clinking the large spirit bottles on the top shelf, as the junior reappeared. His sister crawled under the bench and crooned to herself, "Yak-yak-yak, yak-yak-yak."

"Don't touch my trolley, duckie," said the junior. "This stuff's got such a nasty smell. You'll be able to sniff it from over there in a minute, but if it spills it'll smell and smell. Oh, dearie me!" She put down the half-empty smaller bottles she had brought out. "Aren't I silly? I must have left my funnel in the last room. I'll have to go and find it." She rolled her eyes as she went by me. "Wouldn't I do this, this morning?"

"Gawd! Makes you wonder, don't it?" the youth demanded of his fellows. "You see that bit in the paper about the bloke what had the scissors left inside him when he come out the operating theatre? Packed it in, he did."

"That happened here? In St. Benedict's?" The speaker was a middle-aged man in a dark suit, with the thin, anxious face of a man with a chronic gastric ulcer.

"Not here. But these places is all the same, I reckon." The youth produced a packet of cigarettes and a lighter. There was a huge "No Smoking, Please" notice on the wall directly in front of him and a yard from the room doorway. As if to ram home the message, directly beneath the notice was a row of fire-extinguishers and fire-buckets. "Anyone fancy a fag?"

I glanced round at Robins. Since she was running the Hall, for a junior to protest in her presence was bad manners. She was not paying attention. I guessed she had not heard.

I moved nearer that particular bench. "I'm very sorry, gentlemen, but I'm afraid you mustn't smoke in the Hall." I smiled to include the notice. "That does mean what it says."

The youth looked me up and down. "And what if I can't read, darlin'?"

"Then I'll read it for you, with pleasure."

"Reckon you could, at that." He smiled lewdly. "Reckon you could do a lot for me, darlin', and it'd be my pleasure. So if I put away me fags, what'll you do for me, eh?"

The middle-aged man looked pleasant as well as gastric. He was shocked and cleared his throat uncomfortably. I would have liked to have told him he need not worry. After nearly three years I had met my quota of sheep who liked to imagine they were wolves. I had met them on benches, in ward beds, wheel-chairs. They came in all shapes and ages, and from assorted backgrounds. They were as foolish, and as harmless, as sheep.

"I'll say thank you very much for not risking blowing yourself and the rest of us up. See that trolley? The stuff in one of those bottles is ether. That takes light like petrol."

The youth, inevitably, looked sheepish. The middle-aged man turned on him. "You do like the young lady says and put that lighter away, son! Silly young fool! All the same these teenagers! Think they know it all! Go on, you put it away." He flicked the lighter that was still on the seat towards the youth. It spun and fell on the floor. The children scrambled for it as a new toy.

Everything happened so quickly! Later no-one was able to say which child had bumped the trolley and which had flicked on the lighter. I was so close, but I did not see the ether bottle toppling, or hear the sound of broken glass. Fortunately it did break, which prevented its exploding. The ether vapour ignited with a roar, and simultaneously the trolley was enveloped in a rising, spitting sheet of blue-and-white flame.

The screaming started as I grabbed the nearest fire-extinguisher. I did not remember throwing out my pen and jamming the test-tube in the pen-pocket of my dress bib until I found it there later. It had not broken, and my body heat had kept the contents at the right temperature. I was very hot, and not only because of the heat of the flames. Though Sister had taught us all how to work those fire-extinguishers, it was the first time I had handled one in action, and it was much heavier than I expected. The foam jet was more powerful and effective than I would have believed possible. My one extinguisher was really enough to deal with that blaze, even though I was joined in a matter of seconds by the three more that Old Red, Dr. Jones, and Robins had dived for. Luis, two porters, and three junior C.O.s appeared with others, but they were not needed.

Another staff nurse and the Cas. junior had rushed to attend the two children. Two more nurses and a dresser helped

Sister quietly shepherd the patients away from the benches in the danger area. The patients themselves filed out of the Hall as calmly as if going to take their places in a bus queue. Only the two little children had screamed. Their screams continued for a little while, but they were screaming with shock, not pain. Later we heard it had taken two and a half minutes to empty the crowded Hall. When we practised our fire drill Sister Cas. was satisfied if we were all out in three.

By tea-time my set knew more about it than I did. A girl in the children's ward told me the little brother and sister admitted for shock had recovered so well that they were unlikely to be warded more than one night. Their mother had gone home to get her husband's tea an hour ago. A few other patients had been treated for minor shock. None had needed admission.

"We heard how you did your stuff, Jo!" exclaimed Gwenellen. "I'll bet you're Sinbad's pet, now! What did she say to you?"

"She said, 'Dungarvan, I'll have no gals with lacerated, infected bosoms

231

caused by their own carelessness in my ship's company. So if I ever catch you putting a test-tube in your bib-pocket again I'll have ye guts for garters!"

CHAPTER TEN

THE ACCIDENT RECOVERY ROOM UNIT

A WEEK later I was in the Accident Team. Six days before I was moved Staff Nurse Humber arrived in Casualty.

"The Hall staff nurses are spitting blood," I confided to Margaret when she rang me after my first day in my new job. "Sister didn't tell anyone she was coming to us from Marcus, or that Mrs. Fields isn't coming back as she's having a baby. Humber's been shoved in over all their heads. Robins was so livid it cured her migraine! Usually when she has one it lasts for days. Ruthless type, our Sinbad, but, baby, does she get results!"

"Very necessary, in a complicated department like Cas. Isn't this Humber one of your old mates?"

"God bless her, she is! She even had Sister smiling on me before I left the Hall. What's your news?"

"The General's op. is fixed for next Thursday."

"Poor man!" It was a Monday. "Such a wait! Tell him good luck from me."

"I will. He'll appreciate it. He considers you a most fetching young woman." From her voice she was smiling. "And the Corp. thinks you a real nice young lady with ever such a lovely smile."

"The cute pair!" I was more grateful than I cared to tell her for the kind words. Although Humber had transformed life with Sister Cas. for me, her advent had had no effect on my one-time source of strength and comfort. Richard Leland now seemed ready to spit at the sight of me, and I honestly did not know why. I did not like it either. I had grown so accustomed to thinking of him as my one mate in Cas., and owing to Margaret's habit of using his Christian name, I now found it impossible to think of him by any other name. But when we met he seemed to go out of his way to remind me he was neither the amiably silent Old Red I used to know nor my mildly friendly future Uncle Richard. He was very much our Mr. Leland, the S.S.O.

I asked Margaret how she was making out with the Corp.

"Very well, I think. I had a head start on Dickie's Mum. He calls me 'ma'am', inquires daily after the young master, and when he's not doing odd little jobs for the General he spends all day and half the night sitting practically to attention on a hard chair outside the General's room. When I suggest he goes to a movie or across to the pub for a beer he says 'Much obliged, ma'am, but if it's all the same to you, I'd rather stay.' So he stays, and when the General is snoozing takes me through the Second World War. We reached Alamein last night."

"Was the General in it?"

"Yes. As a major in a tank regiment. The Corp. was one of his tank crew. I now know exactly how General Francis won his M.C., and pretty nearly how to drive a tank. Incidentally, I asked the Corp. what Alamein was really like. He thought for a good five minutes. 'Noisy, ma'am. Bit noisy.' "

I laughed at her. "You sound as if you're enjoying your come-back!"

She said warmly, "I should. Everyone has been so incredibly kind to me."

For "everyone" I read Richard Leland.

235

I should have been delighted. I was, for her. For myself, I was too shaken up by the day I had just worked to feel delight. Recently I had very much wanted to get into the A.R.R.U. to prove myself to Sister, and to myself. One day had been enough to show me my original instincts had been right. I had got what I wanted, but it was not a job I was ever going to like, much less enjoy. That day haunted me all evening, and that night I had the kind of nightmares I had not had since I worked in the theatre. But at least the messiest theatre job was clean, aseptic, impersonal. The most fastidious human being looks the reverse after being mangled in a road accident, and, being in ordinary street clothes and on some ordinary occasion when the accident happens, our patients arrived in the Unit looking like people, not patients. It was that that hit me, and not only me, in the pit of the stomach.

Daisy's friend Mary de Wint was the staff nurse in charge of the nurses in the Accident Team. There were four of us under her. Daisy was the most senior, and I was the junior. We were all third-

or fourth-years. In Benedict's no first- or second-year student nurses worked in the Unit, and only the final-year students, which was why Sister Cas. had been so furious about Charlie Peters.

Nurse de Wint was a small dark-haired, and very quiet girl. During my time in the Hall I had liked the very little I had seen of her, as she was a fixture in the Unit. To call the A.R.R.U. the Unit was something else I had learnt in one day. Benedict's had rows of "Units", but once anyone had worked in the Accident Team, for ever after for that person there was only one Unit in the hospital.

Daisy was off for my first day. Cleaning the already clean Cleansing Theatre together early next morning, she remarked on the extraordinary but accepted hospital fact that throughout one's training one constantly worked with the same people. "Some sets one never meets from the day they start in the P.T.S. to the day they collect their badges; others follow one round and round in the same small circles."

I drew a circle in polish on the spotless metal trolley-top I was working on. (In the C.T., as in the other theatres, we started each day by cleaning the clean, polishing the polished; we cleaned between patients; we cleaned again at the end of the day.) "Even in one's own set one keeps on the same circuit with just a few. I've worked I don't know how often with Gwenellen. Never with Aline."

"Aline Ash? I worked with her in Arthur, and recently in Marcus. She still off sick?"

"Yes. Out in Majorca." I removed my polish circle. "Daisy, in Marcus did she and Humber ever settle down?"

"Hardly. The atmosphere was so thick when the night girls came on a blow-lamp wouldn't have got through."

"I've never understood that. They're both so nice."

"Humber's all right." She gave no opinion on Aline. "Mind you, Humber used to be very taken with Robin Armstrong."

"I never knew that!" Her inference was too obvious for pretence. "You're not suggesting Aline bust it up?"

"I'm not suggesting. I'm stating a simple fact. She did. Right here in Cas. last year. God knows why, as dear old Robin's not her type at all. He's far too slow."

That was true, and, as I did know from Aline, the reason why she had dropped Robin. "Certainly she much prefers the fast-talking fast workers, being one herself." As I spoke I realized I could be describing Bill. "Daisy, she can't have known about Humber and Robin. She wouldn't snitch."

"Jo, I know she's your friend, but that doesn't have to strike you blind. Maybe she can't help being one of those girls who are only attracted by other girls' men—or maybe she just likes playing with fire. Some do. Not me, but it takes all sorts." She had finished and covered her setting. She pulled down her mask, and her face was red from the sterilizer's steam. "Have you really not seen that streak in Ash?"

"No. That is, not until now. Now, hell, yes." I was remembering a couple of tentative romances that had for some reason never got off the ground, and then later how Aline, for a while, had run around with the man in question. Then I remembered a long-forgotten incident that could have split our set wide open but for Gwenellen. It had been in our first year, when Gwenellen first met Tom Lofthouse. Aline had made a very obvious play for him, but Tom, being seriously in love with Gwenellen from the start, had refused to play. Aline had made a huge joke of it all, but to this day had never a good word for Tom. Gwenellen had apparently ignored the whole thing, and had never mentioned it to me, or, as far as I knew, anyone else since. Nor had she let it affect her friendship with Aline. Gwenellen was four months younger than myself and our set's baby. It struck me now that if Aline was our cleverest member Gwenellen was by far the most mature.

My lack of insight infuriated me. "Why do I have to be such a nut? Why do I see people without really seeing them at all?"

"Because you see them as you imagine they are, and not as they are. One hell of a difference? As for your being a nut, that's just something else you've dreamed up to the point where you've kidded other people into believing it so successfully that you're now beginning to believe in the act yourself. Humber rumbled you in Marcus. She's been working on Sinbad."

"That, even I've rumbled."

"If the eyes are opening there's hope yet. Oh, damn the customers! Not this early!"

It was ten minutes to eight. The red light over the door was flashing on and off, a sign that the emergency line from the lodge was ringing the telephone in Mr. Waring's tiny office along the corridor. Nurse de Wint was with Sister, getting the daily staff nurses' briefing. Mr. Waring, his two surgical registrars, two house-surgeons, and the Resident Accident Anaesthetist, plus our four accident dressers, were at breakfast.

Daisy vanished to answer the telephone. "I've had to call for the lot," she said on return. "We've a right packet on the way in."

June Bateman, another fourth-year and next in seniority to Daisy in the Unit, had joined us from the Intensive Care Room. "What's the packet?"

"Two couples. One middle-aged, one

young, and a baby. The baby's only shaken. He was in a carry-cot, between what I guess were his mother and grandmother in the back." She set four emergency transfusion trolleys with the speed and precision of a machine. "The two men have really copped it. The women are pretty bad." She repeated herself as Nurse de Wint came in.

"How?" asked de Wint.

"On the clearway. An empty lorry overtaking got into a skin and spun. Its back hit the car. A closed saloon. Paddy says the cops say the top has been sliced off so cleanly it now looks like an open tourer. It was that drop of rain half an hour ago after the weeks of dryness."

Nurse de Wint surveyed the empty tables. "I thought we'd fill up when I saw that rain. The old dried oil will have made the roads as slippery as when rain falls on snow and freezes. Well, Dungarvan, Table 4 for you. Yates, 2, Bateman, 3. I'll take Table 1 with Mr. Waring." She looked round as the dressers rushed in. "Morning, gentlemen. An early start." She was still briefing them when Mr. Waring and the other men arrived.

Daisy said, "I was sorry to haul you from your bacon and eggs, Mr. Waring."

Mr. Waring, though Senior Accident Officer and of equal status with Dr. Jones, had a very different approach to his juniors. "Nurse Yates. I'll bawl you out for one hell of a lot," he replied amiably, "but not for causing the rain to fall." The red light began to flash. "Here we go again. This'll be 'em."

About a minute later the first special major-accident trolley was wheeled in, quickly followed by three others. These trolleys stood as high as the tables, were fitted with special mattresses through which X-rays could pass, and were so constructed as to allow any part of the trolley to be tilted upwards, downwards, or sideways, without dislodging the occupant. Inside of ten minutes, despite the air-extractor, the scents of oil, sweat, fresh blood, blood soaked clothes, and road grime mingled sickeningly with the scents of ether and anaesthetic.

The young woman I was attending was mercifully unconscious. There was an obvious fracture at the base of her skull, the jagged ends of her right radius were sticking through her blue linen suit-sleeve as well as her skin, and the back of her neck and her shoulders were ripped by flying glass. Of the four adults in that car, she was the least injured. At first I took her for a brunette. She was blonde, and when I washed the caked blood from her face she was pretty and very young.

Mr. Waring arrived at the elbow of the Registrar with whom I was working, together with a dresser. "Any internal bleeding, John?"

"None that I can find. Will you see?"

Very gently, Mr. Waring made an examination. "None. Good. The usual," he murmured almost casually before walking away.

He was not being casual. 'The usual' specific immediate treatment might vary with every patient that came into the Unit, but to the Unit each was a matter of old and much practised routine. The routine was new to me, but as de Wint had briefed me very clearly and everyone else knew his job so well, I found it far easier than I expected to fall in with the routine.

It took me rather longer to grow accus-

tomed to the strange sensation of timeless-
ness. In the wards, even in the Hall,
one was constantly summoned from job
to job. The telephone had always to be
answered. The clock had always to be
watched. Not in the Unit. As we were all
permanent fixtures, no-one had any responsibilities outside. Even Mr. Waring's
emergency telephone was taken over, when
any major accident, as now, came in,
by one of the Hall staff nurses sent to
sit in his office and tell him personally
anything he had to be told. I had always
thought him a nice little man. By the
end of that second morning I never
thought of him as a 'little man' again.

Two hours after they were wheeled in
the two women and the younger of the
two men were admitted to wards. The
older man died on the trolley twenty
minutes after leaving the ambulance.
Table 1 was never used. The Cleansing
Theatre was empty again before I was
aware of this.

Mr. Waring looked back at Table 1
as he washed his hands and arms. "From
the papers the cops found on them and

lying around they were taking themselves and the car to France on holiday. They must have made an early start to get away before the traffic piled up. And then the rain came down. On the just and the unjust."

Mr. Cook, one of the Registrars, asked, "Anyone know what happened to the lorry-driver?"

"Upset, but otherwise not even mildly shocked." Richard Leland had come in. "The cops brought him up for a check up. I've let him go. The baby's all right. We'll keep him in until the other set of grandparents arrive. They've got to come down from Manchester, so they'll be here some time this afternoon." He leant against the door. "I've just been speaking to the grandmother."

Mr. Waring nodded to himself as he mopped his forehead with the towel on which he had just dried his arms. "I'm sorry we couldn't save that older chap, sir."

Richard said unemotionally, "No man can save a man whose face has been pushed through the back of his head. Typical front-passenger-seat injury. But

I've had another look at his wife. I think she and the young couple should do. That's three out of four, Michael. You could have done a lot worse. And the baby's all right," he said again. "His mother was lying on top of him." He glanced up as the light above his head started flashing. "This'll be the boy on a scooter I came in to tell you about. Fractured skull."

"My God? Don't tell me it's another no skid-lid?"

"He had one on, but as he hadn't done up the strap when he came off, it came off." Richard moved from the door and went out with Mr. Waring.

A dresser asked, "Who'll tell that poor old girl about her husband?"

"The S.S.O." Mr. Cook and Nurse de Wint spoke together. Mr. Cook added, "His job."

"Christ," muttered the dresser, "who'd have it?"

No-one answered him.

The boy who had come off the scooter looked about Charlie's age. He was unconscious and already growing spastic from brain damage when he was wheeled in. He was articled to a firm of chartered accountants. He lived in Putney and had had his scooter only a month. He was still in the Intensive Care Room when his parents and seventeen-year-old sister arrived. Shortly after they were joined by the head of his firm. They waited in Mr. Waring's office, and as the most junior nurse in the Unit I was sent to take them a tray of tea. The mother said, "Do you mind pouring, Nurse? My hands are a little unsteady."

Her husband was a plumber. He had been called home from work and was still in his working clothes. He owned a good car, and his wife and daughter wore good clothes. They were a very ordinary little family. They looked as if they cared for each other and for the semi-detached house they were buying with a Council mortgage; as if they always had a joint and two veg. on Sundays, and the only time there was alcohol in the house was at Christmas; as if they did the pools and occasionally risked a few bob of the house-keeping at a betting shop, but never ran into debt, got drunk, had any dealing with the police for anything more serious than a forgotten dog-licence, and regarded violence and sudden death as not really the concern of respectable people.

Later I saw dozens of such little families sitting very close together in Mr. Waring's office. I never grew accustomed to them, and often never learnt their names. The expression they all wore lingered like the Cheshire Cat's grin, but it was no grin. It was an expression of dazed horror, and the horror was tinged with outrage. "This can't really be happening—not to us. Why us?"

Their name was Parker. While Mr. Parker stared at his untouched tea and Jenny, their daughter, crumbled, but did not eat, a biscuit, Mrs. Parker talked to me about her son. "He's always been a good boy, Nurse. I'm not saying he's not had his moods, but all the youngsters have 'em, and he's never given his father and me a moment's what I call real worry. Did ever so well in grammar school. He got his two 'A' Levels. Pure and Applied Maths. he took—though what that means don't ask me, as I'm sure I couldn't say. But you see what I mean, dear?

He's been such a good boy, and he's done so well."

I saw exactly what she meant and knew exactly to whom she was really talking. The head accountant sitting on the other side of the desk in his neat dark-blue suit looked downwards and lowered his head as if he realized he was listening to a prayer.

Jenny had not taken her eyes off my face. She had long, straight light-brown hair carefully arranged to fall forward. Now she constantly pushed it back, impatiently. "Nurse, how is David? They told us he was bad. How bad?"

Her mother said quickly, "Jenny, I told you it's not fair to ask nurses, as they can't tell you. They're not allowed to. The doctor has to tell you. He'll be in soon." She turned to me. "Jenny's not used to hospitals, dear. This is the first one she's been in since she was born. David, too. But I mind what the nurses used to say when I was in St. Martha's for the two of 'em. That's how I know." She looked at her husband and daughter. "We've been ever so lucky. We've all had good health. We never thought"—

her voice shook—"as anything like this could ever happen to one of us." She suddenly stiffened as Mr. Waring came in with de Wint. "How is he, Doctor? How is he? He is going to be all right?"

I did not hear Mr. Waring's reply. A glance from de Wint had told me to go, and shut the door behind me. Mr. Waring's presence with de Wint told me David Parker was still alive, but only just.

The breaking of news to waiting relatives was as organized in the Unit as was every other job performed there. Good news could be given to any member of the Team. The Registrars were allowed to give serious news. When a patient was in a dangerous condition Mr. Waring did the giving himself, with a staff nurse or the senior student nurse if women were present, alone when the waiting relatives were men. When a patient died in the Unit, as this morning, or was a B.I.D. (Brought in dead), the responsibility of telling his next-of-kin fell on the S.S.O., as that dresser had learnt this morning. When a medical patient collapsed and died in Casualty it was the S.M.O. who had to break it to his family. Obviously in certain circumstances it would have been easier and even more practical for Dr. Curtis and Richard to delegate the task to Dr. Jones and Mr. Waring. In the past that had been known to happen occasionally, but never with our present senior residents. As I heard Mr. Waring remark later that day to Mr. Cook about the man who had died, it was not much consolation after one had lost a patient who a few hours earlier had been a healthy man, but it was something to know for certain that when one passed the buck it would never be passed back.

It was tea-time before David Parker was fit to move to Marcus. He was still unconscious. By then we had had in an elderly man with a broken femur; a young man in coma after an acute electric shock; a little girl who had fallen downstairs and broken both wrists, as she had landed on her outstretched arms; a youngish mother of four children who had slipped when hanging new curtains. She had a cracked pelvis. All these accidents had taken place in private homes. We also dealt with five more road accidents before

I went off duty, but none of these were as badly injured as the four car passengers and David Parker.

The number of home accidents astonished me. Mr. Waring overheard me discussing this with Daisy one evening in my second week. "Not really surprising, Nurse Dungarvan, if you remember that as many people get killed in their homes in this country as on the roads. Isn't that right, sir?"

He had spoken behind me. I turned. Richard was with him. "Quite right. I forget the exact figures for last year, but I'm reasonably sure the home figures beat the roads. An Englishman's home may or may not now be his castle," he said drily, "but unless he's careful there's a strong probability it'll now be his death trap." He spoke to Daisy, as if I were invisible. He had treated me like that ever since I moved into the Unit, unless professionally forced to acknowledge my presence. He was only behaving exactly as he did around the hospital with the other girls and had done with me in Marcus. It had not riled me then, yet, stupidly, it did now. I asked myself,

Why care? Was there any law that said one must be liked by one's future uncle? Why bother because Margaret's Richard had for some inexplicable reason ceased to be my mate Richard? It was that particular thought that made me realize I had ceased to think of him as Old Red. I tried to correct that mentally. I did not succeed, and as I could not see that my personal thoughts mattered to anyone but myself, Richard he remained to me.

The Unit opened my eyes to more than the daily holocaust on English roads and in English homes. It was the first place in Benedict's in which I had worked as a near-equal with our men. In my theatre time I had been too junior to be even vaguely aware that under the gowns and masks were young men. I discovered that in the Unit. I discovered the men's feet and backs ached, as ours did, that they fretted about their exams., girl-friends, and professional futures as much as, if not more than, nurses. I also dis-covered that on the job the vast majority were much nicer than they seemed off duty, when out to impress the girls. No-one in the Unit ever bothered to impress anyone. We were too busy, we all needed each other too much, and, working so constantly together, we were all too aware of how much work everyone else was getting through to feel anything but respect for each other as skilled individuals. The work was so highly skilled, and we had to work as such a well-knit team, that it took me only a short time to appreciate exactly why, whilst Sister had doubts about me, she had kept me out.

Though the work continued to appal me when I stopped to think about it, The Unit itself was the happiest department I had ever worked in. At first I gave all the credit for that to Mr. Waring. Later I realized a good bit was due to Richard. Mr. Waring was responsible for all we did, but Richard was responsible for Mr. Waring. Had the two men not so clearly liked each other and trusted each other's judgments, life in the Unit could have been very different.

Mr. Waring was twenty-nine and highly tipped as our next S.S.O. Daisy said, "If Old Red has any say our Michael'll get it. And so he should!"

I agreed warmly. "But isn't he rather young?"

"He's not all that much younger than Old Red. What's six or seven years? Anyway, his job here doesn't end until the end of this year. He'll have to be an S.S.O. in another teaching hospital first, but if he then nips off to a smaller hospital for a year, though that's not as much time as our big bosses like an S.S.O. here to have outside, I'll bet they'll stretch the point rather than lose him. He's much too good to lose, as I'm convinced Old Red'll tell them. As Old Red's next move'll be on to the Staff, his word'll carry a lot of weight."

I thought of Mr. Waring's mobile face, quick manner, and expansive temperament. "I think he's a poppet of an S.A.O., but I'm rather surprised he and Old Red should be such mates. They're so different."

"Physically, maybe. But they've so much in common. They're both surgeons, as near contemporaries in age as makes no matter, and they both like their patients more than they like their knives. Nor is that quite all." Suddenly her eyes danced.

"They are both models of professional discretion."

"Both?" I was puzzled. "How do you mean?"

"Hey, Jo! I wasn't born yesterday. You know what I mean, and you must have seen how Michael's taking no chances either. He knows one look at the wrong moment and Sister'd hear and have Mary out lickerty-split, which is the last thing he wants, and not only for personal reasons. She's a bloody good accident staff nurse."

"Mary de Wint? And Michael Waring? I'd never guessed!"

She laughed and suggested I told that to the Marines. (Just as the Navy had left its mark on Sister, so did Sister's phraseology rub off on anyone who worked with her.) "Not that I blame you for acting dumb. 'No names no pack drill', as Corporal Wix used to say in Marcus."

I had opened my mouth to protest. I closed it without saying anything, as there was really nothing I could say. Thinking things over later, I realized that even had I risked telling her the whole truth and swearing her to secrecy, she would almost certainly have not believed me, as she would not want to believe me. Though so sensible, now we had become great friends, I had discovered Daisy had a glorious unashamedly sentimental streak, and she enjoyed match-making for her friends as much as she did altering the colour of her hair. Time'll sort it out, I thought, weakly, and tried to forget it. I did not succeed, probably as I was having to see so much of Richard.

Seeing so much of him began to have a rather disconcerting effect on me. I found myself missing him when he wasn't there. Thursday evening suddenly became my unfavourite evening of the week. Mr. Tomlin, the Senior Surgical Registrar who acted S.S.O. when Richard was off duty, was a pleasant man and much more civil to me than his boss. Yet I had only to see Mr. Tomlin walk into the Unit to feel peeved. When I realized that, I was as peeved with myself as with the harmless Mr. Tomlin.

Being reasonably good at talking my way out of tight spots, I tried to talk myself out of this one. Being on the rebound, I was ripe to imagine myself in love with any man who caught my eye. I was falling into the common pit of believing the grape-vine. I was over-imaginative, over-impressionable, over-emotional. I was suffering from a father-fixation. I was sex-starved. I was the lot.

I was also, subconsciously, building up a series of mental pictures of Richard's face. Richard smiling at some Unit joke; his intent expression and habit of occa-sionally frowning at the floor when listen-ing to a case history; the kindness that softened the rather austere lines of his face when he talked to an injured patient; and the mixture of sadness, despair, and frustrated rage that lingered in his eyes after examining the battered body of a dead child.

I did not want to watch him so closely or appreciate how much I must have done so, until I found his face was con-stantly in my mind and as familiar as my own in the mirror. Even then I refused to face facts. That was cowardly, but the Unit had taught me to prefer cowardice to folly. The consequences of the former could be unfortunate; those of the latter were almost invariably disastrous.

CHAPTER ELEVEN

A LETTER TO BILL

GENERAL FRANCIS had not had a growth. His first operation proved to have been purely exploratory. He was due to have a second and very extensive operation just as soon as he had recovered from the first.

I was seeing very little of Margaret. Ostensibly, because we were so seldom free at the same time. We knew each other so well. For present events too well. On the few occasions when we ran into each other in the hospital the change in her appearance since her first afternoon back tore me in three. The equal parts were delight, despair, and guilt.

The uniform suited her. The frilly sister's cap with its lace bow under her chin made her face younger and rounder. She had always had a small waist. Her splendidly buckled belt accentuated this the way her black nylons did her neat ankles. But it was not merely the uniform that altered her. She looked more serene and sure of herself than I had ever seen her. As serene as a woman who had come to terms with life and suddenly discovered those terms were loaded in her favour.

I had no idea how much she was seeing of Richard in his meagre off-duty. I guessed as much as possible, though she only occasionally mentioned their private life to me. One Friday in the main corridor she told me of the high-powered dinner-party she had attended the previous evening in the pundit's dining-room. The Dean had been host. "He remembers Simon well and asked most kindly after Dickie."

"Who else was there?" I asked, after being brought up to date on Dickie's prowess in his new school.

"The Remington-Harts, Dr. and Mrs. Curtis, Matron, Richard, and myself. Poor Richard was called away when the coffee came in and never got back. I don't yet know who wanted him. Your Unit?"

"No. At least, not then. The Hall had a spate of P.G.U.s [perforated gastric ulcers]. Three came in inside one hour, then two appendices who couldn't wait, and then just as I was going off at midnight we had in a man who'd been shot in the stomach in some night club. The Unit was buzzing with cops. The gunshot man was in the theatre till three."

She grimaced. "Poor devil! Still alive?"

"I don't know." It was ten to three now, and I was on my way on duty. "He was alive when the night girls came off, and he had a large cop sitting with him behind drawn curtains."

"Three," she murmured. "And then the poor man had all his night round to do. I hope they let him sleep once he got to bed."

"Yep." I hoped that so much I had to be terse. "How's the dear old General?"

Her smile reappeared. "He's not that old, dear! He's doing very well, and looking forward to seeing you and your friend Daisy Yates after his second op. That's next Wednesday."

"Isn't that the dodgy one?"

"Uh-huh. What other news have you got?"

"Not much. The Unit's hectic as ever.

Oh, yes—Gwenellen and Tom Lofthouse have fixed their wedding day in next January. Aline's still in Majorca."

"Still? Her food poisoning is taking a long time to clear up, isn't it?"

"She seems to have had a relapse. Gwenellen had a letter yesterday. There's one thing more," I added more cheerfully "you know Staff Nurse Humber? Well, she used to run around with a houseman called Robin Armstrong way back. It fell apart. Now it's on again. I'm very glad, as I like 'em both. Honest to God, five to! See you." I hurried on, and was deeply ashamed at my relief in being able to do so. It was not that I wasn't very fond of her. But this being torn in three seemed literally to be taking me apart.

Sister Cas. was in the Unit when I reported on. "Back aboard, eh, Dungarvan? Carry on."

"Thank you, Sister." I walked over to report to Nurse de Wint. Sister frequently popped in and out of the Unit to watch us, but she was very good about leaving the entire running of the Unit nursing side in Mary de Wint's very capable hands.

On Thursdays and Fridays Sister was a more constant Unit visitor than on the other week-days, since Thursday, being technically the lightest day of the hospital week, was the day chosen for our dressers to change. The boys—and occasionally the student girls—each worked weekly shifts during which they were on twenty-four-hour call. Being in their final year, by Friday afternoon most of them had settled in to accident work. If Sister entertained any doubts she discussed them with Mr. Waring, and very, very occasionally a dresser was removed. We had a girl dresser that week. Her name was Monica Miles, she was small as de Wint, very fair, and looked sixteen. On present showing she was going to be very useful.

June Bateman, Unit Two, had gone on holiday. Unit Three and I had moved up one. A girl from the Hall called Linda Oxford had come in to take my old place as Unit Four. Daisy was still our team leader.

Linda had joined us on Monday. Sister had been keeping as close an eye on her as she had kept on me during my first week in the Unit. Linda was the only other woman in Benedict's as tall as Sister. She towered over Mr. Waring and de Wint, whom she was assisting. The knowledge that she was the object of Sister's scrutiny made her flush beneath her mask and drop the roll of strapping she was holding. I felt for her.

In a brief slack spell later I said as much.

She said coldly, "Dungarvan, anyone can drop something once. But everyone hasn't your emotional Irish temperament."

"Is that a fact, now?" I copied old Paddy's brogue. "Honest to God, Nurse Oxford, you'll be after telling me next there are no little people to drink the fine saucer of milk I leave out for them every afternoon when I take Mr. Waring in his tea."

She went puce. "Will you never grow up and realize nursing is a serious business?" She stomped off before I could explain that now she was Unit Four taking in that tea was her job. I had continued to do it for the days she had been with us, as I had just happened to be free at the right time, she had been busy, and one of the nicest things about the Unit was the way in which everyone helped everyone else with his job. Daisy had collected the tea-tray for me during all my first week.

Nurse de Wint was in our stock-room. "Yes, get it, Dungarvan. Those men need their tea today. They were called out of breakfast and lunch, and out of their beds by five this morning to deal with that road gang whose lorry overturned when taking them to work. The general theatre was only quiet for two hours in the whole night."

That meant Richard had only had, at the most, two hours' sleep. "Nurse de Wint, what happened to the gun-shot man?"

"Died at lunch-time. Murder charge, now. Got enough money from the petty cash?"

I showed her the usual five shillings in my palm. She added a ten-bob note from her pocket. "Get 'em sandwiches and buns. If we can't give 'em sleep, at least let's feed 'em."

I knew just how de Wint felt, but

266

as she was a very senior staff nurse, I did not say so. I could see from her expression that she understood and did not object at all.

As tea was served in the Doctors' House, no official provision was made for the Unit men to take it in Mr. Waring's office. Whoever drew up that particular rule could never have been a hospital resident, or had any idea of what life in an Accident Unit entailed. The Doctors' House was roughly a ten-minute walk away from Casualty and on the other side of the hospital. No man constantly on his feet would willingly walk for twenty minutes to snatch a ten-minute break. The time allowed for tea, officially, was half an hour. Thanks to Sister's thoughtfulness in badgering our pundits into supporting her "Private Tea Fund", our petty-cash box allowed our Unit residents to take their tea-break packed in Mr. Waring's office, which was far more convenient for everyone, as that way they were always on the spot when wanted.

Mr. Waring was talking to Sister and Dr. Jones in the Hall when I returned with my tray from the mobile canteen.

"That's a welcome sight," he said, as I went by. "Leave it on my desk and round up the others, will you, Nurse Dungarvan?"

Mr. Waring's efficiency and the fact that he treated all nurses in exactly the same friendly way allowed Sister to smile on me approvingly, and even Dr. Jones to look just a very little less pained.

I passed Mr. Cook in the Unit corridor. "Nurse Dungarvan, I'm so hollow my anterior stomach wall is flapping against my vertebral column. I'll gather the lads and our one lass. They're all in the I.C.R. playing with our natty new gadget. Last time I looked in one of the new lads had swallowed a safety-pin to let the others haul it out. There's keenness for you!"

Our new gadget was a machine that removed swallowed metal objects by means of a smallish magnet attached to a specially constructed wire that also had to be swallowed by the patient. Then, with the help of X-Rays, the magnet could be guided towards the swallowed safety-pin, coin, or other metal object, and once contact was made the two could be gently hauled up into the mouth. It was a brilliant and very useful invention, as we constantly had in children who had swallowed the wrong things, and the machine saved many of them from major abdominal operations.

"Mr. Cook, I'm impressed! I just hope the safety-pin was closed? I know the gadget can deal with 'em open, but as old habits die hard, the idea of an open pin still makes me nervous."

"I warned him to shut it. I'm not officially supposed to know about it. I'll go and investigate." He disappeared into the Intensive Care Room, and I opened the door of Mr. Waring's office.

Momentarily, I paused in the doorway. Then I went in, put my tray on a chair, and very quietly closed the door. The sight of a sleeping S.S.O. might have me by the throat, but it was not a sight for curious and uninformed eyes.

Richard had been writing notes at the desk when he fell asleep. His pen had dropped out of his limp right hand and lay open beside it. From the length of the ash on the burnt-out cigarette in the ashtray he had dropped off directly after lighting it. He was sitting back in Mr.

Waring's chair, his left arm hung over the waist-high chair-arm, and his head was tilted back against the wall behind him. His breathing was regular, quiet, and deep. His face was pale with fatigue, and his hair looked darker and lacked its usual glow. His eyelashes were brown, and the shadows beneath his eyes black. He would need a week of sleep to remove those shadows.

In sleep he looked so very much younger that I realized more clearly than ever before how close a contemporary he was to Mr. Waring. Looking at his unguarded face, I remembered how on first meeting him I had written him off as middle-aged and a fine man to make me a future uncle. A fine man, I thought again now, but the last man in the world I now wanted as an uncle.

I hated to wake him, but had to, as the others would be in at any moment. "Mr. Leland, would you like your tea in here today?"

He was too far under. He did not even stir. I poured one cup, added eight lumps of sugar, set it on the desk by him with an intentional clatter. He slept

on. I touched his shoulder. "Mr. Leland."
Still no reaction. I shook him, gently.
"Mr. Leland. I'm sorry to disturb you,
but it's tea-time."

He sighed, blinked up at me, then
smiled sleepily. "What's that, dearest?"
he murmured, and opened his eyes properly. "Oh! Oh, God! It's you, Nurse
Dungarvan! Did I drop off?" He shook
his head violently to clear it. "I do apologize. Do you know, I didn't just drop off,
I was right out. When you shook me I
thought"—he broke off to rub his eyes—
"I'm not quite clear what I thought, except
that you were your aunt."

That I had worked out for myself. "We
are very alike."

"Not very. Superficially, yes." He stood
up. "I've never dropped off before. I
hope I never will again. One feels death
would be a happy release." He smiled
wryly. "I hope you weren't too shocked?"

I had never felt so throttled by etiquette as at that moment. I longed to
tell him that all that shocked me was
the hours he was expected to work, and
work well, without sleep. I said primly,

"No, Mr. Leland," and pushed forward his cup. "I poured this for you."

"Thank you." He sipped it and screwed up his face. "Did you empty the sugarbowl into this?"

"Eight lumps."

"Thank you," he said again. "Nauseating, but I can use it. And thanks for waking me up." He opened the door for me. "Does Mr. Waring know tea's up?"

"Yes. I'll get another cup."

"Don't bother. I'll rinse this one out. I only want one."

He did not close the door after me when I left him. I went straight along to the Intensive Care Room. There was no need for me to do that, but I had to get away fast. "Gentlemen and Miss Miles, your tea is stewing and getting cold."

Monica Miles spun round. "Fancy you knowing my name already, Nurse!"

"Ah, ha!" exclaimed Mr. Cook. "Efficient girl, our Nurse Dungarvan! Come on, you lot! Let's get at it before the customers start rolling in again."

Monica Miles let the others go. "So

272

you're Nurse Dungarvan? Of course! I see the resemblance now! You're Mrs. Ellis's niece!"

I was devoted to Margaret, but my pleasure in our strong family likeness to each other was now wearing very, very thin. "That's right. I take it you know my aunt?"

"Not very well." She explained meeting Margaret in the Wing and hearing of me from her, on her several attempts to call on General Francis. "He's 'No Visitors' at his own request until he's clear of ops. Your aunt has had to break this to me, tactfully. She's been simply sweet."

"I can imagine. You're a friend of General Francis?"

"Not exactly." She had a high squeaky voice that was, oddly, not unattractive. "I met him when he used to visit his son in Marcus. You knew he had a son warded there?" I nodded. "I was a Marcus dresser for his last few days." She hesitated. "He was good fun."

"Yes. He was."

"You knew Bill Francis?" From her tone, I had seen the Holy Grail.

"I was his night special when he was on the D.I.L."

"Were you? I suppose you haven't heard from him?"

I said, "Not since his bread-and-butter letter." I said nothing about his one telephone call. I had a good hunch her feelings had been hurt enough.

"Then you wouldn't know if he's still in Majorca?"

"Majorca?" My mind flashed to Aline's prolonged sick-leave. "I didn't even know he was there."

"Oh, yes!" She obliged with dates. They matched the date that Aline had flown out to join her parents. "He's had his plaster off out there. He sent me a card saying so." She smiled at herself. "I guess he's forgotten my name by now. But he was rather sweet, so I thought I'd look up his father. Not that I don't like General Francis for himself. He's charming."

"I think so too, and so does Daisy Yates. She works here. She's off today. She was Bill's special on days. I expect you'll know her?"

"Not by name. Oh, dear! She's not

tall, fair, and slim, with a tight mouth? An absolute go-getter?"

She was describing Aline. I did not tell her so. Hospital sets were like families, and whatever the individual members might think about each other, to the outside world whenever possible they presented a united front. "Daisy's auburn and not all that slim. She's very nice. You'll like her."

"That's a mercy," she replied frankly, "as, though I like to like nurses, not all nurses seem to like female students. Or have I just got a chip?"

I would have been a liar had I denied her charge. "Some do, some don't. Depends, I suppose, on the nurse—and the female student."

"Fair enough."

We were smiling at each other when Linda Oxford came in. "Dungarvan, Nurse de Wint has just told me I should have got the men's tea! Why didn't you tell me? Don't you consider me capable of doing my own work? Or do you just like getting tea because it gives you another opportunity to talk to the men?"

Richard's reaction on wakening had

left me far too edgy for tact. It was one thing to suspect; another to be certain. I snapped back, "And what makes you think I have to look for opportunities, Nurse Oxford?" I stomped off just as she had done to me earlier. I knew I had just made an open enemy, and was far too cross to care, until my anger cooled three minutes later, and, as always after a childish display of temper, I regretted the fact, as I confided to Gwenellen at first supper that night.

Gwenellen had worked with Oxford. She said, "I can never make up my mind whether that girl's a Matron in the making or a large bladder stuffed with hot air. Her lamp is so bright it dazzles me. She never stops blahing on about wanting to do something really worthwhile with her life. Most people who want that don't blah about it. They just get on and do it. I wonder if old Sinbad's got her number?"

"If she hasn't she will. One may like to believe old Sinbad's making a mistake, but, as I now know, she doesn't. She stands around watching and brooding—and giving one hell in the process—

until she's sure of her ground. She must be pretty sure about Oxford to let her in the Unit, but only pretty, as she's still watching her. She was in again just now. Unless," I added as an idea occurred to me, "she's watching a student girl we've now got. A Monica Miles."

"Monica Miles? Tom's told me about her. Wasn't she in Marcus after I went off sick? Tom said she was very, very taken with your ex-special p."

"You never told me!"

"Why should I? Not my affair, and Tom says she's a nice kid. You won't mention this to her?"

"Don't have to." I explained all Monica Miles had said about Bill. I left out Aline.

Gwenellen glanced round the table. We were sitting alone up one end. Nevertheless, she lowered her voice before filling in the gaps in my explanation. "I've not told you about Aline and Bill Francis before, Jo, as the subject's sheer dynamite. I haven't even told Tom, but as Aline, in the letter I had from her yesterday, said she doesn't imagine she'll be coming back and has just used this 'relapsed' story for Matron's benefit, I don't imagine it'll be long before Home Sister invites us to pack up her room."

I was astonished. "Aline walking out? When we're in a few months of taking State Finals? I've always thought her so bright! This is crazy!"

"Yes and no. You nursed Bill Francis. Wouldn't you have called him a fast worker?"

"Yes. But—"

"Hang on, love. Think. Aline is bright. She obviously thinks she's on to a good thing. I'm not sure I agree with her about the man, but there's no question she's right about his future prospects."

"Journalists don't make all that money!"

"A few do. I wasn't thinking of that. Nor, I'll bet, is Aline. Jo, think! General Francis doesn't run a new Rolls, and pay for Corporal Wix, his bill in the Wing, Remington-Hart's fees, and support a huge stately home in Devon on his pension, good though it may be. To spend money like that you need real money."

"How do you know he's got a stately home?"

"Old Red took some snaps when he

was down there fishing. Tom's seen 'em. So, I guess," she added drily, "has Aline."

"Yes. I guess you're right. And Bill's the eldest son."

"And General Francis not exactly in the best of health. So if our Aline doesn't come back from this holiday as Mrs. Bill I don't know our Aline. I think I do. Don't you?" I nodded, reluctantly. "I wonder if Bill Francis does?"

I did not answer at once. I was thinking of Bill's selfishness in staying away from his father now, and how Aline matched that by letting him stay. She knew all about the General's being in the Wing, if not that Margaret was nursing him, as I had written and told her General Francis was a Benedict's patient only last week. I had given her all the medical details I knew, thinking that since she had known Bill she would be interested. No doubt she was, if not in the way I thought.

"Gwenellen, I feel sick! Really sick! I don't give a damn about them marrying each other—I think they're a well-matched pair—but Bill Francis ought to be with his father now, and Aline knows it!" I explained how. "She must have told him!"

"Not necessarily." Her dark eyes were both gentle and shrewd. "You're as much her friend as I am, and you knew Bill Francis much better than I did, but she never told you she had him on a string. I think she only told me to settle an old bit of business between us."

"Your Tom?"

"Yes." It was the first time she had ever mentioned that tricky period in her life to me. She did not dwell on it now.

I said, "Yet—I like Aline so much."

"She's got some very good points. She can't help being a bitch, and her bitchiness may even be just the job for Bill Francis. He's weak as they come. She's strong enough for two. She may even be properly in love with him, and him with her. Whether he'll stay that way if she lets him off the hook is another story. There's a lad with a roving eye, if ever I saw one. Good thing you ran into Old Red before you got too involved."

I gasped, "You knew?"

"Jo, love, I was right there in Marcus. I have two eyes in my head. Oh, goodness, is that the time? I promised to meet Tom five minutes ago."

I had another ten minutes, but as I did not want any pudding, I left with her. Margaret was leaving the Sisters' Dining-room as we came out of ours. Gwenellen hurried back to the Home to change for her date, and Margaret and I walked slowly back towards Casualty.

I was too furious with Bill and Aline to talk of anything else. Sensibly, Margaret warned me to keep my voice down and thoughts to myself, as Aline was still officially on the staff. "After all this time I doubt Matron would take exception to her getting engaged to an ex-patient whom she just happened to meet again on holiday, no matter how faintly suspect that 'just happened', but she would object very strongly to hearing of a nurse's resignation from anyone but the nurse in question, herself. Who happens to be one of your set—and, I always assumed, one of your great friends."

"That's what I thought!"

She looked at me and frowned. "So you're not quite over it, still?"

"Honest to God, I am! It isn't their romance that sticks in my throat! It's the way this must be hurting General Francis. He was so good to Bill." I told her of those nights in Marcus. I had mentioned them casually, before. Now I gave her the works. "How can such a good father have produced such a lousy son?"

"It worries him. He doesn't talk much about it, but he does worry. Yes, of course he's hurt. Every morning I scan the post hoping there'll be a letter. The most he ever gets is a card. He props it on his bed-table, and we admire the view and say how glad we are Bill's having such a good time in the sun. The other boy's very different. He writes every few days by air from Hong Kong. I wish he was stationed nearer. I did suggest he might ask to be flown home on compassionate leave. I'm sure the Army would give it him. The Army's good about such things these days. His father wouldn't hear of it."

"Why ever not? Doesn't he realize that if he doesn't see his younger son now he may never—"

"Jo, don't be stupid!" she snapped with rare violence. "Of course he knows the score! He's a normal, very affectionate father. Of course he wants to see his boys again! But, like any good father, he's putting his son's future ahead of his own wishes. He says life is hard enough for any serving soldier who has to live down the fact that his father is a Major-General and, even though retired, still in a position to pull the right string, without adding to the difficulties by asking a special concession that would certainly be granted. Consequently, he hasn't even told Paul the whole truth about his present condition. I'm convinced that if he had Paul Francis would be here now."

"Bill should have told his brother. He must know it all." I explained my letter to Aline.

She shared Gwenellen's opinion on that subject, but for different reasons. "You kids are as fiercely intolerant of each other as you are of your elders. Aline doesn't have to have kept the news to herself only to keep Bill to herself. She may honestly believe that's the most sensible thing to do, and there's nothing to be gained by worrying Bill until he has to be worried."

"To hell with Bill! What about his father's feelings?"

She said, "To appreciate another person's feelings requires imagination. Haven't you always told me Aline was the one girl in your set able to view the patients with total detachment? How can any nurse who is able to get under a patient's skin remain detached? To do that you must lack imagination. So Aline lacks it. A pity, but don't blame her for not suddenly producing something she hasn't got." She went on to say that for some time she had been wondering if there was any connection between Bill's long stay in Majorca and Aline's sick-leave, but had said nothing to me as it might only have been a coincidence. "His father's often remarked there must be some pretty girl to add to the attractions of that place, as Bill normally is far too keen to see over the top of the next hill to stay more than a few days anywhere on holiday. And—this is just for you, Jo—Matron the other day told me that I would be astonished at how often her nurses away on a foreign holiday developed the most convenient attacks of food-poisoning a day or so before they were due back. She named no names, but I'd a notion she'd your friend

Aline in mind. It would seem, rightly."

"Yes. You may be right about Aline. I still don't think she's right to keep the truth from Bill."

"Frankly, darling, nor do I. But we are here, and she is out there. It may look so different from out there."

It seemed to me Bill should be given a chance to decide that for himself. I brooded darkly for the rest of my duty, and after midnight wrote to him myself. Not knowing his address, I sent the letter care of Aline's hotel, trusting the desk clerk to deliver it.

I made no excuses for writing, and did not mention Aline or his old promise to me. I wrote that I was prepared to incur his own and his father's wrath for involving myself in the Francis family affairs. Then I sealed and stamped the letter to go airmail, and crept downstairs to post it in the box in our darkened front hall before going to bed.

One o'clock struck somewhere as I drew back my curtains after switching off the light. The general-theatre floor was still lit up. I forgot the Francis family and lay in bed watching those lights and worrying about Richard. I remembered Margaret in the Sister's Home and wondered if she was thinking of him, too. I felt ashamed, miserable, lonely—and went on worrying about Richard. I did not let myself fall asleep until the general-theatre lights went out, one by one, over an hour later.

CHAPTER TWELVE

THE UNIT IS A FACTORY-BELT

NEXT morning I had a letter from the solicitor acting for the Downshurst police in connection with that accident on the bypass. The two men in the black car were now out of hospital, the case was shortly coming to court, and the solicitor wanted to check through my statement with me, if possible in Downshurst, if not in London.

I wrote a note asking Margaret to meet me in the canteen at lunch-time, then stopped a Cas. porter in the yard to ask him to deliver it for me and, if he could, to get an answer. He returned beaming. "The Sister says one-thirty."

She had not arrived when I reached the canteen. Charlie Peters was there, sitting with a crowd of students. We had not seen each other since I moved into the Unit. He waved me over, and when I shook my head and found myself an empty table he climbed over a couple of friends to join me, uninvited. "Meeting someone, Jo?"

"My aunt. Will you mind pushing off when she comes?"

"Sure," he replied amiably. "What's the old lady doing up here? Checking little niecie's being a good girl?"

"Not exactly. She's working here, temporarily."

"You never told me!"

"Forgot," I lied. "How are The Bones?"

"Not so hot. We can't get our sound right."

I laughed. "You are so right! It's ear-splitting!"

"Stuff that! It's dead trendy to be loud. Who cares about the tune? It's the beat that counts. You're way out, Jo. Strictly for olde-tyme, that's you, in music as well as men. How's Old Red?"

Suddenly I had either to scream or snap. "Charlie, do me a favour! Lay off the coy quips!"

"And who's being coy now? Didn't you tell me yourself you'd Old Red like eating out of your hand, man? As all ruddy Benedict's knows by now!"

"It does?" My voice cracked. I was remembering the night General Francis called in Cas. "Charlie! You didn't make with the talk?" His expression told me the worst. "Honest to God! It figures."

He vowed he had only told The Bones in strict confidence. The Bones had six members, and as they were nice boys it was just possible each had told no more than five others in strict confidence. They were junior students, but most had friends amongst the more senior, and most of those friends amongst the housemen. It had to be all round the Doctors' House. I was surprised I had not had this back from Gwenellen, until I recollected her talent for keeping her mouth shut. Gwenellen, I reflected grimly, could teach me a lot.

Charlie looked about to burst into tears. I was making soothing noises when he suddenly leapt up. "Did you want Nurse Dungarvan?"

Margaret was wearing her linen suit and black straw hat. She looked even more attractive than on that afternoon in the car-park. Charlie rocked visibly when I introduced them, then retreated to his friends and sat and stared at her as if she were the promised land.

I said, "The lad's growing up. You've just hit him between the eyes!"

"Nonsense, darling! I'm old enough to be his mother. Sweet boy." She glanced round, smiling, and across the canteen Charlie blushed. "He's the wrong colouring, but very like Richard when I first knew him. He was all arms and legs in those days. Now, why did you want to see me, Jo? Sorry to keep you waiting while I changed, but I'm off to see Dickie at two. He's allowed out tonight and all day tomorrow. Richard's driving me down to collect him and then taking us both on to the cottage."

"So that's why you look so chic. I hope you all have a wonderful week-end." The amount of enthusiasm I had to pack into my voice made me feel like Judas Iscariot.

"I hope so, darling. Richard's staying with the Remington-Harts. Well? What's the problem?"

I showed her the solicitor's letter, and asked if I could borrow the cottage on my next day off, Wednesday. "Then I can see this man in Downshurst."

"You can have the cottage with pleasure,

but won't you be rather lonely? It's very isolated. Why not go down to Downshurst for the day?"

As I could not possibly explain that nothing could make me feel more lonely than I did in the crowded canteen at that very moment, I made some trite excuse about wanting country air. She was in too much of a rush to argue, and promised to leave her key in my post pigeonhole on Tuesday evening, and warn Mr. Sims not to worry if he saw lights in her cottage on Wednesday night. "Forgive me leaving you, Jo, but this rain is going to slow us down. Have a good week-end."

"Sure. And you. And give my love to Dickie."

It was still pelting when I went on duty at three. I wore my cloak for the first time in weeks, and though the subway was now officially open, preferred to cross the road under an umbrella.

The rain and the sudden drop in the temperature gave the Unit its quietest week-end in weeks. By Sunday evening Mr. Waring had caught up with his arrears of paperwork, every instrument in the Unit had been repolished, every gown mended, every rubber glove repaired, every stock emulsion bottle had a new linen collar, and every old Unit hand was jittery.

Linda Oxford and our dressers took another view. Linda Oxford said it just proved what an unnecessary song and dance the Unit staff normally made about their constant pressure of work. Monica Miles said she wished no-one any harm, but, as she was with us to work, she would much rather work.

"If you are really interested in work," retorted Linda patronizingly, "you should be a nurse—if not a Unit nurse. Now, ward nursing is nothing but hard work! It's non-stop, but so worthwhile! One gets such satisfaction from it. One grows so close to one's patients. One forgets oneself completely. But then, obviously, one has to have a vocation."

"Obviously," echoed Monica Miles politely. I winked at her. She looked faintly startled, then winked back. Later she inquired, "Has one no vocation, Dungarvan?"

"God knows. I just enjoy nursing." I

sniffed the air. "I'm not enjoying this week-end."

"Naturally." Linda had rejoined us, smiling thinly. "The S.S.O.'s off."

I was missing him so much I could have been missing an arm or leg. I grinned as if she had made a huge joke. "Sure, now, and isn't my poor heart aching and breaking for himself!"

Linda's reaction astonished me. "My God! Is there nothing you take seriously?"

The light over the theatre door was flashing for the first time in an hour, so I did not have to answer her.

Our patient was an eighteen-month-old boy who had fallen head first out of his cot. He was fat and cheerful despite two black eyes and a swollen nose. He had no fractures and very much enjoyed the fuss we enjoyed making of him.

His mother was very young, pale, and harrassed. Mr. Waring glanced at her thoughtfully after attending to her baby. "Let's see that cut on your wrist, madam. It's new. How did it happen?"

"It's just a scratch from the teapot spout, Doctor. I dropped it, washing up. Always dropping things, I am." She

293

sighed. "It's wearing them rubber gloves."

Mr. Waring examined her hands. "You wear gloves because of this rash?"

"Yes. I thought they might help. They don't. Not really."

The cut on her wrist was clean and minute. Mr. Waring attended to it himself and very slowly. Whilst he did so he let her talk.

She shared one room in her in-laws' house with her husband and two babies. The baby she had left at home was three months old. She admitted to headaches. "But it's this rash that's the worst. Comes up every time I do the washing, and with the two children and Frank working up the garage there don't seem no end."

Before she was allowed to take her baby son home Mr. Waring fixed her up with appointments to see the Eye Specialist, Ear, Nose, and Throat Specialist, Skin Specialist, and Out Patients' Lady Almoner. She left looking very much happier with a sheaf of prescription forms and Monica Miles as escort to show her to the dispensary. "Those three pundits are going to be out for my blood," said Mr. Waring, "as I'm sure they'll find nothing more amiss with her than I did. But I'm not infallible, and she needs a little fuss to be made of her."

Nurse de Wint asked, "Those headaches weren't her eyes?"

"Not as far as I could see. Headaches very seldom are caused by eye trouble. Either they're caused by sinus trouble, or, far more commonly, emotional stress. Like that skin allergy. Laying off the washing won't clear it. The stuff she's getting now will help a bit, but until she gets out of that one room and into a home of her own it'll blow up again and again. What really ails her, my lads," he explained to the dressers, "is a chronic attack of in-law-itis. You'll see a lot of that, and don't underestimate the physical damage it can do. And that seems to be"— Nurse de Wint had caught his eye—"no— as you were. One thing more I must explain about that girl. You've just seen me do the kind of job more usually done by Dr. Jones in the Hall. Not true accident work, you may have been thinking, and and up to a point correctly. Only up to a point. If any patient comes in here with an injury and I observe he or she needs special attention for some other condition, then obviously I'm allowed to do something about it, and would be one hell of a lousy medic. if I did not. As you all saw, I treated that girl first, because she had cut herself on a teapot. That's in the log. Nurse de Wint?"

"Yes, Mr. Waring. I entered it myself"

Mr. Waring grinned. "That'll keep the boys who keep the books in the backroom happy. Never forget to see everything's written down, signed, and dated with the time of admission as well as the date, lads. Then if anyone tries to query anything you do you point to the given line and say —take a look—that's why! I did what I did because, in my opinion that, was the right thing to do." He raised a finger. "Don't forget that 'in my opinion'. Stick on that, and you'll have the whole bloody medical profession lining up behind you. And providing you keep to union rules and keep your books straight, you'll find no man in the world has a tougher or more solid trade union behind him." He turned to de Wint. "I hope you don't object to my bringing a soapbox into your department, Staff Nurse?"

"Not at all, Mr. Waring," she replied gravely, and we all laughed.

I enjoyed seeing those two together. They were such professional professionals, and never allowed their pleasure in each other's company to affect the high quality of their work. Their discretion was brilliant as well as admirable. Daisy was still the only person in the hospital from whom I had heard one word about their being in love. That amazed me until I recollected they were very senior, Mr. Waring had nearly as little off-duty as Richard, and, being very popular with his Unit men, could rely on their complete discretion in their turn—if they were in the secret, and it was quite possible they were not. As he and de Wint worked only in the Unit, the rest of the hospital forgot their existence. When they met off-duty it was obviously far from Benedict's, and they were probably careful to return independently. Such discretion might seem unnecessary to an outsider, but not to anyone working in a large hospital. Let the news break, and then one small error be made in the Unit, and the consequent wagging of tongues could seriously damage both their Benedict's careers.

Knowing Sister Cas. to be so shrewd, for a little it puzzled me that she should never have had any suspicions. Then I remembered that the one thing that mattered above all else to Sister was the welfare of her beloved Casualty. To admit to suspicions could entail breaking up a first-class team. As long as the team remained first-class I suspected Sister would remain willing to look the other way. In her place I certainly would.

The manner in which their affair had managed to evade the grape-vine explained something else that had been puzzling me. No-one, apart from myself, seemed aware Richard and Margaret were meeting off duty, and only my set appeared to know they had trained together and were old friends. So much for my ill-made schemes to fix the limelight on myself. A boomerang, no less, I reflected, and an unnecessary boomerang at that. They hadn't needed my help. Theirs was no boy-meets-girl romance. They were mature adults who knew all the rules of the game, and hospital life inside out. As I should have appreciated had I not been so blinded by the mental beauty of myself as Cupid.

The quiet lasted another thirty minutes. At nine, when an unconscious attempted-suicide arrived, only Table 1 was empty, and that only because the schoolboy who had fractured both ankles jumping from a high wall for a dare had been moved to a ward.

"It's in a terrible mess he's in, Mr. Waring, sir," announced Paddy laconically, "and in a terrible mess he'll be until you've stitched his poor foolish head back on his neck."

"Had a real go, has he?" Mr. Waring raised the sterile towel Sister Cas. had added to the ambulance men's first-aid dressing. "Good God Almighty! The things they get up to! But his clotting time's good."

Nurse de Wint watched from Table 4. "Can you manage, Mr. Waring?" She meant without a nurse.

"Pro tem. He'll start off again soon as I start mucking those clamped-down vessels about."

Nurse de Wint was helping the second

Registrar with a small girl who had fallen from a third-floor window on to a concrete path. Her head had escaped, but she had multiple fractures and was being examined under anaesthetic. Her parents were too shocked to explain, if they knew, how she got out of the window. They were having supper when they heard the thud outside. Linda came back just then from taking them tea in the office.

Mr. Cook, a dresser, and myself were at Table 3. Our patient was an old man who had been knocked down by a bus. He had three fractured ribs, one of which had pierced his lung, and a fractured pelvis. Shock had collapsed his veins. Mr. Cook had been unable to insert a blood-transfusion needle and was having to cut down to put in a cannula.

Monica Miles and another dresser were working with a houseman at Table 2. Their patient was a man who had been stabbed in the chest by the shaft of his steering-wheel. He had skidded his car into a post-box.

Our other houseman was at supper. Mr. Waring asked Paddy to call him back. "You might also give my compliments to

Mr. Tomlin and say I'd be obliged if he would stop in here. I'd like him to see this chap."

"Then I'll be after ringing the general theatre, sir, seeing as himself'll just have got started on the strangulated hernia we'd in not an hour back, and in a bad way he was, the poor man."

"Right. Let it go, Paddy. I'll shout later if I have to. Just get my houseman. I need more hands."

Linda was hovering officiously. "Shall I help Mr. Waring, Nurse de Wint?"

De Wint surveyed the room anxiously. She looked at me and then at Mr. Cook. Then she looked at Table 2. "Right, Nurse Oxford. Miss Miles," she called quietly, "will you also go and help Mr. Waring?"

"That's it," grunted Mr. Cook. "Speed it up to start with, Nurse Dungarvan."

I was still adjusting the screw of the drip-connection set in the transfusion apparatus that regulated the flow of blood when the crash came. Linda Oxford had fainted. She would have knocked over Mr. Waring's dressing-trolley had he not switched it speedily aside with a flick of one foot. "You'll have to leave her on the floor, Miss Miles," he muttered as Monica had turned to bend down, "as I need you. Pass me those snaps—" He glanced up. "Christ! Not you as well? Beat it, stat!"

Nurse de Wint looked round again, without moving her hands. "Mr. Cook, can you manage with just a dresser? Thanks. Dungarvan." She jerked her head at Mr. Waring. "Gloves."

That told me not to wait and wash my hands, but to put on one of the many emergency pairs of sterile gloves and help Mr. Waring. Linda came round as I had on the first glove. Her colour was dreadful, and her eyes were appalled. Richard came in as she sat herself up. He helped her to her feet and out of the room, without exchanging a word with anyone. He wore a dark suit and was without his white coat. He reappeared almost immediately. "Sister's taking care of her." He came and stood by Mr. Waring. "I hear you wanted Mr. Tomlin, Michael. For this chap?"

"Yep. Didn't know you were back."

"I've just driven up from Downshurst. Paddy told me." He watched what we were doing. "How much do you think he's lost?"

"Four, five pints." Mr. Waring clipped off another gaping blood-vessel. The wound itself was like a second nightmarish mouth grinning garishly in the unconscious young man's neck. "A right messy job the poor bastard's done of it, but as he's missed the jugular and the common carotid, he's still with us." His hand shot my way, as it had been doing since I joined him. I placed another pair of Spencer Wells in his open palm. "That's the lot." He looked up as the pathologist on duty returned. "Not a rare group, I hope, Henry?"

"Moderately. But we've enough to top him up with all he'll need." The pathologist held out a card on which was written the patient's sex, approximate age, time of admission and date, and blood group, in large block capitals. I copied these quickly into our log-book, then fixed the card with the special clips provided to the clean accident gown the man wore over his own blood-soaked clothes. These would be removed after he had been transfused.

Mr. Simons, our absent houseman, had arrived. Mr. Waring nodded at the waiting transfusion trolley. "In his left ankle, and try not to hack him about too much. He's been hacked enough for one day."

The houseman tried to get in the needle. The young man's veins were as collasped as those of the elderly man on Table 3. "I'm afraid I'll have to cut down, sir."

"Shall I try?" Richard had removed his jacket, rolled up his sleeves, donned a mask and apron, and scrubbed up. "Yes. Very tricky. However"—he got in the needle at his first attempt—"I've been dealing with the tricky ones rather longer than you have, Simons." He set the rate of drops himself, watching Mr. Waring's stitching. "That's a neat job, Michael."

"H'm. Think he'll thank me for it?"

"Possible, if not probable. What do we know about him?"

"Damn all! He had locked himself in some public lavatory. The attendant saw the blood under the door and broke it down. There was a nick opposite, so the cops whisked him straight here in a car. Nothing on him to identify him. He obviously meant to do the job properly, and if our head-shrinkers can't find out why, next time that's what he'll do."

The room had cleared as the other patients had been moved into the I.C.R. Monica Miles had returned and was standing watching with the three other dressers. One asked. "Do they always try again?"

Richard said, "The ones that mean business, do."

"Even after psychiatric therapy, sir?"

"You can psycho-analyse a man until you and he are blue in the bloody face," muttered Mr. Waring, "plug him with everything in the book, and shock him half out of his wits with electro-therapy, but if he's really determined to do himself in, soon as you let him out he'll have another bash."

"Then, if you'll forgive my asking, sir," drawled the student with mock humility, "is there really much point in trying to save 'em? I mean, isn't it all rather a waste of time and blood and so on?"

Until then I had never suspected our amiable S.A.O. had a quick temper. He flushed dully beneath his mask. Richard shot him a calming glance before facing the student himself.

"What's your name, boy?" he asked gently.

"Frampton, sir."

"And you feel, Mr. Frampton, that we should start taking over from God?"

"I—? I'm sorry. I don't follow you, sir."

"Surely you must? Since you are suggesting that we are qualified to sort out whom to save and whom to reject, doesn't it follow automatically that you must consider us capable of assuming the mantle of the Almighty?"

The student was now as flushed as Mr. Waring, and very persistent. "I didn't exactly mean that. I just thought that if a chap like this is likely to repeat the performance, wouldn't he prefer to be allowed to get away with it?"

"Possibly. And just as possibly not. Why did he do it? Do you know? No. Nor do we. All we know is that his life needs saving, and we can probably save it. To save those we can is our job. If it isn't a job you care for, don't take it on. If you do it'll be your job. As for time being wasted—what the devil do you suppose our time is for? Or, for that matter, the

306

blood in our blood banks? Do you imagine both are there to be used sparingly and only on those we deem worthy of saving? And just supposing that obtained, how would you like to be carried unknown and unconscious into a hospital? Yes, you, Mr. Frampton. This lad here could be you. Every patient carried into St. Benedict's could be you. Ever thought of it that way? If not, just you start thinking along those lines, boy." He pointed a finger at the figure under the towels and blankets. "That's how you look, after hitting the bottom of the pit on one wet Sunday night in London. That's how you look" he repeated, "after carefully locking yourself in a public lavatory, taking a razor-blade out of your pocket, hacking away at your own throat, and making as much of a bloody hash of the job as you must have felt you'd made of your life to pick up that razor-blade in the first place. But what if you were wrong? What if tonight you want to die and tomorrow to live?" The student did not answer. "While you've still the hope of a second chance, has any man the right to deny you that?"

I could not wait any longer. For the last hour I had been fighting back nausea. The mental pictures his words had sparked off in my mind finished me. I managed to say primly, "Excuse me, please," and to walk sedately out of the Cleansing Theatre. Then I ran.

Monica came into our changing-room as I washed my face in cold water. "I've been sent to see if you're O.K."

"I am, thanks. Now." I retied my mask. "De Wint send you?"

"No. The S.S.O. Faint?"

"Nothing so elegant. I vomited plus."

"Me too. Only I wasn't quick enough."

"Poor you! Don't worry. One's timing improves, with practice." Richard's concern was no comfort. After his week-end he was probably having another avuncular bout. "Anyone else coming in? That sounds like another stretcher." I opened the door. "Yes. Back we go."

The incoming stream of accidents continued all night. There was no let-up next day. That evening the dressers were drooping with exhaustion. Mr. Waring stood first on one foot, then the other.

"One's used to black Mondays, but this is ridiculous. This isn't an Accident Unit, this is a factory-belt. God help my fallen arches!" The light was flashing. "Back on the job, slaves!"

Linda Oxford was off that day. When de Wint sent me to second supper she told me to come back five minutes early, as Sister Casualty wanted to see me.

"What have I done, Staff Nurse?"

She smiled wearily. She had been on since 7.30, and though officially off at 4 p.m. and scrapped her own off-duty. "Relax. It's only about some change in our rota."

I looked in my post pigeonhole en route to the dining-room. There was a note from Margaret. It glowed with content. Dickie had looked well and happy; the weather in Sussex had been far better than in London; they had all enjoyed their various long drives; General Francis had been delighted to get a cable from Bill that afternoon. Bill was flying back to-morrow to see his father before his second op. "It would seem we've all much maligned your friend Aline."

Yes? or had Bill had my letter this

morning? Either way, I was glad of the result. I had always liked General Francis, and the more I heard of him from Margaret the more my liking had increased.

Richard was with Sister when I knocked on the half-open duty-room door. "Ah, Dungarvan! Come aboard. No, please don't disturb yourself, Mr. Leland. This won't take a moment."

He had risen from his chair by hers. He stayed on his feet and went over to read the notices on the wall behind her desk, with his back to us.

Sister said briskly, "I'll tell you straight, gal, I'm about to alter any private arrangements you may have made for your next trip ashore. I'm sorry, but I've no alternative. I refuse to allow my senior staff nurses to work themselves into early graves, or any student nurse inside the Unit, until I consider she's got her sealegs. I don't often make mistakes." She met my eyes, steadily. "But I can make 'em, same as anyone else."

That was no small admission, to a junior and in front of an S.S.O., even if his back was turned. My respect for her took another leap upwards. I said nothing.

She explained she wanted me to stay on the late, late shift until Thursday, to have all Friday and Saturday morning off, and from Saturday to work 1.30 to 10, instead of the day shift, as expected. "Any objections, gal?"

"No, Sister." That was true. All this meant was another letter to that solicitor and a note to Margaret.

"Thank you, Dungarvan. Carry on."

I ran into Daisy in the Unit corridor, and asked if she knew what was going on.

"Humber's coming to us, temporarily, as Oxford's not coming back."

"She's been chucked out for fainting? That's hellish tough—"

"Not for fainting. For throwing a full-blown attack of hysterics, and when she came out of that for flatly refusing ever to set foot in the Unit again. She saw Matron at her own request today. I gather Matron and Sinbad were very decent. Sinbad offered to have her back in the Hall until her nerve recovered Oxford won't even hear of that."

"Honestly? How about her bright, bright lamp?"

"It's gone out," said Daisy. "Just like that."

The rush continued until Wednesday evening, when it stopped as suddenly as it had begun. After supper and standing around waiting for an hour Nurse de Wint, Daisy, and I sat down to mend gloves, the dressers vanished to their rest-room, Mr. Cook doodled on the desk blotter, while Mr. Simons and our anaesthetist shared an evening paper.

Mr. Waring propped himself against the C.T. doorway. "Here's a sight to unnerve the most case-hardened S.A.O. Never have I seen all my nurses sitting down to their tatting together." He smiled on us, then looked back into the corridor. "Here's a sight even you won't have seen often, Mr. Leland."

Richard looked us over. "A pretty picture," he observed drily, "if a slightly ominous anomaly."

"Not the lull before the next storm already, please Mr. Leland!" exclaimed de Wint.

"I'd like to say that's too obvious, Nurse de Wint." Richard's glance rested on me. "But life has such a tedious and hackneyed habit of repeating itself." He leant against the other side of the door. He looked as tired as I had ever seen him, and something more than tired. His face had grown much thinner lately. It was all angles and shadows, and the weariness in his eyes seemed more than just physical weariness. Something bad had happened to him. I did not know what, but that it had I was as sure as I was that he was standing there. I thought instantly of Margaret, and then of General Francis's op. this morning. From the grape-vine I had heard it had so far been a great success. But there was nothing successful in the manner of the man who had sent General Francis to Mr. Remington-Hart originally.

Mr. Waring glanced backwards again. "Here comes Paddy looking busy. What's up, Paddy? My line not working? Come to tell us you've a customer for us?"

"Indeed I have not, Mr, Waring, sir. Isn't it a grand sight for a man to see yourself and himself with not a patient to the pair of ye? Quiet we are, as quiet as we were on Sunday, before we had the poor lad who'd cut his head off. And making a fine recovery, they tell me?"

Richard roused himself to smile briefly. "He's going to do, Paddy."

"I'll be lucky if he doesn't do me," put in Mr. Waring. "I hear he's after my blood."

"For saving his life?" queried de Wint.

"For not leaving him with a neater scar."

"No!" Momentarily de Wint's indignation gave her away. She controlled it instantly. "Something I can do for you, Paddy?" she asked, as the old porter was still waiting.

"Well now, if you've the time to spare I'd be obliged of a word with you, Staff Nurse." He looked at me as he spoke. "Would you care to step this way?"

She went out with him, and they disappeared. Mr. Waring looked after them, then turned and spread his hands at the rest of us.

"Nurse Dungarvan, a moment please," called de Wint.

She took me to the very end of the Unit corridor before explaining why she had called. "You've put me in a spot, Dungarvan, but as it's not your fault, we are so quiet, and Nurse Chalmers won't object, just this once I'm going to let you take an outside call. I've told Paddy to put your caller through to Box 9. Make it snappy, and tell him never to ring you again on duty. We both know what Sister would say if she were on, to myself as well as you, despite the exceptional circumstance, which Paddy's just explained."

"Exceptional—Staff Nurse, who's ringing me?" But I had guessed, and rightly, before she answered. There was then another question I had to ask. "Do you know the official report on General Francis's op.?"

"Very satisfactory. If the graft takes he should be up and out in twenty-eight days."

"Thanks." I walked on to Box 9, to talk to Bill. "Jo Dungarvan speaking."

"Jo, is it really you?" I barely recognized his voice. It seemed years, not months, since I had heard it. "It's me, Bill. Bill Francis. Oh, my dear girl! You don't know how glad I am to speak to you!"

He was right. I didn't. "How are you? And where are you?"

"Ringing from that box outside your

main gates. I had to ring you, Jo. I tried to see you. The porter was hellish sticky. He didn't even want to put through this call."

"He's not allowed to. I'm on duty, and—"

He cut me short. "To hell with that! I had to talk to you! I've just seen the old man again. Jo, you must believe me"— his voice shook—"until I got your letter I'd no idea this was all so serious. I knew he was in Benedict's, but from his letters I thought he was just having a kind of rest-cure. Even yesterday when I flew back and came straight up here, he seemed so merry and bright. But tonight, Jo, he looks—God, he looks like death. He's too ill to talk—too ill to move. He's just lying there, flat out."

I would have had to be inhuman not to have a rush of sympathy. "Bill, listen. After a big op. people do look quite terrifyingly ill. The way he looks tonight isn't anything to go on. His op. went well —as they must have told you?"

"Yes. They all said that. The sister nursing him was sweet. She reminded me of someone—don't know who."

I did not explain that one. This was not the moment. "You're staying the night in the Wing?"

"No. They said I could. Jo, it's no good, I can't do it. I can't bear to see Dad like that. And it's not as if there's anything I can do. That Sister said that for the next next five days he's got to be dead quiet. I'd only disturb him. I can't sit around. So I've booked a seat on a plane to Madrid tomorrow morning. I'll get one from there to Malaga."

"Tomorrow?" I thought I must have misheard.

"I'd have gone tonight if I could have got on any plane, but they're all booked. I don't know what I'm going to do to-night. That's why I wanted to see you. I can't stick this on my own, Jo. I just can't."

I took a deep breath. It was very necessary. "You're not going to stay around whilst your father's on the D.I.L.?"

"Jo, I know how this must sound," he retorted petulantly, "but face it—what good can I do Dad by sticking around? I'm just not the type to sit still at bedsides. Old Wix is with him, of course.

And Dad couldn't be in a better place, or better hands, could he? Didn't you tell me yourself Benedict's is the best hospital going? Aline says the same. She understood when I managed to ring her this afternoon. She's going to meet me in Malaga tomorrow, we'll pick up my car—it's been there weeks—and drive straight back here with it together. We'll make it easily, inside the five days." He paused and, when I said nothing, added rather uncomfortably, "You—er—do know about Aline?"

"Vaguely. You engaged?"

"Since this afternoon. I had a long talk with Dad about her yesterday. He was very decent."

There was so much I wanted to say, but as he was unlikely to understand any of it, I only said briefly, "I can imagine. Congratulations! Give Aline my love when you see her tomorrow."

"But I want to see you tonight. Now. I must, Jo, I can't take this alone."

I said, "I'm very sorry, Bill, but I'm afraid you've got to. I'm on until midnight, and there's no possibility of my getting off. I'm really sorry."

He said, "I never thought you'd let me down, Jo!" and slammed down the receiver.

I replaced mine very carefully. No doubt it was not really his fault he had never been taught to give as well as to take, but he must have been taught the elements of good manners. He had not even said "Thanks for writing". Momentarily I felt nearly as sorry for Aline as I did for General Francis. I walked slowly back to the Unit, and when I reached the C.T. the light over the door began flashing again.

CHAPTER THIRTEEN

A VISIT FROM RICHARD

I was still in bed when Margaret brought the key of her cottage up to my room in her lunch period the following day. I offered her in exchange a cup of stone-cold tea from my uncleared breakfast-tray. "Gwenellen nipped it over hours ago. It'll be black and stewed as hell."

"Never mind. I can always drink tea." She sat on the side of my bed, cradling the saucerless cup in her hands. "I'm getting old, Jo. This post-op. strain is getting too much for me."

She was looking older again, and as tired as Richard last night. And either my imagination was playing me up again, or there was something very wrong with her too. She looked positively haunted. "How's your General?"

"Not very well."

"That's a relief, since I know of nothing more worrying than a D.I.L. who's too bright on his first post-op. morning."

I said unnecessarily, as she knew that far better than myself.

Yet she turned to me with an almost pathetic eagerness. "It is quite a good sign, isn't it?"

I studied her anxiously. "Margaret, how much off-duty have you had this week?"

"I had three hours on Monday. None since then. That's why I took the week-end off."

"A day and a half is hardly a week-end!"

She sipped the cold tea. "I knew what this would entail when I agreed to take this case. I've enjoyed it—until yesterday." She looked at me. "Jo, has that wretched boy been in touch with you? You know he's gone?" I nodded. "John Francis isn't up to asking questions, yet. What am I going to say—when he starts asking?"

That had been one of the problems that had prevented me getting to sleep before dawn. I had not solved it then, but sleep had cleared my mind. "Did Bill explain why he couldn't bear to stay and had to keep on the move? Then, if I were you, as soon as your General's up to asking questions, I'd tell him the truth. He must know his own son. Presumably he loves him, warts and all."

"That's much what Richard said last night."

"When last night?" I thought of Richard's expression when he came into the Unit. "After supper?"

"Thereabouts," she agreed absently. "But how can Richard, or you, begin to understand how something like this must hurt a parent? If Dickie did something like this to me—" She broke off. She was very close to tears. "Jo, being a parent myself, I know how this is going to hurt John Francis. I just can't bear even to think of hurting that man."

I grew tense, inwardly. "You say this to Richard?"

"Of course I did!" She turned on me with the impatience of acute anxiety. "Jo, I've seen that man sweating with pain, without making a sound. All this time in the Wing, and he's never once, day or night, rung his bell. He's never made one single demand of Beth Kateson or myself. He's been in pain for years. He's been hurt so much. I know life has given him a lot, but, God! Has life sent him in a bill! If that sounds like a hideous pun I can't help it! How can I hurt him more?"

It was a strange reversal of our normal rôles to find myself giving her advice. "Won't it hurt him more when he discovers—as he's bound to—that you've lied to him? You've been with him weeks, all day, most every day. By now he must trust you. You must be his friend."

"Yes. Yes, I think I am."

I said, thinking aloud, "Richard must understand that."

"What the devil has that got to do with Richard?" She sighed wearily. "My God, Jo! You're not still trying to marry me off to him, are you? Haven't you yet realized—can't you see—I could no more marry Richard Leland than you could marry—what's his name? That gangling child you introduced me to in the canteen?"

"Charlie Peters. But—"

"But, NOTHING! Enough's a bloody enough! I'm sorry, darling, but I'm far too worried about John Francis to have any patience left for your infantile attempts to find me a husband! When I want one I'll find one for myself, thank you very much! At present I'm just not interested! All I'm interested in is—" She paused abruptly. "I want to get John Francis well," she added in a small voice. "Do you see what I mean?"

I saw exactly what she meant. To give myself time to get my mental breath I asked if Corporal Wix knew Bill had gone.

"I had to tell him. He said, 'Not worth his father's little finger he isn't, ma'am, and never were.'"

"You couldn't let him break it to the General?"

"That wouldn't be fair. Anyway, I think he'd rather hear it from me."

"As you are both parents of sons?"

"Yes."

"That must make quite a bond between you."

"Yes." She flicked back the neatly folded corners of her apron skirt and stood up. "I must get back. I'll be so late for lunch."

"Before you go, if all goes well, how much longer will you be here?"

"Three to four weeks. He won't need me his last few days—if all goes well."

"It will! Everyone says his op. was a great success!"

She leant against the door and grimaced queerly. "As far as the op. went, yes, I suppose it was a great success. But successful surgery doesn't automatically mean a successful recovery. These first five days'll be crucial; the first fourteen, not much better. After the fourteenth—we'll see. How I'll last out I don't know. As I said, I'm getting too old for this job. Up to now I've been able to carry any professional strain. Now, suddenly, the weight seems to be forcing me into the ground."

I said carefully, "I don't believe this has anything to do with your age, and I don't believe the strain's only professional. I do believe that if General Francis is as much in love with you as you are with him you can stop worrying. He won't die on you."

She went white. "Jo, forgive my reminding you of your own mistake, but it seems I must. Let me also remind you I've been nursing on and off for nineteen years. I'm a long way from being an impulsive, impressionable girl. And John Francis is no weak, frightened boy. So will you kindly forget what you have just said and never repeat it to me, or anyone else, again!" She sounded and looked nothing like my Aunt Margaret and exactly like a Benedict's senior sister, and the starch in her skirts crackled as she swept out of my room, closing the door quietly after her. But she had not denied my real charge, and we both knew it. She had always disliked lying to those she loved as much as she disliked hurting them. Her senior-sister act was good, but, as I knew her so well, it was not quite good enough.

She must have hated hurting Richard. I saw now very clearly that she had had no alternative to doing that, but the thought of his hurt cut me like a physical pain. If I had needed to find out how important he had become to me I found out then. It was some time before I could think of anything else.

If only he could have been spared this hurt I would have been simply delighted. Though General Francis was on the D.I.L., London was filled with healthy people who had once been on our D.I.L. He had a long way to go, but he was on the way. Yet though I liked him and he had so many good qualities as well as material advantages, how she could prefer him or any man on earth to Richard was beyond me.

For once, I was delighted it was Thursday and Richard's free evening. I prayed nothing caused Mr. Waring to call him to the Unit between three and five-thirty that afternoon. Mr. Tomlin would be on from then until eleven, when Richard returned for what was officially and euphemistically described as "the S.S.O.'s final round before retiring". That left me only one more hour on duty to worry over before my day and a half off. Saturday afternoon and the future, I would face on Saturday afternoon. I could not face seeing Richard again just yet, and seeing that same hurt in his eyes.

The Unit was moderately busy when I arrived on duty. I watched the clock and breathed out at five-thirty. At five to six a maintenance mechanic was wheeled in from a local factory. He had been on the shift that worked from 4 p.m. to midnight. An ammonia explosion in the refrigerating plant had started a fire. He had been on the spot and helped put out the fire, burning his chest and hands badly in the process.

I was working with Mr. Waring.

"Get the lodge to get hold of the S.S.O., Nurse Dungarvan," he muttered, once the saline drip was running well into the anaesthetized mechanic. "This chap'll have to come in."

"Excuse me, but don't you mean Mr. Tomlin? It's Thursday."

"No, lass. If I'd meant Mr. Tomlin I'd have said Mr. Tomlin. But he's off this evening, and the S.S.O.'s on. Make it snappy," he added amiably.

When I returned from phoning, de Wint had sent Daisy to take my place in the Burns Room. She wanted me in the C.T. "Another motor-cyclist's on the way. The ambulance men have just called back to say they've found a diabetic's card on him, so he may be in coma because he's got a head injury, or he may have a head injury because he went into a coma first. Set for intravenous insulin and/or glucose."

We were very busy before I went off.

Richard was in, constantly. I was aware of that even though we were so busy.

I had never been so glad to leave Benedict's and London as next morning. My interview with the solicitor in Downshurst took much longer than I expected. He stood me lunch, then I spent the entire afternoon and half the evening at a very bad, very long movie. I caught the seven-thirty bus out to the cottage. It was quite dark when the bus dropped me at the top of the lane. There was a stiff breeze and the country darkness was a blanket at first, after the street and building lights in London, and then, as my eyes grew accustomed to it, I could see fairly well. The lights were on in the farm, half a mile from the cottage, and they were the only lights apart from the stars that kept appearing and disappearing behind the scurrying clouds. The darkness and the isolation suited my mood. After night-duty being alone in the dark never had bothered me, and as I let myself in to the cottage I decided to ring Mr. Sims at the farm in case Margaret had forgotten to let him know I was arriving today, and not Wednesday. It was a point I had forgotten to check with her, and if he saw lights and had not been warned he would probably call to investigate. I did not want any visitors. I wanted to be alone. Loneliness was so much more bearable when one was alone.

I turned on all the downstairs lights. I had just gone upstairs when I heard a car draw up outside, a car-door slam, and steps. "God damn all helpful neighbours!" I cursed to the spare bedroom, and went down as there was a knock on the door.

As the cottage was isolated, I put on the chain before opening the door, although I was pretty certain who was calling. "Sorry to keep you waiting, Mr. Sims—" My voice stopped abruptly as I opened the door. The hall light slanted out, illuminating the man outside. "Oh! Oh!" I swallowed. "It's you, Mr. Leland." My voice sounded as strange as I felt. For the first time ever my imagination failed me. All I could think was, it's Friday. He was never off on Friday evenings.

"May I come in, please?"

I removed the chain and held open the

door like a zombie. He came in, closed the door for me, then looked round the hall. His face was taut and curiously expressionless. I was dimly aware I had seen him look like this before, but too astounded to bother placing where or when. I was also too occupied in trying to control the white-hot wave of happiness that threatened to overwhelm me. God knew why he had come, but just to have him with me alone was enough to carry me to the stars.

He said, "I'm afraid you must be rather surprised to see me?"

"Yes." I smiled foolishly. "It's Friday."

"Mr. Tomlin and I have switched round this week."

"Oh, yes. Of course. You were on last night."

"Yes. Can we go into the sitting-room? Then I'll explain why I've called."

"Yes, do come in." I led him in. "Would you like some tea? Or coffee? I expect Margaret's left some. I haven't yet had time to look."

"I think tea would be a good idea." He spoke very deliberately, as if the choice of beverage was of immense importance. "Want any help?"

"No, thank you, Mr. Leland."

"Mind if I smoke?"

"Please do." He was patting himself. "I'm sorry, I haven't any cigarettes as I don't smoke," I apologized.

"I've got some somewhere, thanks." He produced a packet and matches. "You're sensible not to start. I wish I hadn't. I'm always advising the patients against it, and trusting they don't smell the tobacco on me. I'll have to cut it right out one of these days. I smoke far too many."

"Couldn't you just cut down?"

He shook his head. "I haven't the right temperament. I can practise abstinence, not moderation." He lit one. "You're sure you wouldn't like some help with the tea?"

I took the hint and went into the kitchen. When I carried the tea-tray back to the sitting-room he was standing by the fireplace looking at Margaret's wedding photograph. He turned from it at once, to accept his cup. "Thanks. Won't you sit down?"

I sat on the edge of the sofa. "Won't you?"

He put his tea on the mantelpiece. "If you don't mind, I would rather say what I have to say on my feet. Let me tell you first, that it in no way concerns your immediate family."

Suddenly I remembered where and when I had seen him look as he had in the hall. It had been when he walked down the Unit corridor before facing the waiting relatives in Mr. Waring's office. I jumped up. "Bad news?"

"Yes," he said simply, and his eyes were compassionate. "Sit down again. I'll tell you."

"Not the family?"

"No. Two of your friends." He came closer and stood in front of me. Then, gently and without wrapping the truth in a cocoon of unnecessary words, he told me Bill and Aline had been killed outright when their car ran off a Spanish road and hit a tree in the early hours of that morning. The news had first reached Benedict's at lunchtime, via the Spanish police. During the afternoon Matron had had a cable from Aline's parents. He said,

333

"From the report there doesn't seem to be any reason for the accident. The road was empty. The night was fine, and there was a good moon. There was nothing wrong with his tyres, but apparently he ran straight at that tree for about ninety feet, which should have given him time to pull out. I can only guess he had been driving too long, and perhaps drinking a little too much, and dropped off." He took an unopened half-bottle of whisky from his pocket, opened it, and added some to my tea. "Have this."

Stunned, I obeyed mechanically. "Aline and Bill? Dead?" I muttered. "Aline and Bill? Dead, now? But they only got engaged on Wednesday. They—dead?"

He sat by me on the sofa, switching sideways and leaning against the arm as he faced me. "I'm sorry. Yes. They are dead. As they were killed instantly, at least they knew nothing about it." He hesitated. "I didn't know they were engaged, though I had heard that was in the air. Matron doesn't know. She told me she had no idea what Nurse Ash was doing in that car. She thought her in Majorca on sick-leave."

I could not bear to take any of this in yet. I knew I would have to shortly. As talking might help postpone the inevitable, I talked. I told him how I had written to Bill, and Aline, and all Bill had said to me in that telephone conversation. "They met in Marcus. He followed her out to Majorca."

"I know."

"How? Tom Lofthouse?"

He shook his head. "I know she won't mind my telling you. Maggie, here, last Sunday. I had asked if she knew how we could get hold of him. She knew he was in Majorca, but not his address, as his father always gave Wix his letters to post. I got that out of Wix on my return, and wrote to Bill that night. I had intended following it up with a cable. His arrived first. When he himself arrived on Tuesday he told me he'd not yet had my letter."

"So you wanted him back, officially?"

"Obviously. We'd have liked him back some time ago, but his father refused to allow us to send for either son, as he was within his rights to do, so we had to respect his wishes. That is, we had to do that until the question of his next-of-kin's rights arose. If we are given a next-of-kin, and know we are about to do an op. that'll slap a patient on to the D.I.L., then, whether the patient likes it or not, in Benedict's we have to put his next-of-kin in the picture. That's a Benedict's rule. But we don't have to tell the patient. I didn't tell John Francis I had written." He lit a cigarette. "Maggie didn't tell me you'd written to Bill. Nor did he."

"I meant to tell Margaret. I forgot. I expect he forgot to tell you. Did he tell his father?"

"I didn't get the impression he had from John Francis. He seemed to think Bill had heard about his coming op. indirectly from some of his various contacts in Benedict's. I gather Bill was a great sender of postcards."

"Yes."

He looked at me keenly. "His father was touched and pleased by his return. I could be wrong, but I'm convinced he had no idea anyone had actually sent for his son."

The whisky was removing some of the anaesthetizing effects of shock. I wished

I had not drunk the stuff. "I had to spell it out loud and clear. Having specialed him, I knew the only way in which to get any action out of him was to give him the whole works. I did that." I paused. "And kicked off what ended early this morning."

"Jo, skip the dramatics." He was stern, but not unkind. "This is too serious for that. Yes. It was your letter that brought him back, but almost certainly only thirty-six hours earlier than mine would have done. Once back, I'm quite certain that in the event the final pattern would not have varied in one iota from that which now obtains."

I wanted to believe him. If not, that letter was going to haunt me for the rest of my life. "How can you possibly be certain? You can only guess."

"I'm not giving you a guess. I'm giving you my considered opinion."

"But you can only have reached it by guessing."

"My dear girl," he retorted still more sternly, "I know you're shocked and distressed, but that doesn't provide you with an excuse for talking childish rubbish.

337

I'm a surgeon, not a physician. A physician may be able to get away with, and even have a talent for, inspired guesswork. Surgeons deal in facts. They have to, as you are very well aware, since ultimately surgeons have to translate their opinions into actions. You don't rely on an inspired guess when you pick up a knife and cut into a human being. You have to be bloody sure of your facts before you even reach for that knife. As, again, you well know!"

"Yes, but, I still don't see—"

"You will. Listen. I based my opinion on two main facts. One, Bill Francis's character. Two, a fact I've observed about human nature in general. I'll explain that first, as it may make it easier for you to follow me." He stubbed out his cigarette, lit another. "Have you never noticed that every adult has his, or her, specific pattern of behaviour, and that when confronted with any acute physical or emotional crisis, that pattern instantly manifests and repeats itself?"

"I'm sorry. I don't follow."

"Then let's use you as an illustration. When you are suddenly faced with a crisis you instantly react with speed, common sense, and efficiency. Remember that road accident? That ether fire? Innumerable recent occasions in the Unit?" He waited until I nodded. "Each time you repeat your own specific pattern, and each time wait until it's all over for the shock to hit you. Each time, between crises, you return to your other established pattern. You are gay, kind, sensitive, sometimes foolish, occasionally bloody childish. With me now?"

"Yes," I said flatly. "Go on, please."

"When Bill Francis met a crisis his immediate reaction was to try and pretend it hadn't happened. That's why he walked round with pneumonia for twenty-four hours rather than see a doctor who might frighten him with the truth. That's why, when he first heard his father was in the Wing, he instantly persuaded himself it was for a rest-cure. His father! The man who, he had himself told us, disliked hospitals, doctors, and making any fuss over his own health. Was John Francis the man to meekly take a rest-cure? Is Benedict's a convalescent home? Bill knew his father and, having been one of our patients, Benedict's. He knew the facts, but refused to face them. When forced to return and forced to face up to them he was emotionally incapable of carrying the burden. He could no longer pretend his father wasn't gravely ill, so he got round it by pretending he was thinking only of his father's good, and that the best thing he could do for his father was to leave him in our hands." He walked over to the mantelpiece and frowned at the floor. "As the emotionally immature can persuade themselves into believing anything that suits them, he probably believed he was doing the best thing. Undoubtedly that must have seemed best for himself. Once he got right away, collected his girlfriend and his car, he wouldn't have to think about what was going on in Benedict's." He looked up sombrely. "One can alter circumstances, not a man's character. In nearly every event it's the character that shapes the circumstance. Yet, though I knew that perfectly well, I used every argument short of brute force to try and get him to stay in the Wing on Wednesday night. I didn't get anywhere."

"Was that just before you came into the Unit? Was that why you looked so— so sort of black?"

"When I looked in during that brief quiet spell after supper? Yes. I'd just come from talking to him. I looked black?"

"Yes. Yes."

"I felt black. I didn't realize it showed. I did realize I'd seldom been so bloody sickened by the human race. God knows, by now I should be accustomed to its nastier habits, but every so often, when a son walks out on a father on the D.I.L., a husband on a wife, or vice versa, or a mother on a child, I reach the pitch of thinking that the sooner someone pushes that bloody button the better. I don't generally stick on that pitch long. It lasted longer than usual that night, as John Francis has become a friend as well as a patient, and, consequently, I was more involved. I'm no more supposed to grow involved in my job than you are in yours, but obviously on occasions it's impossible to avoid that. I try to avoid that, as it does affect one's judgment. Without much success," he admitted tersely. "I attempt to console myself with the reflection that even Homer sometimes nods, but I nod so frequently it's a wonder my bloody head doesn't fall off. That nearly happened on Wednesday night. My one consolation then was the thought that John Francis still had Maggie—" He stopped suddenly. "You have at last realized that situation?"

"Since yesterday."

"Only then? Of course, you've not been seeing them together as I have. I've always thought it a good thing. Now it's not just good, it's essential. For a very ill and not particularly young man to recover he must have something to live for. Something more than an empty house, no matter how large and well appointed, and a devoted old batman, no matter how faithful. And the fact that Maggie and Dick need him quite as much as he needs them will be an extra shot in the arm. Women talk a great deal about their necessity to feel needed. The same applies to any man who is a man." He glanced again at that wedding picture, then sat back on the sofa. "You didn't administer the kick-off. That was done years ago by whoever it was was the main figure in Bill Francis's early childhood. Probably his mother. There are few more destructive forces in life than an overdose of maternal love. In illness he behaved like a spoilt child, but no child spoils himself. That pneumonia was the catalyst. It changed the course of his life, Aline Ash's —poor girl—his father's, and, shortly, unless I'm much mistaken, and I'm sure I'm not, Maggie, and young Dick's. Bad out of good. Good out of bad." He rubbed his eyes with both hands, stifling a yawn. "I've talked far too much, and I'm afraid I've been rather rude. I didn't intend that. I came down as I thought to hear of this quietly might cushion the shock, if not the blow." He could not stop yawning. "I do beg your pardon."

There was so much I wanted to say and ask. I only asked if he would like fresh tea.

"Very much. If it's not too much trouble?"

"Not at all."

I got off the sofa, collected our cups, picked up the tray. "I don't suppose you've had supper, Mr. Leland?"

He was having to blink to keep his eyes open. "I'll get that when I get back."

I did not press the point. He was now looking even more exhausted than that afternoon in Mr. Waring's office. I left him sitting on the sofa and took the tray out to the kitchen. Little Ben was in my handbag upstairs, so I slowly counted one hundred and twenty seconds. Then I went very quietly back to the sitting-room. As I expected, he was asleep.

CHAPTER FOURTEEN

THE SLEEPER WAKES UP

I KNEW I should wake him. It was nearly half-past nine, and even if he left immediately after having tea he could not be back in Benedict's until well after eleven.

He had shifted himself in sleep. His head rested against one arm of the sofa, his legs stretched along the seat, and his feet dangled over the edge at the end. He was as far under as that other afternoon, but, being on the sofa, looked so much more comfortable. When he woke he had a two-hour drive and a night's work ahead. If any food had been kept for him, by the time he got to it it would be uneatable—if he had time to get to it.

I just could not make myself disturb him, yet. I retreated silently to the hall to think things out, and the sight of the hall telephone reminded me of Mr. Sims.

I closed the sitting-room door, huddled the telephone and myself in one of Margaret's old coats, and dialled the farm. Mrs. Sims answered.

"My Harry was just coming over to see why the lights are on, dear. Your auntie told us Wednesday, not Friday. Changed, were you? There, now! Still, makes a nice break, I expect. Your friend bring you down? We noticed his car. Come down after you, did he? That's nice! Going back, tonight? Well, I expect he thinks it's worth it, eh, dear?"

When she rang off I replaced the receiver carefully, then sat on the bottom stairs staring at the sitting-room door.

As he had swopped evenings with Mr. Tomlin and taken out his car, even if no-one but Margaret knew he was here —which was highly probable—the porters would have noticed his car was missing. Paddy and Co. noticed everything. If he was late back they would tell Mr. Tomlin he was somewhere on the road. Anyone could be held up on the road. I winced, as my mind shot to Bill and Aline, but for Richard's sake refused to shelve my train of thought. He might just have had a puncture? Or his battery had failed? That could happen to anyone, even an S.S.O. Mr. Tomlin was a very capable deputy. He could carry on as such for an extra couple of hours, and, to give him his due, I was sure he would not mind doing so, particularly if he knew the truth. I thought of the ~~two~~ extra hours Richard had put in last Sunday night and the countless other occasions when he had worked whilst officially off. If he now had an hour's sleep he would have time to ring Benedict's from here before eleven to warn Mr. Tomlin he would be late back, and to eat a proper meal before he left.

I made up my mind. If he was annoyed with me for letting him sleep I would be sorry for his annoyance, if not the cause.

I moved into the kitchen, helped myself to Margaret's store of tins, and cooked a casserole hot-pot that would be ready when wanted, but not ruined if it had to sit in a low oven. The mechanical movements of my hands did nothing to soothe the deep sadness that settled over me like a cloak. My thoughts drifted from the struggle to save Bill's life in Marcus, to his father sitting by his bed, to Aline, the brightest girl in our set heading all our exam. results, to General Francis again, this time lying flat in the Wing, waiting hopefully for a message or a visit from the son he did not yet know was dead. Margaret would tell him, I thought, and the thought made my heart lurch against my ribs.

I thought of Margaret, and then Richard. I thought how he had looked and sounded when talking about Margaret's future. He had been far too tired at that moment to maintain any act. He not only didn't mind, he was glad.

I sat on the kitchen table and breathed as if I had been running hard. Then I thought on the reason he had given for coming down here tonight.

It could be sufficient for a kind man who was an old friend of my aunt, who understood how sets felt about each other, and how nurses felt about patients they had once specialed through and off the D.I.L., and who was himself a member of Benedict's. Today would have been a black day in Benedict's. All hospitals were forced to accustom themselves to the deaths of patients and a climate of illness and grief, and yet maintain a routine composure. The unexpected death of any member of a hospital staff invariably, and automatically, shattered that composure. Patients died. Not doctors, nurses, or medical students. We were invulnerable—until something like today happened. Benedict's had a huge nursing staff. There would be hundreds of girls who never knew Aline. There wouldn't be one who had not some time today thought, God, it could be me. And as most of our men had nurses for girlfriends, at least for the next few days Benedict's men would drive that much more carefully.

All that could have been sufficient—had I not been over sixty miles from Benedict's, and had it not been a Friday evening. Everyone's reserves were low by then. This last week had been one of the heaviest, surgically, I had so far experienced. What the extra effort had cost him was now plain to anyone who walked into the sitting-room. Out like a light. Yet he'd come.

Up to his final remarks before he dropped off I would have sworn on oath any help he gave me was for Margaret's sake, whether or not she loved him. He didn't have to love me for me to be willing to do anything I could to help him.

My mind went back to our first meeting in the subway; to Marcus; to that morning on the bypass and how he had driven me back here to change; to the little chats he used occasionally to have with me in the Hall; and the night General Francis called. Then I went back to tonight.

If not for Margaret, for—me?

Somewhere in my inside a star flared. Then I got it under control. I made myself remember how I had managed to kid myself Bill loved me. I asked myself savagely when I was going to grow up and stop dreaming up fairy-stories with myself as heroine, and was it any wonder he thought me occasionally bloody childish? Had he known me rather better he'd have dropped that "occasionally".

It was time to wake him. I made fresh tea, took it into the sitting-room, set the tray quietly on a small table, then stood by the sofa, studying his unguarded face exactly as on last Friday afternoon in the office.

It cost me a conscious effort not to sit in the space beside his legs, not to touch the very slight wave of red hair above his forehead, not to take in my hands his right hand that lay so limply on the seat. Having to stand primly by last Friday had been bad enough, but at least then I had had my uniform, his white coat, and the facts that we had both been on duty and were in the hospital to add to my defences. Hospital etiquettes and hospital traditions might be throttling, but they did provide a magnificent invisible armour. Then it had been tea-time. Here it was night. Here we were alone together, off duty, from Benedict's in an isolated country cottage. I held my hands behind my back in the approved position for any Benedict's nurse when about to address her senior. "I'm sorry," I said, "but I'm afraid you must wake up."

Exactly as last Friday, nothing happened.

I remembered how I had had to shake him, gently, and how he had mistaken me for Margaret, and whilst still too drugged with sleep to control his sub-conscious had given himself away.

But he wasn't in love with Margaret. And he wasn't a man to "dearest" and "darling" even old friends.

Not just one star. A couple more flared. I took a deep, calming breath, gave myself another pep-talk, then shook him gently. That was now not enough. Having slept longer, his sleep was that much deeper. I used both hands on his shoulders and shook him really firmly. "I'm sorry, but you must wake up! Come on!" I patted his face. "Time to wake up!"

"M'mmmm?" he murmured without opening his eyes and reaching for my hand. Momentarily, he held it against his cheek, then slid my open palm over his mouth and kissed it. "Dear Jo." He dropped his hand as he went straight back to sleep.

For a few of the most wonderful mo-ments of my life up to then, I did nothing but stand and smile at his sleeping figure. Then I had to remember the time, his job, and the fact that it was possible to be as drunk with fatigue as with alcohol, and that to set too much store by a kiss on the hand from a sleeping man was as foolish as to take seriously a pass made by a drunk, or, again I reminded myself intentionally, a delirious patient. Yet though that impressed my judgment, it had no effect at all on my instincts. In fact, every instinct I possessed was behaving so strangely that it took all my willpower to give him an even more violent shake and not to kiss him.

That did it. He blinked, frowned. "My God! I didn't drop off again?" He squinted at his watch. "This thing right? Why the devil did you let me sleep so long?" He was as annoyed as I had anticipated. "Didn't you realize the time?"

"Yes. I'm sorry. You looked so tired. Here." I handed him a cup of tea into which I had again emptied half the sugar-basin. "You'll feel better after this." He had swung his legs to the floor and was sitting on the edge of the seat, rubbing his face. "I'm afraid you are going to be very late back. Do you want to ring Benedict's and warn 'em?"

"That won't be necessary, thanks." He sipped the tea. "God! More syrup! This seems to be getting quite a habit for us both. I do apologize for my appalling manners, but I wish you'd woken me sooner." He drank the tea, stood up. "Forgive me if I go out to the car. Run out of cigarettes." He vanished before I could answer. On his return he went into the kitchen, and I heard a tap running. When he came back his hair was damp and newly combed. "No therapy like cold water for removing muzzy edges. Plus strong, sweet tea. I've drunk so much of the stuff since I qualified that if I ever need a transfusion and have to be grouped the path. lab.'ll send down a couple of vacolitres of strong tea. May I help myself to more?" Again, he did not wait for my answer. "I've just noticed you've been cooking."

He must also have noticed the two supper-trays I had set and left on the kitchen table to bring in here, later. "I thought you might like supper before you left. Can you stay for it? It's ready when you are."

"It's kind of you"—he had another

354

look at his watch—"but it is getting late."

"And you want to be off?" I had realized this might happen. That did not mean I liked it, but because of his job I understood it. I stood up. "If I get yours now and you eat quickly, surely another ten minutes won't make all that difference?"

He stiffened. I could not conceive why. Then he said, "Jo, do you seriously imagine I'm going to leave you here alone tonight after the kind of news I've had to bring you?" He glanced round. "I'm not sure I think much of the idea of your staying here alone on the best of nights. This cottage is far too isolated. There's going to be no question of my leaving you behind on this night. You must come back to Benedict's with me, as I know your aunt would agree, were she aware of the present circumstances."

It was ages since he had called Margaret "your aunt" to me. She had been "Maggie" as before he fell asleep. It was probably unimportant, yet it puzzled me quite disproportionally. "Margaret doesn't know you're here then?"

He was chain-smoking again. He shook his head over a lighted match. "I didn't know, when I saw her this afternoon, that I could get the night off."

"You're off all night?" I demanded.

He straightened his head and shoulders and looked at me with the expression he used on students who rashly stepped a little out of line. "Until 9 a.m. tomorrow. Mr. Tomlin's taken tonight for me. I'm taking Sunday night for him, as he wants two nights away this week-end. It's a matter we're entitled to arrange between ourselves when it suits us. It so happens this arrangement suits us both."

"I see," I lied, being too confused to see anything clearly. My confusion was not unpleasant. After nearly three years in Benedict's I knew these arrangements were permissible and never affected the patients, but as they involved a detailed handing-over report on roughly half the hospital, they were only suddenly arranged for urgent personal reasons. Had that reason just been Mr. Tomlin's, Richard would have taken his Sunday without asking him to do tonight in exchange. I remembered two occasions when Mr.

Tomlin's mother had been ill and he had done the two extra nights in double-harness without having even one off himself in return. "I wish I'd known you were off, before!" I exclaimed.

He raised his eyebrows. "Why?"

"I needn't have woken you. You could have had a whole undisturbed night, for once." His eyebrows remained up. "Look —I know how that would sound to anyone who didn't know the true set-up, but I do, you do, and I'm sure Margaret wouldn't object. And she's my aunt, and this is her cottage, and you are one of her oldest friends."

"I hadn't forgotten." There was a touch of grimness in his tone.

Suddenly I realized what I had said and why it had turned him grim. As I could not go back, I went on: "Did you guess I wanted to marry you two off?"

"A blind man could have guessed. So John Francis has finally opened your eyes?" He was still grim. "Right?"

"No. It was first Margaret, yesterday. Then you, tonight."

He flushed slightly. Mentally, I held my breath, but he only asked how I had got hold of the impression there had ever been any chance of my plan succeeding.

"Originally, from you."

"Would you care to enlarge on that?" He might have been asked for a case history. I answered as I would have done in that event. I kept it brief. Even so, it took some time. He listened in silence, and was silent when I finished.

I could not take that silence. "Look," I said, unnecessarily as his eyes were fixed on my face, "I know I'm a moron to get these fixations. I know now that you and Margaret were once the sort of chums I am with Charlie—"

"Charlie—"

"Charlie Peters. He used to be in the Hall."

"The boy with all the hair who runs that unspeakable group and used to follow you round knocking things over?" He smiled slightly. "So he's Charlie? Carry on."

"There's not much more to say, as I've said most of it. Like I said, I see now that you just dropped in down here because you and Margaret like each other, and you probably went fishing with Dickie because you like fishing and Dickie."

"That's true. But I had another reason for accepting John Francis's invitation. I wanted to get to know him, and his background, better. From the afternoon I brought him here I got the idea that he and Maggie were attracted to each other. As she's always been as willing to treat me as a spare brother as you've been to consider me as a future uncle, I decided on that occasion to avail myself of my adopted rights and, bluntly, vet him. I liked very much what I saw of him in Devon. I like him even more now."

"Was he why you advised Margaret to come back to Benedict's?"

"He was one of the several reasons I had for giving her that specific advice. My main one came from my conviction that it was high time she did come back."

"She told me you said sometimes one had to raise ghosts to lay them. You were so right. She looked ghastly, her first day back. Then she started looking younger and so serene. Till yesterday."

"As she was labouring under a great personal anxiety and forced to maintain an outward professional calm, that's hardly surprising."

"I guess not."

We were silent again. It was worse than before.

Again I broke it. "You two weren't my only moronic fixation. For a while I had one about Bill. Did you ever guess?" He nodded, reluctantly. "It wasn't his fault. He didn't know what he was saying. I knew that at the time. That didn't stop my persuading myself I loved him, and in a way I did. I've loved other patients, women and kids, as well as men." I told him about Mrs. King, Violet, and David Grant in Arthur. "I wept most of the next day after that boy died. Too emotional, that's me."

He was watching me clinically. "Too soft-hearted."

"Or it could just be, too bloody childish."

"I shouldn't have said that. I've seen how you've worked in the Unit. It was most unfair and uncalled-for. I'm sorry I made that remark."

"You needn't be. You did qualify it with 'occasionally', and if that isn't true enough I don't know what is. Would you like to eat now?"

"If it suits you."

"May as well." I had to push myself out of my armchair. My energy seemed to have drained away. My legs were heavy and my hands were cold. "I'll bring the trays in here, as the kitchen's so small. We generally use that table."

"Wait a moment." He came closer. "You're not feeling right. You're far too pale. Sit down again." He stood over me as I flopped back into my chair. "Get your head over your knees."

"I'd much rather not, if you don't mind." I lay back, half closed my eyes. "I hate the feeling of blood rushing to my head. I'm just a bit cotton-woolly. Shock, I guess."

"You were over that before I went to sleep. I watched your colour return to normal whilst we were talking." His concern was obvious and wonderful. "This is a reaction to something that's happened in the last half-hour." He hesitated, then reached for my wrist. Directly his fingers touched my pulse he looked quickly at my face, then checked the beat on his watch.

"Conflicting symptoms?" I asked.

He gave me a politely blank, professional glance. "Why do you ask that?"

"Because I can feel I've got a touch of tachycardia, and I've always been taught that in shock the rate goes down, not up."

"In general, yes. There are always exceptions to every rule. You must be one."

I watched him through my eyelashes. "Did my pulse go up that morning on the bypass?"

"Not, as I recall. The circumstances were, of course, very different."

"Yes." Someone had to say it, and since, being the man he was, his job, his being Margaret's old friend, and above all his now being alone with me at night in this cottage would prevent him from saying it first, I said it. "I wasn't in love with you, then. I was all set to have you as Uncle Richard. But please don't turn yourself into him now, as you've been threatening to do ever since you woke up, and say, 'There, there, little one', as if I was all of eight years old. I'm not eight. I'm not waffling because I'm feeling rather lousy. I'm twenty-one, old enough to work in the Unit, old enough to have to cope with grief, mutilation, and sudden death, every day of the week. I've often felt lousy in the Unit, but I've still known what I was doing and saying. I know what I'm doing now. I know exactly why my heart probably shot up to one hundred and something when you touched me. As I'm in love with you, it would be very odd if it didn't. And please," I added breathlessly, "don't turn yourself into the Big Doctor you've treated me to recently whenever we've had to work together. I'm just not up to dealing with Old Red of Benedict's right now."

He was very still. His expression nearly stopped my heart. "You love me, Jo? Since when?"

I smiled weakly. "Honest to God, I don't know. I discovered it in the Unit. I think it started before that, but I was so busy marrying you off to Margaret I hadn't much time for my own problems."

"I've been one of your problems? Have you any idea of the problem you've been to me?"

"Till tonight it never crossed my mind. I was quite sure that first you just saw me as a carbon copy of Margaret—and later that you didn't much like what you saw."

"And it was only when I turned up down here that you guessed my motives for coming were not purely altruistic? I did want to help you by breaking the news gently, but I did want to see you. I wanted to look after you and then take you back with me. For myself as well as yourself. To have you to myself just for once I'd have driven treble the distance from Town gladly. And then I wasted a precious hour and a half sleeping like a bloody log!"

"It wasn't quite such a waste of time as you think." I felt myself redden. "I'm not sure how you're going to take this—"

"Jo, from you, I can now take anything. Well?"

I explained.

"So I kissed your hand? That doesn't surprise me. I was dreaming of you. I think I dreamt that kiss. When I woke to find you shaking me I thought it just another dream about you."

"You've dreamt of me, very often?"

"Very, very often. My subconscious

and you are well acquainted—as I would have expected you to appreciate that afternoon in Waring's office. It was the hell of a Freudian slip to make. Were you honestly that much fixated by your notion that I loved Maggie? You really thought I mistook you for her?"

"Yes." His smile warmed me like a caress. "I know I've been bloody silly, but it's not all my fault. You've been horried to me lately."

"That bloodyminded bastard, Old Red?"

"Just about. Why?"

"As usual, mixed motives. The first time I met you I knew I wanted to see more of you. I knew, hospitals being the places they are, that wasn't to be as simple as it would have been had I been a houseman, or even Registrar. I knew I'd only to take you out on one date—that is, supposing you had accepted my invitation —and Benedict's would have us in bed together inside of twenty-four hours. I didn't give a damn about that for myself. I gave several, for you. Then, as you know, we met again in Marcus, and you didn't see me."

"Not then. No. I'm sorry."

"Jo," he said unevenly, "after what you've said to me you don't have to apologize to me for one bloody thing. Want the rest?"

"Please. Please."

"Maggie turned up in that car-park. You came here on holiday. I came down to lunch with the Remington-Harts, intending to call in here in the hope of seeing you during that afternoon—and saw you sitting on the grass verge covered in blood. God," he muttered, "that did it! I've never cared for the sight or smell of blood, and when I was a junior dresser it used to turn me as pea-green as your friend Charlie on his first visit to the Unit, and as you still go at the mere mention of a burns admission. I've long passed that stage, yet one look at you that morning and I could have done with a double brandy. That was when I discovered I was in love with you."

I had dreamed so many daydreams. Not one approached the wonder of reality. "You were very kind to me. You lent me your shoulder as a back-rest."

"You remember? I didn't think you'd

even noticed. When you began to notice me on the drive back here you were hard put not to call me 'Uncle Richard'."

I smiled. "That's true."

"Didn't I know it! It froze every attempt I made at getting close to you in Benedict's, in the nicest possible way. You were so bloody keen to have me join the family—as dear old uncle! I knew that had I tried to date you you'd have regarded the suggestion as a cross between disloyalty to Maggie and incest. So I had to wait."

"Until I discovered for myself about Margaret and her General?"

"I hoped that would help, but that wasn't why I waited. Bluntly, dear heart, I was waiting for you to grow up. You've done that in the last month. Everyone grows up in the Unit, and fast. Do you mind me saying this?"

"No, since, again, it's dead true. Though I'm still not clear why you've been so tough with me, in the Unit? Because you had to wait?"

His smile was tender. "You've grown up faster than I thought. Yes, partly. It was also because before you moved out of the Hall I noticed you had begun to have a difficult time with Sister Cas., and it was about then that Michael Waring first tipped me off on the rumours circulating about us. Being a very old hospital hand, it occurred to me that my efforts at getting better acquainted with you could be doing you, personally a lot of harm. So I restrained them so bloody pointedly that I wouldn't have been too surprised had you refused to remove that chain tonight. I've never been clear just how those rumours started. I presume through my occasional chats with you?"

"Yes and no. Richard, you may not like this—"

"What have you done now?"

When I explained about Charlie he grinned. "Fair comment." He tilted my face to the light. "You've recovered. Good. I can kiss you, now." He drew me out of the chair and into his arms. "Dear Jo, do you make me wait!" He caught his breath. "Dear Jo, do I love you! Have I loved you! Will I love you!" He kissed my mouth, my face, my neck, and then, again, my mouth. He kissed so hard and he held me so tightly I could neither move nor breathe properly. Neither bothered me at all.

He lifted his face a fraction to look at me. "Darling, have I hurt you?" he demanded anxiously.

I smiled. "I hate to think what my pulse is doing, but I'm doing fine. Please kiss me again."

He did, but more gently.

Afterwards, after supper, we sat on the sofa. We talked of John Francis. Richard said, "I think he'll be up and out inside the twenty-eight days."

"And good to Margaret and Dickie?"

"I'm sure of it. God knows the poor girl rates a happy marriage after her first go! She'll get it, with John." He read my expression. "You didn't know?"

"You're saying she wasn't happy with Simon?"

He got up, took down the wedding photograph, and handed it to me as he sat down and lifted me back on his lap. "Take a good look at Simon Ellis."

It was years since I had looked at that photo properly. I gasped. "He's not as good-looking here as the Francis men, but he's the same physical type."

"The type that attracts Maggie, and vice versa. He wasn't very like, just vaguely similar. But he had a lot in common with Bill Francis. You don't remember Simon?"

"Only dimly. What was he like?"

"In small doses, very amusing and attractive, particularly to women. Fundamentally, he was more immature as a grown man than his son is at twelve. He always wanted his own way, but was incapable of accepting any responsibilities that involved. He wanted Maggie, so he married her, as she wasn't a girl he could get any other way. He wanted neither wife nor kids, but having married her he did not want to let her go as she was his possession. Ever tried to take a toy away from a spoilt child?"

I winced. "She'd no idea? Before she married him?"

"Her Benedict's friends, myself included, tried to talk sense into her—and met with the usual response on such occasions. She was too much in love to see or think straight; she then had your quick temper and your independent streak, but not your strong vein of common sense that serves you so well in any crisis."

"She's so sensible now!" I protested.

"Now, yes. Dick's birth jolted all the sense she needed into her. I've seen childbirth transform a good many women, but none more totally than Maggie. She was a sweet, patient, but still bloody stupid girl, until she held her son in her arms. You knew Dick was born in our Mat. Unit? I used to visit her. In those days mothers were kept in ten days. I saw Maggie grow up during those ten days. Simon was then an orthopod registrar. He was in the same hospital. He visited his wife three times."

"He didn't want Dickie?"

"A son? A rival in his own house?" He shook his head and was briefly silent. "At the time I thought his attitude inexcusable. From this distance I realize he could no more help being what he was by then than Bill Francis could help doing what he did on Wednesday night. He was running round with a physio-student then. The hospital knew as the hospital always does. She was a nice kid. And so was the girl with whom he went off on what proved to be his last week-end. She was a fourth-year in the orthopaedic theatre. Simon," he added bitterly, "knew how to pick his women."

"Did Margaret know?" He nodded. "Why did she put up with it?"

"I asked her that about six years ago. She said she had loved him when she married him, he needed her, he was her husband, and she had been determined to make it work. It never would have worked. The baby was the last straw. Things after Dick went from bad to worse. Maggie knows that now, and that's why she's been so scared of any repeat performance."

"I never guessed! I should have!" I explained why.

"You might have guessed from that letter, had you been old enough to remember more of Simon, and had Maggie not taken such care for Dick's sake that no-one outside of her old small circle in Benedict's should guess. There are very few of us left, now. Matron, Bernard, myself, and a couple of pundits or so. As you know, Benedict's is too large for anyone to know well anyone outside one's immediate circle. Twelve years is a long time. If anyone—take Sister Cas.—now remembers Simon Ellis it'll be as a good party man who genuinely had a good brain and a talent for orthopaedics. Had he known how to use his many gifts he could have done very well. I've noticed Maggie's stressed his gifts to Dick and left out the rest. She's dead right. A boy needs to be proud of his father, dead or alive." His eyes softened. "Thanks to the climate of love and security Maggie has built up round him that child's a normal, well-balanced, highly intelligent, dirty little monster. He's going to enjoy having a Major-General for a stepfather. He'll take all his pals through his stepfather's wars and medals. He's already got old Wix under his thumb. John Francis, being an over-indulgent father, will probably try and spoil him a little, but at Dick's age that won't hurt him. And thanks to Maggie's early upbringing he'll take for granted, until he's much older, the affection and very considerable security John Francis will provide for his mother and himself. It's only unhappy kids who are wary of affection. Those accustomed to being surrounded by it take it as their birthright, which, of course, it is. Unhappy kids," he repeated, "and emotionally scarred adults."

That thought was in my mind. "You don't think Margaret'll lose her nerve at the last minute?"

"Though she has been looking so much happier, up to this afternoon I've not been too sure that wouldn't happen. That's why I drove her down to Dick's school on Saturday, even though I knew she'd rather go alone, as naturally she wanted her son to herself. But I wanted a long, uninterrupted talk with her. I told her, in so many words, not to be a fool and chuck away happiness through cowardice. She kept protesting about the ethical position. I told her I thought on this occasion ethics could go jump in a bloody lake. Some of it got through. Not all. But after today she'll marry him. She appreciates what the loss of a child must mean to a parent. Bill Francis may not have seemed to us the best of sons, but his father loved him for what he was, and not for what he didn't possess. Remember how he sat out those long nights in Marcus ?"

I began to cry. I cried on his shoulder, and he held me gently and stroked my hair until I stopped. Then he kissed me, at first gently, and then as when for the first time.

Suddenly he lifted me off the sofa and stood me on my feet. "Jo, I think we should go back now."

"Richard, must we ? Already ? Of course, I'll come back with you when you go, but must it be right now ? And anyway, I haven't got late leave. How'll I get in ? It's midnight already, and the Night Super.'ll be furious if I turn up at two in the morning and ask for a key."

"She won't be furious if I turn up and ask for one for my fiancée and explain we've been delayed, unexpectedly. Naturally, I'll apologize, though I won't explain, and she won't expect any explanation from me. There aren't many compensations to being an S.S.O., sweetheart, but there are a few. My request won't surprise her. The only people in Benedict's who'll be surprised by this turn of events are our two selves." He kissed me once more, then let me go. "Now's the time, Jo. What with one thing and another, you've taken a tremendous emotional beating and look as if you've had as much as you can take for one night. In a rather different context, my darling, so have I. Understand?"

"Now, yes. Sorry. I was being bloody childish again."

"No. Just a little dim and very, very sweet." He put his hands back in his pockets and smiled at me. "Right, Jo! Come along! Uncle Richard is about to do what he has always intended doing with you. Uncle Richard is going to take you home. Later, he's going to keep you there—and not much later. Uncle Richard has done the hell of a lot of waiting. And Uncle Richard, though you may not have realized this, is not by nature a patient man. It's that red hair," he said. "It's that damned red hair."

THE END